THE UNDERGROUND GAME

Other Books by Françoise Mallet-Joris

THE
UNDERGROUND
GAME

Françoise Mallet-Joris

TRANSLATED FROM THE FRENCH BY
HERMA BRIFFAULT

E. P. DUTTON & CO., INC. / NEW YORK / 1975

This work was first published in France under the title *Le Jeu Du Souterrain*. © Editions Grasset & Fasquelle, 1973. It was subsequently published by W.H. Allen in Great Britain as *The Underground Game.*

Published simultaneously in Canada
by Clarke, Irwin & Company Limited, Toronto and Vancouver
ISBN: 0–525–22587–0

Library of Congress Cataloging in Publication Data

Mallet-Joris, Françoise, 1930–
    The underground game.

    Translation of Le jeu du souterrain.
    I. Title.
PZ4.M252Un3   [PQ2625.A7124]   843'.9'14   74–30249

Contents

I

The Treasure

AFTER DINNER

After dinner, Robert liked to settle down in his study for a long evening of conversation in which he took the lead, doing most of the talking.

Comfortable in his tweeds and in his roomy old armchair, he smoked his pipe as he talked, becoming expansive in the presence of his mother-in-law Germaine and his sister-in-law Vivi, who were always ready to listen and admire. They were there this particular evening, and so was his wife Catherine. Less comforting, she. Yes, quite often in the evening after dinner, he was, as now, settled down in his study, a glass of brandy within reach, the floor lamp lighting up the bookshelves and the peaceful old furnishings that had belonged to Catherine's parents. Here he was, at ease in his fifty-some years, a little too stout, but not terribly so, a warmhearted, likable man, fond of billiards, good food, and anecdotes—in short, a writer.

He was narrating a strange anecdote. They were listening —Germaine, Vivi, and Catherine. Germaine, her round hazel eyes wide open and glistening as usual, large-mouthed, a veritable frog's mouth; hard to believe she had been a beauty in the 1920s, for she was now sunk in a mountain of flesh and clothed in the baggy garments "suitable to her age." A good soul. And Vivi, blue-eyed and fair-haired, her features fine

9

but irregular, a little faded but still attractive, very modern, known to everyone as very avant-garde. Then, there was Catherine, his wife.

He was telling them about his subject—that is to say, about the subject of the novel he would eventually write, perhaps.

"Good Lord!" said Vivi. "It's hard to believe that such things happen in the twentieth century!"

"Yes, exactly," said Robert.

That was exactly the element of interest in the story, the fact that it occurred in the twentieth century. In a village bristling with television antennae, in the age of the pill, real estate developers, Women's Lib—a world undergoing a transformation more rapid and astonishing each day.

Catherine remarked rather dryly that, after all, even in the twentieth century, there were ethnologists digging in the earth for relics of the past and sociologists carrying out investigations. In fact, there was a renewed interest in such research.

"But that's not the same thing at all!" Robert fumed.

"Absolutely not," said Germaine.

She always backed up Robert, which sometimes got on his nerves—but not too much. His mother-in-law adored him, bestowed upon him an instinctive trust and unreserved admiration. She believed in his subject for a book so utterly that if she could have conceived it herself, she would have torn it from her vitals. All this, of course, without discernment.

"How can you talk about your book projects to Mamma?" said Catherine. "In such matters, she doesn't understand a thing at all!"

No, she didn't understand a thing at all about writing, but still—

"It's not the same thing, that man digging down there in the Cotentin. He's the guard of the museum in the little town, and for years he's been burrowing under the earth at night like a mole, hoping to find some treasure, a tomb, or a temple of the Templars, or I don't know what, and I don't care. He's doing this all alone; he's not a sociologist or an ethnologist; he doesn't have a university backing him. He had this one little idea all by himself; he did some research, collected some information all by himself—and one wonders what notion of history a self-educated man might have. Yes, all by himself, down there in that remote part of Normandy. To get to the nearest library—it's at Valognes—he has to take a bus. And for more than ten years, he's been digging. I think it's admirable."

"Admirable!" Germaine echoed.

"But not merely admirable, it's also farcical," said Robert. "Tragicomic, if you like. Exactly because, as Vivi says, it takes place in the twentieth century. It's both admirable and foolish, like a lengthy serialized novel, as if I were to write a long episodic novel in an age when no one reads the stuff."

"But is it a good subject for a novel?" Germaine timidly inquired.

"Subject, subject!" Vivi scoffed. "As if there were still subjects!"

Catherine said nothing. In the presence of her mother and elder sister, who were always so eager to admire Robert, to play up to him, she simply kept quiet. Her slanty eyes were expressionless. Something like a smile hovered on her lips. But he guessed her hostility, or rather, a secret disapproval.

And I know why, he ruminated. I know what she's thinking: Since you'll never write the book, what's the use talking about it? Well, to begin with, because I enjoy it. And then, who knows—

True, it was a long time since he'd written a novel. He was a writer who had stopped writing. And interestingly enough, those writers who don't write any more are the most likable. Because they have time to read the manuscripts of others, to sit on committees, be members of round tables, write this or that article, pay attention to a beginner, have a circle of friends—in short, time to live. A writer who has stopped writing is treated more gently by the critics. He's proved himself. And I've proved myself, with my published works:

11

the first novel a little scandalous, the third one a prizewinner, the fourth one arriving five or six years later, a little out of breath, but there it is, to show the rest of the writing tribe that I can still write, I've not given up; I've pulled off the trick and earned my right to breathe now. No one can earn a living writing good literature, but one can live pretty well on its perimeter—on the staff of a publishing house, writing magazine articles, doing radio and television broadcasts. You write an article on Woman, broadcast a piece on proletarian poets or Bulgarian folklore; you lecture on folk art and folk songs. (Oh, what about that lovely trip Reine and I made to Languedoc!) It's a good life; you have friends, and you render services. You even discover now and then that you have readers; for instance, that short article I wrote on agriculture for that northern provincial paper, *Voix du Nord,* giving it little thought, was actually read and liked by a number of nice simple people, a village postmistress, a graduate in engineering; and they wrote letters praising it and complaining that Lille was a boring place to live in; and there was a schoolmaster who said in his letter, "I, too, am a writer," and a self-educated miner, and a museum guard—like the one in my novel, or rather, in the novel I just may write. I've not given up that old dream of mine that one day I will suddenly appear on the scene with a book that will astound serious writers and disillusioned critics, a book that will justify to others (Catherine) all those idle conversations, the apparent wasting of my time and talent at ceremonial banquets and in writing all those prefaces and letters of recommendation, in reading and putting to rights all those manuscripts, all the countless occupations that others (Catherine) call wasted time.

But why was he trying to justify himself? Was there really any need? And then the old dream loomed up again: How wonderful to be the ugly little duckling that turned into a swan! How wonderful to be the man who has fooled everyone with his disguise of a rather corpulent, beer-drinking, superannuated citizen who turns out to be Bach, or that good-for-nothing who turns out to be Verlaine or Villon—It was a metamorphosis Catherine had been expecting and perhaps expected no more.

He shook himself out of these dismal reflections. Melancholy was not in his nature. A good story is always a good story, whether you write it or not.

"Just listen to this," he said with enthusiasm. (And this kind of enthusiasm deserves a footnote. It's not fake; it's not brainwashing stuff; but it is hesitant, uneasy, uncertain; and that is how Robert's voice sounded despite the peaceful setting, the aroma of pipe tobacco, the glass of brandy, the glow of the standard lamp.)

"Listen to this passage I'm going to read to you in this old book; you'll see, it bears on the same subject exactly."

And he read aloud:

One of the astronomers, Monsieur Le Gentil de La Galaissière, departed on a voyage to India in the month of March, 1760 and, unable to land because of the war with the English, he remained for eight years at Pondichéry, waiting for the next transit of Venus, due in 1769. By so doing, he lost his official position with the Academy of Science which, having had no news of him for so many years, had replaced him with another. He also lost his patrimony, having left it in faithless hands; and it seems that his wife had remarried and, to top all these misfortunes, he had failed to attain the goal of his voyage. For, during the transit of Venus in 1761 he had been unable to land and thus to join other astronomers in an observatory, he had been unable to observe it, and in 1769 a heavy cloud cover made any observation impossible.

"But what advantage is it," said Germaine cautiously, "that your subject has already existed?"

"No advantage. It's merely interesting."

Already a pricked balloon, Catherine told herself, already his enthusiasm is dampened. His heartiness and warmth are illusory. "But what an imagination!" as his humble correspondents say. He's interested in everything, always from his own point of view, and it all boils down to what? To wasting his time, his talent, writing those magazine articles, those prefaces for his pals' books, those late nights out that leave

13

him empty-headed and thick-tongued next day, using up his energies in rendering services to acquaintances, for instance to that one who is starting a new literary review, or in radio broadcasts or writing lyrics for that nightclub singer. No matter who or what provides him with an escape, a means of avoiding coming to terms with me, his wife. I'm becoming embittered. No, disillusioned. I ought to encourage him; I ought to back him up this time, perhaps. But then, he has Mamma—

"Essentially," Robert was saying, deriving courage from the sound of his voice, like a child whistling in the dark, "essentially, the curious thing about La Gallaissière's experience is that his absurd action—picturesque in that epoch— was in the cause of science. To risk one's life and married happiness in a long wait for an eclipse—that was an act of folly incomprehensible to the general public. Today, tell anyone down there in that remote Cotentin that you've spent ten years peering through a microscope or talk to anyone about atomic fission or microbes or cosmic rays, anything bearing on science, and you will be respected. Today, it's the seeker after buried treasure and old myths who is called a madman."

"And novelists—" said Vivi.

Vivi always comprehended things too quickly, with her nervous sensibility and curiosity always on the qui vive, aware of the least change in fashion or art or happenings. And all this without any real discernment. Nonetheless, a nice person.

"Is that honestly true?" asked Germaine, anxious to understand, to be of help, to put her hand to the plow.

"Yes, to a certain extent. The novelist is a madman. For in the twentieth century, we no longer have a common language, a common set of symbols. This means that the novelist has to choose between realism and subjective solitude if he doesn't want to be called a madman. All he's left with is—"

He stopped short, realizing that he was floundering.

14

"Well, thank goodness you're not a madman," said Catherine.

"That's not nice," said Vivi, as usual coming to the defense of her brother-in-law.

"Not nice? Why?" asked Germaine, never able to keep up with what was being said. "Not nice to say he's not a madman?"

Well! After that, there was nothing more to be done except to turn on the television.

Catherine, who is Robert Guibal's wife and teaches literature at the lycée in Chartres, has an oddly Oriental look, with her clear, pale gold coloring, her slanty eyes, and straight black hair, indeed she looks like a very young Eurasian girl. But not at all; she is French, absolutely. Her aloof, almost hostile attitude allows one to think she does not love her husband. This, too, is a mistaken assumption. She does love her husband, but in a yes-and-no way. One might conclude that she loves him in spite of herself.

Whenever Catherine complained about Robert to Germaine, her mother always said, "He's a man—and an artist."

The first attribute an extenuating circumstance, the second being thrown in as a bonus. But the two seem to be in contradiction, since "a man" implies a giant in whom everything should be forgiven because of his strength and the security it offers, while "an artist" implies a kind of child whose thoughtlessness is more to be pitied than blamed.

In short, Catherine told herself, women are the only ones in whom nothing can be forgiven.

GERRY WANTED TO BE A WRITER

All this had come about because Gerry aspired to be a writer.

"Oh, dear, and he's such a nice boy!" said Vivi in a pitying way when she heard of his ambition. Gerry was both hand-some and young. He was the staff photographer on *Modes et Loisir*, the fashion and travel magazine for which Vivi also worked. Robert was fond of him; Catherine didn't like him; Vivi felt compassion for anyone so perfect but at the same time so out of date.

Gerry had been sent down to the Cotentin to get some shots for a picture story on that remote part of Normandy; almost an entire issue was to be devoted to the region. There he made friends, as he always did everywhere he went. And he had heard the talk about the guard of the château-museum who was convinced that a chapel of the Templars was buried somewhere nearby on the peninsula. For close to fifteen years, he had been secretly digging at night, hoping to discover it. But only a year ago, the municipality of Boissy had found out his secret and was hesitating over what to do. Should they order a bona fide archaeological expedition to investigate the region, or should they risk being laughed at and join in the work of this self-educated man who was per-haps crazy and was certainly behaving in a foolish way?

Gerry had become chummy with the mayor of the little town, with the parish priest, with the owner of a bistro, and with the château-museum guard himself—and with every-one. This affair had intrigued him. He called the old guy a good sport to have spent so much time on this uncertain project; after all, it was like climbing Annapurna all alone, wasn't it? And he felt it would be a good subject for an article he himself wanted to write. He had in fact written it, but *Modes et Loisir* rejected it, wouldn't let him give up photog-raphy; so he'd come to ask Robert to read what he'd written and tell him what was wrong and maybe touch it up a bit. Robert was his god, and it was really because of this intense admiration that he wanted to try his hand at writing.

And in the presence of Robert, Catherine, and Vivi, he had read his article aloud, standing between the handsome bookcase and the floor lamp:

In this quiet village where, all the same, the rooftops bristle with television antennae, reminding us that we are in the twentieth century, life unfolds between the church and the bargain store (the *Prisunid*), between the town hall and the garage, the cooperative food store and the factory, not far away. This routine seems very contemporary. The farmers of the surrounding countryside have set up a system of buying their agricultural implements and machinery in common, and the cooperative store has now functioned for five years very satisfactorily. This was revealed to us by Monsieur Guimard, the genial agent for the firm, and was verified by Monsieur Graff, the president of the cooperative, who showed us around his model farm where the Louis XIII window copings and an adorable dovecote have been preserved intact by this family of rabid traditionalists. But this does not preempt milking machines and up-to-date chicken coops equipped to furnish maximum egg laying. In short, this little village of Boissy, which, thanks to the efforts of its inhabitants, its dynamic parish priest, the mayor, too, who is also the community butcher, seems to be in line with progress.

But it was not progress that we came to look for here, traveling by the local buses down the rutted roads of the Cotentin. Mystery is what we came to find, mystery that our contemporaries laugh at, thinking they've gone beyond it, but missing it all the same. Who can say how much nostalgia lingers in the hearts of so many human beings who appear to be mechanized, who no longer find the mystic impulses of medieval faith, and whom the sexual liberation has deprived of the romanticism of our ancestors and no longer cherish the dreams to which they have a right? Has the pill destroyed romantic love? Is it scientifically proven that cats die when deprived of their dreams? It would be premature to answer these questions. But everyone today asks them like a nagging anxiety. Stuffed with information that is often tragic, enamored of science and statistics, does the world yet know the recipe for those dreams that enable us to live?

Vivi sighed audibly.

Gerry valiantly continued:

That is the recipe we hoped to get from Monsieur Pierre Sorel, guard at the château-museum of Boissy, who for many

17

years, with a perseverance and obstinacy worthy of a better fate, seeks in every moment of leisure in this château that is entrusted to him, and which in olden times served as a refuge for the Templars, a treasure. A treasure! How many times, in the dreams of childhood—

"Is there much more?" asked Vivi.

"Why? Does it seem stupid to you?"

"It's not stupid," said Catherine, "but it's rather silly."

"Well, you see, it's because I don't know how to write," said Gerry.

"It's not that you don't know how to write," said Catherine in an effort at generosity, "it's because you use platitudes, turns of speech that everyone uses."

"But if everyone uses them, then they'd be understood, wouldn't they?"

"Yes, of course," said Catherine, giving up. "But one doesn't write so that everyone will understand."

"Well, for my part," said Gerry, "I think that old duffer is tremendous. But then, I've always liked stories about buried treasure; haven't you?"

"Why, yes, but—"

"And I think everyone does. So I'll go ahead and write it."

"But, Gerry, you're writing it so badly. I'm sorry, but, for instance, one simply can't say nowadays 'childhood dreams.'"

"Why not?"

"One just can't, that's all."

"But didn't you have dreams when you were a little girl? And now, don't you believe that most people dream at night of winning the top prize of the lottery? And that Brigitte Bardot will fall into their arms, or that they will somehow bring peace to the world—things like that?"

"Possibly, but you simply can't say 'childhood dreams.'"

"To begin with, it's reactionary," said Vivi, who had remained quiet as she sat in a corner of the study, her crocodile handbag on her knees.

"It's reactionary to write—?"

"Yes, it is!" Vivi fairly barked, for the whole thing was getting on her nerves. "It's reactionary journalese and in the worst possible taste! Think of all the atrocities that are being perpetrated in the modern world, of the sensation of the absurd that is overwhelming all of us, think of the necessity of struggling against so much oppression, against all the taboos that are strangling our consumer society; and here you are, talking about 'childhood dreams'!"

"It's more a question of vocabulary," said Catherine, as usual annoyed at her sister's vehemence.

Robert made no comment, merely puffed away at his pipe, that weapon of the weak.

"Well, what I'd like to know," said Gerry sulkily, rumpling his hair, "is why, if you want to say 'childhood dreams,' you can't simply write: *'childhood dreams'*?"

Three groans were the only reply he got. The question remained unanswered.

All this had come to pass because Gerry was Gerry. And just what is that?

According to Catherine: "A happy imbecile."

According to Vivi, more gently: "He's inconceivable."

"Because he's sincere," added Robert by way of rectification.

Vivi, in her own way, was also full of sincerity. Which no doubt explains her rapport with Gerry. But their vocabularies were not the same.

When Gerry read the lonely-hearts columns in the newspapers (and he did read them), he was likely to say, "That woman must really know a lot about suffering." And at sight of the headache pills advertisement in the metro, the one that pictures the tormented face of a man with a wagon crossing right through his skull, his comment was: "There's a good idea in that!"

Vivi had once congratulated him for having quoted Engels very aptly ("Woman is the proletarian of *Homo sapiens*"), and he beamed with pleasure. But then he said,

"Yes, I ran across it in a book of quotations."

Vivi was absolutely floored.

"We'll never make anything of that boy," she told her brother-in-law.

Now, many people do read books of quotations, and they do consult their horoscopes; some remarkable women write to the lonely-hearts columns; scholars must occasionally read serialized trashy novels; musicians may find their inspiration on the airwaves of Radio-Luxembourg—at any rate, all this is possible. But Gerry was the only one who talked about these things without embarrassment. In a sense, he was a cripple; something was lacking in him. An acquaintance with the social proprieties? Gerry read Dale Carnegie's *How to Win Friends and Influence People*. He had found the book in a public toilet. His comment was: "There's a lot of good, sound sense in that book."

"He drives me crazy," said Catherine. "Gerry, you drive me crazy."

He took no offense. He was never offended. Good-looking, well dressed, conscientious, with a sterling character—all this Catherine conceded and could not account for her detestation of the boy. She couldn't bear him. "He's not stupid," they said of him in the magazine office. And Catherine had to admit that in addition to his many good qualities, he did have a certain shrewdness (with that word she was taking him down a peg or two!), even a kind of intelligence. And he was disinterested. He never tried to put himself forward. When he suggested a layout, when he had an idea for an article, it was just for amusement or to give pleasure, artless ingeniosity. "Everyone adores Gerry," one heard on all sides. "Everyone but me," was Catherine's private comment. One case in a hundred.

"He has personality," said Robert. Oh, yes? A hero for little factory girls, the seducer in picture stories, with his thick curly hair, his white teeth, his blue eyes holding such a frank expression. And Catherine argued with herself: At least he's not a pederast. His stereotyped reactions, his kind attentions to old ladies, his pluck, that quality so much touted in books for juveniles under fifteen. Perfect. Smooth as a marble statue. As upright as Saint George. Nothing secret, nothing hidden. The "great girls" he met, his romances with them unfolded in full view. The girls were as good-looking as he, and as nonexistent. Fashion models, salesgirls, stewardesses—they knew "how to make love"; and then, at a later stage of the idyl, they were "very busy with their work"; and still later, "they seem to have found someone better than I am." And these pale plots ended always with the no less inevitable formula: "We're still good friends." And he said, "I still photograph her," adding, like a hero in a Paul Morand novel, "I'm a good sport."

"You fail to realize," Robert told his wife, "how rare a person of his kind is. No second thoughts, no ulterior motives. It's because Gerry is that kind of person that he gave me my subject."

His subject, his subject! Catherine fumed to herself. He's full of it at present. His subject will keep him in good humor, will give him something to talk about and will give him a raison d'être for a few months. Then his subject will gradually become diluted, will disappear little by little, fade out like an old photo, emptied of substance, emptied by the Gerrys, the club friends, the devotees of billiards, the meetings of literary circles, the restaurant dinners with his pals, all those people he says can't be avoided, the aspiring young authors, the episodic mistresses. (Catherine always knew about them, sensed their existence, and never could resign herself to them.)

"Did you notice how pleased Gerry was when I told him, 'It's absolutely a subject made to order for me'? He will be so proud and—"

"But what does that amount to? For heaven's sake! You don't write just to please Gerry, do you?"

"Well, yes, among others."

He really wanted to give pleasure to Gerry.

And to please others, as well. He would like to please his amiable concierge, who treasured his articles she clipped from the magazines and who treated him with such consideration. He would also like to please that student who stole one of his books, the first one, naturally, right out of the display window of Gibert's bookstore. He wanted to give pleasure to his readers—he still had a few—who had written to ask him why he had stopped writing novels, especially now that modern literature was so depressing, while his books were "so fresh." He recalled the plaintive housewife who had used the phrase in a letter: "Your books, Monsieur Guibal, are at least fresh. But what is there to read nowadays?" He knew what many of his colleagues thought about them. But he was resigned to that as he was resigned to so many other things. "A picture should be like a good armchair." Matisse's words, more or less.

To give pleasure.

To Reine, for whom I must write a new song, he reflected. To please Bernard, whose *Magazine des Arts* was on the brink of bankruptcy, despite all his efforts, and who had asked him to write an article.

"I say, you who have something of a name," Bernard had said, "won't you write something about the Etruscan exhibition at the Grand Palais?"

Why, of course.

In spite of that "something of a name." Funny how I can't seem to take offense at things like that "something of a name" and "your novels are so fresh and clean." Or that word "polygraph" used to describe him in a recent issue of *L'Express:* "Robert Guibal, that polygraph, that ubiquitous but likable writer."

"That word 'likable' doesn't help at all," Catherine had said.

"It proves that the critic wasn't being mean."

"As everyone knows, it's not a good sign not to have enemies," said Catherine.

No doubt. But that doesn't bother me either. That tinge of condescension is present in the most sincere friendships. "He's a good soul, Robert." "He's a great guy—a bon vivant, but not without talent, you know; he's written some charming things, for example, *The Imprisoned Fox*, very fresh." Well, why not? All the same, I'd like to write this book that would fool its readers. On the surface, it would appear to be an illustrated episodic story, but beneath that surface of extravagant adventures (he was very fond of the brocade of passionate love, the silken presence of young girls, poisons and daggers, the word "damascene," sudden conversions, betrayals, children lost and found, false and real incest, Balzacian gangs and groups, Dickensian social indignations, the erudite digressions of Hugo—in short, beneath all this), while *giving pleasure*, I could say one or two things—No, that's still too much. It wouldn't be saying; it would *be*, if one weren't too modest—Beneath all this, I would sing, would make people feel, let something secret appear on the surface. Yes, the secret he had borne within him ever since his novel *Café of the Friends*, no, ever since his childhood, a secret he had always, shall we say, been too timid (strange word to use in connection with this big, hearty man with the vibrant voice) or too discreet to display.

But does that secret really exist? he asked himself as he peered at the grimacing potteries of the Etruscans on exhibition at the Grand Palais. Or is it a feeling everyone has of possessing a key, an inner music, something precious and secret that shame—or laziness—renders incommunicable? And if everyone possesses it more or less, doesn't that take away its value? He didn't know what to think.

"Well, well! There's Robert!" said Geneviève to Bernard. (They, too, were paying a visit to the Etruscans.) "And how gloomy he looks!"

Bernard smiled.

"Poor Robert, it's my fault. I asked him to do an article on the Etruscans for the magazine. He must be meditating on it now. Having to think hard on any subject is the only thing that depresses him."

"Then you shouldn't have asked him to do it," said Geneviève sweetly.

"Oh, it does him good; it shakes him up," said Bernard a little cynically.

"But you're delighted to find him when you haven't anyone else to help you out," said Geneviève.

"Oh, of course. Robert's extraordinary; he can write on any subject. He missed the boat in his career as a novelist, but he's extraordinary. Well, if he can go on living like this, it must certainly be thanks to Catherine."

"And to his character, too. He does have character."

"Oh, a sterling character. And that may be why he's not a success. He doesn't know how to say no."

"Especially to you."

"Especially to me," Bernard agreed. "He's a really good friend."

"With a heart of gold? Shall we go over and speak to him?"

"Heavens, no! Do you want to knock out my article? Just when he's mulling it over?"

Laughing, they slipped into another gallery.

VIVI TELEPHONES

At half past seven in the morning, Vivi telephoned.

Catherine, who was in the bathroom, ran to take the call. "Hello. Vivi?"

Robert overheard what followed.

"What did you say? You say it's nothing serious? Then you could have postponed telephoning until later. You woke me up. . . . Very well, it's for Manuel; I'll tell Robert, but if it's nothing serious—"

Then they seemed for a moment to be quarreling. Catherine, childless, was a little jealous of Vivi's children, Manuel, aged fifteen, and Marina, fourteen (but the two were always dubbed "the twins"). Above all, she was jealous of the role the twins played in Robert's life, as Vivi well knew. Vivi behaved something like the second wife in a Chinese ménage, taking advantage of her children, so Catherine thought, to possess herself of Robert, who lent himself to this maneuver. Vivi telephoned at all hours—as, for instance, this morning—asking him to repair the drains or to get one of her weird friends out of a hole (she had some preposterous friends: unemployed Peruvian journalists, Spanish refugees, Russians without identity papers), or she wanted him to advise her and Marina on their wardrobes or on Manuel's studies, "which are giving him all kinds of trouble"; or she wanted him to drive one of the children to dancing class, the other to a meeting of the Friends of Zen, which this time was to be held some distance away near Malmaison. Her requests were endless.

Of course, Robert dragged himself out of bed to speak with Vivi. Catherine sometimes told herself, I'd rather he had a mistress—as if she didn't know quite well that he did have one.

"Good, I'll see him this evening," she overheard Robert tell Vivi. "Have him meet me in the office of the *Magazine des Arts* at seven. . . . Oh, he knows where it is. . . . No, don't bother to put him in a taxi."

That Robert should have a mistress was a profound grief to Catherine. But it thoroughly exasperated her that he should let himself be imposed upon by Germaine, by Vivi and Vivi's children.

"Well, Robert? When can I expect to see you this evening?"

"Oh, I'll not be much delayed. After office hours, I'll have a drink with the boy, that's all. He's having some difficulties with a classmate. You know how it is. At that age, the least little thing takes on importance."

She felt like asking, "How could I know?", but did not. How could she know, childless as she was? He would answer her with the exasperating patience he'd developed in dealing with authors and journalists, all of them slightly crazy. "But you yourself were once a child, weren't you?" And she wanted to avoid the dispute that might follow, when she would be put in the wrong once more. She said nothing.

"I forgot to tell you, I'm not coming home to lunch today," he said in that assumed abstracted way he had when he was going to visit Reine. "I'm having lunch with Bernard [this wasn't a lie, but the lunch would be at Reine's apartment]; we've got to talk about my radio broadcasts on the provinces. You know, I told you about them."

One never uses so many words when telling the truth, Catherine told herself cynically. Why did he feel he had to make up a lie, since he knows perfectly well that I know what's going on? Married people always say too much or too little. And as for her, it would be too little, not enough.

"Then I'll see you tonight," she said with a barely perceptible effort to maintain a serene expression.

"See you tonight, my dearest."

His voice was cordial, but he was obviously embarrassed. He was even affectionate. Yes, as he was with Manuel, Marina, Vivi, Germaine, and as he doubtless was with Reine and with all the others, the journalists, the musicians, all the parasites who consumed his time and made it impossible for him to write—and, she told herself, made it impossible for him really to love. And she didn't want that kind of affection, that universal fellow feeling. And everyone knows that I'm not a good mixer (she knew this was what her pupils at the lycée said of her), and moreover, I prefer not to be, rather than to be universally liked, as Robert is. (And how could she be easy and generous in her affections, since she was not loved?)

26

Despite Reine's perfection (she was only human, after all), she sometimes asked Robert if he loved her. To which question he always responded with, "Why, yes, naturally." And Reine, with that gravity she always demonstrated in theoretical matters, responded with, "What does that mean, 'naturally'?"

Oh, the word came to him just like that, by chance, but it expressed his thought. Naturally. Because he loved Reine without affectation; he didn't have to force it or worry about whys and wherefores. Because Reine suited him; he could relax with her; he liked her profession (a nightclub singer). And because she was good-hearted. He liked her friends and her apartment. In short, he thought that when a man is attracted to a woman and she is attracted to him, then there's no reason not to make love.

He could have added that he loved her because she lived not far off; the distance between the Gare du Luxembourg in his neighborhood and the rue Saint-Séverin, where she lived, was short and could be covered in an agreeable stroll. For he always walked to her apartment, taking his time, pausing to look at the bookstore window displays or the haberdasher's, or the Chinese grocery on the rue de la Harpe, sometimes stopping in the Saint-Séverin cloister to smoke his pipe. The stroll was pleasant, and it added to the pleasure he took in Reine's company. He liked to hear the sound of her piano as he climbed the greenish stairway to her apartment on the fourth floor, which he reached just a little out of breath. There was a lovely, cool light in the stairwell, like the cool glimmer of an aquarium. The building was ancient, and the stairs had originally risen from an open court, which was now roofed over with glass. The steps were of stone, with, at every landing, a balcony with a handsome wrought iron balustrade. The fact that the first two floors were inhabited by large families who left plastic buckets and basins on their Renaissance balconies did not bother Robert;

indeed, they rather delighted him. Reine's balcony-landing on the fourth floor was adorned with potted plants and a small fountain, a water jet that splashed into a stone shell (its provenance was the Bazar de l'Hôtel de Ville), and a small stone statue, very ugly, brought up from Provence. Robert was fond of that little statue; it revealed a desire for beauty and order in Reine that a faulty education had not encouraged. This very imperfection was appealing.

He liked just as well that yellow plastic bucket and the enamel basin on the lower balcony. The poesy of the stone stairway was thus as if veiled in and excused by the presence of life: that stray bath glove, that salad basket, that utilization of the Renaissance balconies for the humble necessities of existence.

"I love you on account of your stairway, the little statue, and the sound of your piano," he told Reine.

"Then if I moved to another apartment, you'd not love me any more?"

He didn't know what to say. For him, Reine was the sum total of the stairway, the aquarium light, the pleasant stroll, each item as important as her abundant red hair, the popular songs she sang, the beautiful timbre of her voice, her warm bed, her scent of carnations. How to disassociate these things?

"Why should you move?"

Reine shrugged.

"Why should I stop loving you tonight?" he asked.

"Well, you've stopped loving your wife," she said without acrimony.

Had he stopped loving Cathie? He had never gone farther in his thoughts about her than to tell himself that Cathie and he were not suited to each other. Their union was unsuccessful. His apartment was pleasant; he liked his study, his mother-in-law, his sister-in-law, his nephew and niece; and in all this, Cathie was like the wrinkle in an otherwise smooth sheet, a dripping tap that keeps one awake at night, one of those trifling annoyances—tax forms, telephone calls that must be made and are always postponed—that hounded him and were rather unpleasant but didn't make him really unhappy. However, he was too fair-minded to blame her. He loved her, but as one loves a memory, as one remembers having been very fond of chocolate or *blanquette de veau* and having given them up after the umpteenth liver attack, for one's liver must be taken seriously. They were just not suited to each other, nothing more.

"But why do you love me in particular?" Reine said, not agitatedly, but gravely. "Why me?"

Her face was very close to his as she asked the question, peering at him with her piercingly blue eyes. Those high cheekbones gave her a Slavic aspect. Her glowing beauty was statuesque; she was tall, broad-shouldered, with lovely breasts. It was a beauty both feminine and masculine, and in her character, there was the same duality. Warm, choleric, impulsive, she was at the same time calm, dependable. There was something eternal about her. She carried off her name well: a woman, but queenly and bearing a scepter that gave her gravity, weight, a function. And that gravity was with her in the humblest moments; when she was sorting out the lettuce, or going into an ecstasy over a towel rack hand-painted with roses, or stammering out tender words, she was indeed queenly. And with her large white body, she could figure in an allegory as Woman, with nothing to individualize her. She was a body, a voice when she sang, and sovereign because she was no one.

"I don't like my Christian name," she once said.

"Then why didn't you take a stage name, as everyone does?"

"Well, because that's what I'm called."

Her lovely round forehead. Not to change what is. Her wisdom. Some people find Reine stupid, but then, that is all too easily said about singers. Reine is quite all right.

"I love you because you are Woman," he said tenderly.

Reine didn't argue. Her conclusion was that Robert's wife must be frigid.

Sometimes Robert wondered if Reine's lack of interest in his work—his magazine articles, his broadcasts, and now this still-nebulous book he'd told her about—might not be a proof of her love. And always her comment, even on the songs he wrote for her, was, "It's such fun to work together!" But if he were to stop writing them, then what? She'd find another librettist. And were he to stop seeing her, would this be a tragedy for her? No. She'd find another lover equally peaceable, affectionate, undemanding, a man she could trust, could talk to, a man with whom she could go to the movies, make love, sleep. And as for himself, were he to lose Reine, along with the big colonial bed, the stairway, the little statue, would he have the sensation of an irreparable loss? He believed not. But all this did not imply that they didn't love each other. No. They loved each other just as they could love someone else. Was this rather sad or very beautiful? He couldn't decide.

A MEDIEVAL COUPLE

Like a medieval knight, Bernard lived according to a strict code, which can be described in one word: elegance. In every meaning of the word. Laugh if you will, but this rule of conduct, which on occasion had cost him some real sacrifice, had its beauty; such strictness is admirable in this fluctuant century. For three years, he had preferred to live in a kind of garret at "a good address" (the rue de la Faisanderie) rather than in a more comfortable apartment at an address not so "good." Robert recalled seeing Bernard emerge from his uncomfortable studio apartment as impeccably attired and as self-possessed as if he were leaving a posh residence in the avenue Victor Hugo. He always said he was looking for a decent apartment, and he did find one almost immediately when Geneviève inherited a tidy fortune from her Uncle Maurice.

It was while Bernard was still living in the makeshift apartment that Robert came to compare him with those valiant medieval knights, panting and sweating in their heavy armor under the hot sun of the Crusades, no doubt laughed at by the Arabs of Saladin in their airy garments of silk. But they maintained their dignity (it is difficult to bend down in armor), evidently considering (at least before the mixed marriages and the trade in spices) these Arabs a rabble beneath contempt, if only because they conformed to the necessities of the climate by dressing lightly and comfortably.

Thus, Bernard preferred to walk in town so long as he couldn't afford to buy a sufficiently good car. He surely deserved a coat of arms engraved with a noble motto: *Ne faut point*, or perhaps *À tout seigneur, tout honneur*. Robert formed the habit of hailing him jokingly, "Behold, Sir Bernard in his helm!" The joke remained a complete enigma to Bernard. He considered asking Geneviève but didn't, for even if she understood, she'd not give a sign. Geneviève had the self-possessed, aloof, abstracted bearing of a girl whose family has at one time had a great deal of money. That time was in the past, but this changed nothing in her attitude. She adhered absolutely to Bernard's credo and would die of hunger wearing a dress bearing the signature of a top Parisian dressmaker. She had always remained the medieval lady in the conical headdress. An almost perfect woman, was Geneviève. Almost perfect, for in spite of her tacit vow of allegiance to Bernard and his credo, this had not deprived her of a surplus of intelligence and a sense of humor. (Bernard labeled this "Geneviève's absurd side.") Try as she would to suppress her inherent attributes, they rose to the surface from time to time. There must have been a Jewish ancestor in her family tree, and that's fatal.

Robert liked them as they were. Catherine said, "They're odious." And that was why, after carefully feeling out the terrain, Robert had formed the habit of inviting them to Reine's apartment. Not without some apprehension the first time. And to his surprise, the evening had been a success!

They had obviously thought they were going to dine with Zulus and were happily surprised. The dinner was good; Reine did not eat with her fingers; there were chairs to sit on! And when, after dinner, Robert had taken off his jacket, revealing his suspenders, and when Reine had sung *"J'aurais voulu jouer l'accordéon"* and served the Benedictine (Benedictine!) in colored liqueur glasses she had inherited from her grandmother, they had almost felt like applauding, as children applaud circus acrobats. And when, upon taking leave, Bernard thanked them for "a most pleasant evening," the words had rarely been so true.

When Bernard and Geneviève talked about it afterward, they made some caustic remarks, although not really spiteful. "But goodness, Benedictine! How funny!" And when one knew Bernard well, his closing remarks were nothing short of benevolent: "After all, it must be easier to make love to a nightclub singer than to Madame-Express and pleasanter to live on the rue Saint-Séverin than on the boulevard de Courcelles."

And surely it was better to be the author of a ditty such as *"Ah, mon chou, mon loup, mon petit lapin"* than to be the author of quite a few other things. (That song had unexpectedly become a best seller among popular records.) Many of Robert's friends agreed on this point. Those songs he had begun to write for Reine a few years ago were now making money. It was a success that hurt no one. And no matter what Catherine said to the contrary, in the narrow world of literature, there was no one who did not regard with indulgence the author of *"J'aurais voulu jouer de l'accordéon,"* an indulgence that would not have been granted the author of a more ambitious work.

Because he was aware of all this, Robert could have cursed Reine when she referred, quite naturally, to "that book Robert wants to write" as they were having their coffee after dinner.

"What's this, old chap?" Bernard exclaimed with exaggerated cordiality. "You're going back to serious writing?"

Geneviève smiled the absent smile with which she greeted any ill-timed remark. The smile said, "I will disregard this blunder, but do please quickly change the subject." Apparently Bernard did not see the smile.

"After all, why not?" he went on. "An author who has been silent for a time is often treated in a more friendly way by the public. And you do have friends, thank heaven! And of course you can count on me." (This was true, Robert reflected, but my goodness how Bernard was taking charge of the affair!) "Well now, the subject?"

"*Well now, the subject?*" Exactly like a professor at a lycée addressing his pupils: "Well now, these exams?"

"Oh, you see, that persistent man in the provinces. . . . his continuing to dig for ten years all alone, and this in the twentieth century. . . . The gap between modern writing and the public. . . ."

But the book was not shaping up in his mind, and he was beginning to wonder why he had been thrilled with sudden excitement when Gerry had first told him all about the affair.

"But who do you think would be interested in that underground story?" said Reine as she took out the liqueur glasses under the amused gaze of the medieval couple. "Since no one really knows if there is a treasure?"

"I don't imagine that Robert intends to stick close to the reality," Bernard explained with the rather patronizing patience he always employed with Reine. "He must see in that prolonged effort, that inefficient and amateurish endeavor a form of physical and moral dedication—"

"Yes, yes," said Reine, whose stubbornness was both peaceable and formidable, "but all the same, when a man has been digging a hole for ten or more years at the risk of being buried alive, of losing his wife, his money, everything, it's important to know whether it's worth while, isn't it?"

"Not necessarily. No."

"Yes, Reinette, of course it is," Geneviève chimed in.

"But you see this from the viewpoint of a news item—I'm not criticizing you. But I don't believe Robert intends to write a suspense story."

"Oh, you're wrong; that's my intention, to a certain extent."

Bernard laughed.

"Robert, you're incredible. Do you really mean you're going to play that game? You're headed for a terrible fall, my friend! The mysterious Templars—is it the Templars?—the ghost of Queen Blanche, the buried chapel, the secret of the alchemists, the wizard's book of spells? You'd be on terribly dangerous ground. Either you take only what the man in the street knows—in which case it's melodrama, popularization, and you set a whole corporation of Catharistic poets and historians of occultism against you. The French radio and television organization is full of such erudite people! Or else you go deeply into alchemy, with all its jargon and symbolism, and you will bore everyone to death."

"And if you abandon that and go in for pure symbol," said Geneviève, "then it's Samuel Beckett or Le Clézio."

Bernard frowned at her—the remark was too intellectual for their hostess—and she fell silent.

"Bernard's right," Reine exclaimed with the ardor she reserved for ideological arguments. "Either your book is serious and no one will understand it, or it's not and the result is no good."

"If you two gang up against me," groaned Robert, "then I surrender!"

"Reine has admirably summed up the problem," said Bernard, holding out his glass. "Reine is always the incarnation of good sense. A little more Benedictine, Reine, if you please."

He and Geneviève treated Reine as if she were an old family retainer, a servant of long standing; that is to say, they treated her with more than ordinary politeness.

They were right, of course; he'd have everyone against

him. Reine and Bernard. The news items amateurs and the ones addicted to "good literature."

"But you're discouraging poor, dear Robert!" exclaimed Geneviève. "Let him write the book he wants to write!"

"Oh, if both Reine and Bernard are against it—" said the helpless victim.

"Obviously you risk going from one extreme to the other," said Geneviève.

The farewells were prolonged and embarrassed.

"I'm not going to the office this afternoon," said Bernard. "I have to see Bérenger. You'll make my excuses."

"Then, do you mind if I use your office for interviewing two authors?"

"Not at all," said Bernard. (He detested the idea but suddenly felt sorry for the poor devil who wanted to return to novel writing and so had to be treated with the care one gives to chronic invalids.) "Use it all day long if you like."

"You were insupportable today, Geneviève," said Bernard as they settled themselves in the Mercedes.

"But you were the insupportable one! If your good friend wants to write a book, let him!" (Geneviève was in one of her "absurd" moods.)

"But he's heading for disaster, my darling! I'm quite fond of Robert. But he needs to be held in check!"

"Perhaps he wants disaster," said Geneviève.

Bernard disregarded this absurdity. There were days when Geneviève must not be contradicted. As a rule, and of her own accord, she recovered her good sense. With most people, horse sense usually prevails.

GOOD LITERATURE

Everyone felt sorry for Robert, who had to read all those manuscripts. Even Bernard did, and sincerely. Reading those manuscripts was obviously the most boring part of his life.

"Mind you," he said to Geneviève, "with his present earnings from his song records, he could afford to drop the job he has with us. He keeps on working just to be of service. Robert is a great guy! Reading those manuscripts is an act of charity."

Bernard could be rather caustic in his judgments of Robert, his capacities, his occupations, and he doubled up with laughter at the thought of Robert and Reine making love. But he had a real admiration for Robert on account of those manuscripts that he conscientiously read and reported on to the authors.

"And besides," Bernard went on, "he has real taste, knows good literature when he sees it, has judgment, so it must be a real chore to ingurgitate all that tosh. Of course, it gives him a small fixed income; but even so, I pity him."

Robert didn't pity himself. He was losing his faith in good literature. Indeed, he had once scandalized Bernard by proclaiming this fact. Bernard was scandalized, although he himself revered little else but well-cut clothes, good addresses, and cars one could be seen in without shame. Bernard had brought up the subject of French belles lettres, and Robert had bluntly said, "I can think of nothing more boring than the French classics!"

Bernard knew that Robert wasn't merely being argumentative but really meant what he said, and this so nonplused him that he was struck dumb.

And he did mean it. Those classics bored him; those perennials revived each season, those pieces of fine writing on coarse subjects—they made him gag. For example, Madame de La Fayette's novel *La Princesse de Clèves*, 800 pages of fine writing on—what else but incest? Then, the moralizings of Lautréamont, and all those catechisms on debauchery, dull, stilted, that were constantly reprinted. He'd prefer any day to read the traveler's tale of that old spinster who was the first to visit Lapland, some fifty years ago. Or the adventurous provincial priest who told about his hunting of the chamois. Or that director of an orphanage who was so preoccupied with shower baths and football fields. Or even *The Story of My Life,* by the aging actress who had enjoyed great success on tour in Libya and Transylvania.

Robert paused in his self-examination. Was there such a place as Transylvania, or had he got it confused with a country mentioned in a juvenile book he'd read with Manuel? No matter. In sum, he preferred any kind of writing not in the category of belles lettres. Was he growing old? Was he behaving like those old people who say, "I only read memoirs nowadays"? Or like those who say, "I no longer read; I re-read"?

Perhaps "good literature" now took, for him, second place to something that was not literature, was more than literature, a form of creativity which he felt but could not yet define, which had a close relation to life itself—Sheer laziness, Catherine would call it. And she was not completely mistaken. He was indeed lazy. He was lazy because, little by little, he had come to think that Catherine was right.

MÉLUSINE, THE BRETON SPRITE

"Our editorial committee has concluded, Madame, that the book project you have offered us falls between two stools. Scholarly in concept, it is really a kind of vulgarization—"

"Oh, Monsieur! Vulgar? Mélusine vulgar?"

"Mélusine," a Breton romance, was a book she, Madame Synge de Coufontaine, had dedicated her whole life to writing. The author's name was obviously a pseudonym and sat rather grotesquely upon this woman of a certain age, nervous and skinny, rather comic, too. But then, as Claudel said, perhaps one must often be ridiculous in order to be occasionally sublime.

She could not be rich, this lady, who was probably a spinster. There was something skimpy about her dress—her coat was too tight at the shoulders, and the color was rather outlandish, a mixture of green and brown—skimpy and at the same time foolish, rather disturbing. Her hands trembled slightly as she argued her case. Her face was fine-featured and wrinkled with nervous tension rather than age; her hair was drawn back tightly into a thin little bun. At twenty, she had been pretty, no doubt; but now, at anywhere between thirty-five and fifty, she was so no longer. Impossible to judge how old she was because of that slight trembling and something wild in her gaze. She might be slightly crazy, but not yet a derelict, although on the verge of becoming one, halfway between straitened circumstances and poverty, halfway between inoffensive manias and delirium, chosen and accepted. Mélusine.

"You must understand, Monsieur, that I propose to demonstrate by means of first-class documentation—I was research assistant for twelve years at the Colonial Ministry in Brussels—I will demonstrate that Mélusine the Sprite represents the persecuted minorities, Jews mainly, and perhaps the Cathari, and that her transformation into a fabulous animal on Saturdays signifies the celebration of the Jewish Sabbath—or else—"

"Why, certainly, I quite understand the interest—"

"What in this could give an impression of vulgarization, Monsieur? That word hurts me very much, for my research is sound; after all, I studied at the School of Paleography and Librarianship. What could give the impression of vulgarization is perhaps the subjective element I introduce to give color and life to the book. A childhood friend, a Breton girl called Mélusine. . . . No, her name was Annick, but. . . . Raped in nineteen forty-two in her family's small manor house. . . . The German authorities claimed that. . . . the guilty one or ones were never found. . . . and all our papers, all our documents that represented ten years of work, were burned, Monsieur! Think of it, the fruit of ten years of labor gone, vanished. . . . I had tackled the Round Table and the Holy Grail. . . ."

All this reminded Robert of something (he couldn't recall

exactly what), and anyway, he was listening with only one ear, fascinated by her hands, very slender and white, the hands of the young girl she had been long ago, as she fiddled with the paper knife on the table.

"Ban and Bahor, you know, the two brother kings, the double of each other, no doubt. . . . Well, Annick and I were like that with our research, and it was because of the passport —rather, the laissez-passer paper—that I was unable to accompany her in August nineteen forty-two and so these tragic events. . . ."

Oh, yes, now he remembered. Saint-Pol Roux, the poet, whose daughter—she had a funny name he couldn't remember—had been raped—papers burned—But such coincidences do occur. She was still fiddling with the paper knife, which rather worried him.

". . . almost my double, or else perhaps I was the one who. . . . Are you interested in supernatural happenings?"

"Oh, my goodness—"

"I know, you have your doubts, like many people. But, you see, I'm absolutely convinced, absolutely, that it was Annick who dictated my book to me, from the Beyond, my book about Mélusine. . . ."

Robert reflected that her arguments were not arguments that would convince a publisher's committee of readers. Her hand that held the paper knife no longer trembled but grasped it convulsively. What an idea to make paper knives in the form of daggers! And what bad taste, and dangerous, too, for you might hurt yourself thoughtlessly.

". . . and it's just possible she wanted—I'm referring to Annick—to give me a message which would evidently have given the book a slightly nightmarish quality, inconsistent with pure erudition—"

"Yes, there is certainly that element, she must have—"

"I agree with you, but don't you think I could enlist the reader's greater interest if I were to write a short preface describing the climate of our friendship, which was so exceptional, and the promise we made to each other to remain faithful beyond the grave and the signs I have had—oh, subtle signs, but very clear to me—of her survival?"

"But then it would be quite another book, Madame."

"You mean, there would be two levels of understanding my work. As in life, moreover. Haven't you ever noticed—?"

"You think so?"

She had dropped the paper knife.

"Yes, I'm quite sure of it," he said with more assurance. "It would take a long time to do, a very long time, but then perhaps it would—"

"Stand a better chance here?"

"I mean, it would perhaps touch the reader more than a work of scholarship, which, necessarily. . . ."

He knew he was being cowardly. But how to get rid of her, otherwise? And then, after all, those stories of double identity, of life in the Great Beyond, did find a public. He could recommend her to *Planète* or to *La Petite Bibliothèque Fantastique*. But he also knew what this would entail: countless telephone calls, a number of letters, useless efforts. However, his craving to be left alone, in peace, was too great. Also, his urge to be of service. And if she set herself to work again on her book, she would perhaps have some months of happiness, poor creature.

"I still believe you should reread your book from beginning to end and accentuate those passages you mention as, er, nightmarish."

"Yes. Perhaps."

She put on her gloves; they had once been of good quality, green lizard, but now were scraped and skinned. He sighed with relief and stood up. But she was not quite ready to go.

"I am deeply touched by what you have said, Monsieur; it shows a great deal of comprehension. Perhaps I was not sufficiently receptive to the message of my beloved Annick —Mélusine may not have been sufficiently crystal-clear." She giggled like a roguish little girl. "I will think over what you have advised. And I will come to see you again. You have been of great help. Are you, by chance, also in communication?"

"Beg pardon?"

"Do you, too, perhaps, have someone in the interplanetary sphere?"

"No, no, I think not," he said briskly.

"One can never be sure, you know. You discover—Well! We'll talk more of all this in the future. At present, I'm taking up too much of your time."

At last she stood up. She was wearing some strange buttoned shoes. An attempt to be in the latest fashion? Or shoes she'd fished out of a trash can?

"I will accompany you to the door, Madame."

"Mademoiselle. I never married. I couldn't, not after being raped, you see; eleven times, can you imagine it, eleven times?"

"Obviously," said Robert, indicating the stairs.

He felt greatly relieved as he returned to his office. All the same, he wondered if Annick had ever existed.

CATHERINE ALONE

When Catherine returns from the lycée, she goes through a routine that has become a ritual. First of all, she changes into more comfortable clothes: Arabian babouches replace her street shoes; brown velvet slacks replace her skirt. Since she always wears a white knitted pullover, that item remains. Next, she goes into the kitchen to set a kettle of water on the stove. While the water is heating, she sets the red lacquer tea tray with the finest white porcelain tea set. Three cups, never just one, for supposing Robert were to come home? And two cups look sad. When the water boils, she makes the tea, then carries the tray into her bed-sitting-room and places it on a low table. While the tea is brewing, she turns on the record player for some soft music. Sometimes, not always, she burns a cone of violet-scented incense. Then, she switches on the green lamp in the corner, where it gives a subdued glow. Then, she settles down on a big floor cushion beside the table. The cushion is velvet and almost the same brown as her slacks.

The decor is becoming to her, and she knows it. A crackled mirror—magic object—is opposite her and reflects a strangely Oriental-looking young Frenchwoman: petite, with rather slanting dark eyes, black hair parted in the middle and with bangs; clear, pale golden complexion; small, well-kept hands with some beautiful rings on the slender fingers. This year they are silver; last year they were coral; before that, carnelian and jade.

The room also has an Oriental look, more East Indian than Chinese, with its walls covered with woven hemp; and hanging on one of the walls is a rare East Indian rug that had belonged to the Colonel, her father. Opposite it hangs a quaint old print. On the dressing table, in a far corner, are aligned all the dolls of her childhood, carefully preserved, including the little pickaninny doll given her when she was seven.

The room, her ritual preparations, those relics of the past, are portions of a secret. And often, as she pours herself a cup of tea, she says aloud, "Everything is ready." As a child, sitting at the enamel dinette table in the kitchen (for this had been her childhood home), she had often said aloud those same words: "Everything is ready." And tears had filled her eyes then—as now.

Vivi tried to shake up her sister.

"Me, too, I work, but I also go out in the evenings; I keep myself informed; I don't shut myself up in my apartment as if in a convent. Grief is not a vocation."

"As to that, I'm not sure," Catherine responded one day.

Seven months, that's the same as seven days or seven years. They were in no hurry. Time had stood still because at every moment—or never—there could be a miracle, the discovery of the buried treasure. Three men—let's say three—to whom seven months, more or less ("Give me seven more months to reach the gallery," Pierre Sorel had pleaded), are one and the same thing; the gallery will be found. Poets, seekers, lovers, misers, meditators, dreamers, idiots. Also peasants. Monsieur Graff ("who competently manages the agricultural cooperative") is a peasant. Preoccupied with seeds, fertilizers, the weather, always too cold or too hot, too dry or too wet. The blessed year when a man can take a rest with the granaries full to the brim—that's always next year. The three men are simple folk. Georges Guimard is "agent for prefabricated hangars" (they exist and are quite ugly). He is a simple and kindhearted man but something of a drunkard, something of a spinner of yarns, who lives in the present and doesn't worry about the future. Then there is Pierre Sorel, the man who burrows underground at night. But this one is hard to figure out; he doesn't know who he is.

Three men who share the idea of a buried treasure. They are in no hurry.

They are in no hurry and haven't been since the beginning. The beginning lasted a long time: four or perhaps five years.

During those four or five years, they must have resembled almost any group of peasants, merchants, workingmen who come together on Saturday nights in any grocery and wineshop in the countryside.

This licensed grocery, this *épicerie-buvette* where our three men habitually meet, is the good, homely color of gingerbread. Balzac might have described it; Rembrandt might have painted it. A single window with small panes of violet-colored bubble glass looks out on the road that leads to Monsieur Graff's farm. The shadows behind the bar are flecked with faint glints, the golden light reflected on cans of peas and sardines. The exposed beams in the ceiling are brown; the counter, a reddish brown; the two tables beside the counter are of a more Venetian brown. A Tintoretto, broken up with lights. Card games are played under a modern hanging lamp. From time to time, a young girl, far too thin or far too fat, comes into the store to buy a package of Gauloise cigarettes or a pair of shoelaces.

The door opens with a faint tinkle, supplemented by the barking of a little black and white dog with the common name of Mirza, whose barking is worthy of a place more frequented. Guimard pats the dog as he enters. Monsieur Graff passes stiffly by; his jacket is too tight perhaps to allow him to bend down? He ignores Mirza, a typical *buvette* dog, hence a town dog, alien to a peasant. Pierre Sorel enters, carrying his gold-braided museum guard's cap in his left hand, extending his right to pat the dog, then pulls it back just in time. Had Mirza not been tethered to the counter, jumping and barking there, Sorel's hand would surely have been bitten. Georges Guimard guffaws.

Mirza. The marquesses of the eighteenth century, infatuated with anything Oriental, always called their lapdogs Mirza. Just as Médor was a novelistic hero. But if you asked Madame Bâton, the proprietress of the licensed grocery, why her dog was called Mirza, she would say, "Because that's a name for a dog."

She turns on the suspension lamp that is equipped with an all-too-weak light bulb. The three friends have ritually grumbled about that weak light, while really being quite fond of the penumbra. The massive armoire, the counter, and the tables, all waxed and polished to perfection, try their best to reflect the feeble illumination. Thus, the *épicerie-buvette* on Saturday nights resembles those English jigsaw puzzles that depict, in a ship's cabin, men with weathered faces, who have lit only one kerosine lamp and are smoking

44

up the atmosphere with their pipes, complicating the task of the patient jigsaw-puzzle player.

No doubt it was Georges Guimard who offered the first round of drinks. An agent. Yes, it is easy to imagine.

"Well now, Madame Jeanne," he says to Madame Bâton, the fat storekeeper, "won't you join us?"

She only shrugs. If it were anyone else but Monsieur Guimard, she would take offense. But he sometimes brings her a bottle of Calvados (a gift to him from a customer), or some eggs, or even a box of candy, which he presents while patting her bosom as one pats a cow.

"As much a beauty as ever, Madame Jeanne? Here's a little gift for the queen of storekeepers!"

The shrew (for she is one), limping on her enormous legs, a smidgen of a moustache on her large, pale face, unhealthy, unwashed, possessing some of the talents of a witch, an abortionist—she blushes self-consciously and twists a corner of her apron like a communal schoolchild.

"Oh, Monsieur Georges! You are *too* kind!"

Pretty phrases like that have penetrated the countryside with television, and if a television actress can say, "You are *too* kind!", there's no reason why Madame Jeanne Bâton, proprietress of a grocery and wineshop in Boissy-la-Forêt in Basse-Normandie (Manche), can't say it as well.

The three men spread out their papers on the table while Madame Bâton, at the counter, spreads out her tarot cards, studying them with such concentration and seriousness that any hint of mystery or doubt is definitely denied. Thus, the scientific spirit has filtered in everywhere, and the humblest clairvoyant would not dare to talk to you about a dark lady or a letter on the way without first invoking atomic radiation and the fusion of metals.

"When we're within fifteen meters, we must shore up," declares Monsieur Guimard with the gravity of a chief engineer.

45

"In the Rayat woods, there's some good timber for that," says Monsieur Graff.

"At eighteen meters, I excavate toward the right," states Sorel, whose self-consciousness has disappeared. "Horizontally. This will bring me under the main gallery in about seven months' time. Something may be found."

"Another round of Calvados, Madame Jeanne."

Guimard says this without raising his voice, for they all know that Madame Bâton, who has retired to the back room, is listening from behind the door and hears everything they say. They would be glad to invite her to sit down with them, but this would spoil her pleasure.

Another Calvados. This can be indulged in on Saturdays. Georges Guimard is tall and broad, very self-confident in his checked jacket (the checks rather too big), and comfortably installed in his fifties. He has the air of sitting for eternity when he sits down—jovial smile, shoulders slightly bowed, eighty kilos of flesh, attaché case full of prospectuses, with plenty of time on his hands, knowing everyone within a hundred kilometers—no farther, because it's not worth killing yourself.

Monsieur Graff, who has never been addressed by his Christian name, sits stiff and straight on his chair, as if enduring an appointment with the photographer. He, too, will always be the same, a thin little man, ageless in his jacket of shiny alpaca, cap always on his head, a front tooth missing.

Their conversation turns now to timber, to shoring up, to floor resistance, to stone. They drop phrases such as "according to my calculations" and "the ancients must have left by the river or maybe by the Pré-Coupé?", and Sorel says, "Even the etymology indicates—," and the others listen to him respectfully, for they do not know the meaning of that word "etymology." They are visionaries. But they look like realists.

"How many meters of rope do we still need?" asks Guimard, who is taking notes.

46

"Oh, I'll guarantee that timber," affirms Monsieur Graff. "It won't buckle like the other planks did."

They talk and act realistically, but Monsieur Graff firmly believes in the buried treasure, and Georges Guimard offers his apparatus at half price.

Later on, they are a little drunk as they part. Monsieur Graff lives close by. He will walk down the road slowly, looking up at the sky, not to estimate the weather, as people think peasants do, but reflecting on that treasure buried in the earth and on those men who in bygone times excavated there to hide the treasure, in this calm landscape, and thinking about himself and how he never stops for a minute in the week and takes glory in the fact ("On my feet or lying down, but never sitting," he says with the pride of a Spanish grandee). He stops at the entrance to his farm, listening to the sound of Guimard's car starting up, after which silence closes in.

Georges Guimard is the last to leave. Pierre Sorel has gone off on his motorized bicycle, having sold his car years ago. Georges has paid for the drinks.

"I've got to go now, Madame Jeanne," he says. "If I stay on, they'll all be jealous of me; they'll say, 'There he is, always hanging round Madame Bâton!' That's what they say about me in my district, as far off as Flers. And why not? We're both free, aren't we, Madame Jeanne?"

Of course he's joking, but with such a kind smile on his flushed face that she actually believes he's not joking all that much; and when he leaves, she will stand at the window, watching until his car is out of sight, her forehead pressed against the violet windowpanes, a pensive young girl, captive of a monster.

As Georges starts off, he sees in the distance ahead of him the red taillight of Sorel's bicycle.

"That crazy Pierre Sorel!" he comments aloud, with a smile that tries to be self-mocking. Four or five years have passed during which they have met on Saturdays, four or five years during which nothing has changed, during which "the treasure" has been more present in their minds than it will ever be in reality.

"I say!" says Gerry.
"What?"
"You're not listening! I might as well not tell you anything! You send me down to the Cotentin, and when I tell you about it, you don't listen!"
"As if the Cotentin mattered!" says Robert, annoyed.

FRIENDS

"Have you heard that Robert is writing a book?"

Bernard, in his office at the *Magazine des Arts*, was having an idle conversation with Jean-Francis Roy, who occasionally did some work for the Larousse publishers.

"Ah, yes, I've heard about it," said Jean-Francis. "It's a book about picturesque Auvergne, I believe!"

"Not at all!" Bernard spoke with assumed nonchalance in an effort to conceal his delight at being able to disclose some astounding news. "He's writing a novel!"

"A what?"

Jean-Francis was only slightly astounded. This tall, slender, blond young man with a rather handsome face, was the very picture of an esthete as imagined in 1910 by Romain Rolland and his readers. He played the flute, wrote poetry, wrote biographies of musicians, and like everyone else, did occasional broadcasts. He had very ethereal, very platonic love affairs that caused a lot of gossip. His manner was gentle, aloof but kindly, with occasional outbursts of spitefulness that were so brief they could be blamed on absentmindedness.

"A novel. Set in the age of the Templars," said Bernard, speaking calmly.

"Is his wife being unfaithful to him?" asked Jean-Francis with solicitude.

In the past, he had courted Catherine; and he still, from time to time, besieged the fortress.

The imperturbability of Jean-Francis was positively offensive; he seemed determined not to get excited over the news.

"His wife is faithful, his mistress is in good health, he doesn't have cancer of the throat, and he is writing a novel!"

"I would not have thought that of him," said Jean-Francis with moderate severity.

Their eyes met, and they began to laugh.

"Perhaps he needs the money," said Jean-Francis, trying to find a meliorating circumstance.

"No. With what he earns on his songs, he's not in great need."

"Fair enough!" said Jean-Francis.

Those songs, and Reine—it was all very funny, almost surrealistic, they agreed, and were rather flabbergasted. It proved that Robert had a sense of humor, an imagination. But after all these years, a novel!

"Essentially," said Jean-Francis, revising his values, "he's a failure."

"And perhaps he wants to prove the contrary?"

"Exactly. It's the proof. Too bad. He was happy, and so rarely do we find among us a happy man."

Bernard was inclined to take all this as a joke. All that talk about the Templars he considered simply preposterous. But Jean-Francis was determined to drag everything into the realm of melancholy, where he was at an advantage. A happy man so rarely found among us. The flight of time, the autumn of life—these had been his themes ever since he was twenty. A late-born romantic, with his talk about extinguished romances and disillusionment.

Bernard was at heart a dandy, with a tinge of fascism. His credo was: Be hard, be pure, and regardless of what happens, be well tailored. Jean-Francis, on the other hand, wore his

49

collar open—very becoming, this—and affected loose and shabby cardigans of first-quality cashmere. To each man his own style. For twenty years, people had referred to Jean-Francis as "a charming young man," just as they called Robert "a great guy." Nuance. Bernard took a rare delight in the fact that he could not be qualified by either one of those terms.

"And what about you?" he asked with false heartiness. He was suddenly very annoyed with Jean-Francis, who had refused to play the game and thus left him with a whole series of unused, exquisitely witty remarks on the Templars. "What about you? Are you writing?"

"I don't see the connection," said Jean-Francis in absolute fury. He had flushed like a schoolboy suspected of sucking up to a professor.

"After all," said Bernard, enjoying the effect his words had had, "Robert isn't devoid of talent, and so, who knows, he may pull if off. I admire him for having the courage to risk being ridiculed. Not everyone can do that."

He kept on in this vein until Jean-Francis could stand it no longer and left the office.

That's what comes, fumed Jean-Francis, from having a reputation for kindness! It leaves one defenseless, disarmed, which isn't a paying proposition! After all, Bernard went too far. A childhood friend! They had known each other all their lives, each one secretly judging himself to be the superior, without ever having a showdown. And now, on account of that crazy idea of Robert's—And how unfair to use Robert against him and him against Robert! Bernard was like that. The worst of it was that he, Jean-Francis, was more furious with Robert than with anyone else. For how ridiculous of Robert to play at being a real writer at this late date!

VIVI TELEPHONES AGAIN

Once more, Vivi telephoned at an early hour: eight o'clock in the morning.

"Did I wake you?" she asked in a tone of feigned apology.

She knew very well that on Tuesdays Catherine had no classes and so *might have been* asleep at that hour.

"No, but I was in my bath," said Catherine with some satisfaction, for she knew what would follow.

"Listen, I'm terribly upset about Manuel. He missed Robert the other day, and he really does have a problem. Just imagine—No, it would take too long; I won't go into it. Could you call Robert to the phone?"

"Robert has gone out," said Catherine.

"What? This early?"

"His book," said Catherine soberly.

"What book?"

Vivi was horrified. To her way of thinking, Robert should always be on tap.

"The book he talked about the other night, when you and Mamma came to dinner."

"Oh! Then it's serious?"

"For you, perhaps not. For him, yes."

She knew she was triumphing prematurely, that it would backfire, but she could not resist the temptation.

"But don't worry," she went on, "I'll tell Robert to telephone you or Manuel as soon as he can."

"That's right. But don't forget."

Vivi sounded as if she had lost all hope.

Putting down the receiver, Catherine returned to the bathroom resolved to continue her bath undisturbed. But the water had cooled, and already she was remorseful, knowing full well that she would telephone Vivi within the hour.

Poor Vivi! Once so pretty, but now, in her forties, just a faded blonde, thin and nervous. Some days she looked ten years older than her age. Hyperactive, always determinedly in the vanguard of some kind of movement. She regularly reported on fashions for a newspaper—oddly enough, considering the way she dressed. Her divorce did not seem to cause her any suffering. But then, as Catherine and their mother said, echoing each other, "After all, Vivi has Robert."

Catherine could have been really fond of Vivi, who was at heart good as gold, had it not been for the fact that Vivi represented to her the very incarnation of the injustice that caused her perpetual grief. It had begun in their childhood when Germaine had shown a definite preference for Vivi, her elder daughter. Strangely enough, since no two women could be more unlike. Germaine, with her charities, her pious widowhood, her half-mourning clothes, her economical recipes; and Vivi with her countless love affairs, her futile occupations, her canary-yellow ponchos, her miniskirts, her scatterbrained cultural activities. But Germaine saw other qualities in Vivi. She remembered that day when Vivi had an inflammation that disfigured her, causing her such pain that her whole face was distorted; this, however, had not kept her home from an op art exhibition in Boulogne—or was it a happening in Nanterre? She had attended it, regardless. And Germaine had said, "Even though I don't always see eye to eye with Evelyn, I must concede that she has great courage." And Germaine was not mistaken. Any woman who will go out on a cold February night, regardless of pain, and attend an exhibition in Boulogne-Billancourt, miles away, is a person with principles. Even though, instead of visiting the hovels occupied by the wretchedly poor Portuguese who live in that neighborhood, she had attended an exhibition for the benefit of New Zealand sculpture. Germaine had remarked on this with a hint of scandalized admiration: "Vivi is the woman of today. She has her own perspective."

Catherine didn't have a perspective; all she had was a grief. And giving way to grief shows a lack of self-control, a lack of principles. At least so Germaine thought. Anyway, Vivi had stacks of friends who left her bathroom in a frightful mess; her children adored her in spite of the crazy way she'd brought them up. Marina at thirteen was already wearing eye shadow and going about in shorts, while Manuel was taking a course in sculpture and, at the same time, classes in Spanish dancing! And Vivi constantly dragged her sister along with her to lectures on health foods or tried to persuade her to take lessons in tap dancing. Vivi imagines she is only eighteen, Catherine told herself, and she's ridiculous. She follows diets to reduce or put on weight; she borrows money from Robert; she isn't even intelligent—Oh, Vivi, I adore you!

Catherine left the bathroom and phoned her sister back.

"She's not at home? She's at the School for Oriental Studies?"

Marina had taken the call and was speaking with that impeccable diction she had adopted when she decided to have a theatrical career.

Vivi had gone to a lecture on Zeno. Catherine didn't know who Zeno was. Well, that was Vivi! Presumably worried to death at eight in the morning, and half an hour later, Zeno! It really wasn't worth while to be nice to her.

PHOTOGRAPHS

Gerry spread out his photographs on the carpeted floor of Robert's study and threw down his gear. Robert was too fond of him to object, but he really found the boy irresponsible.

"So you're letting me down?" asked Gerry.

"After all," said Catherine, "you're old enough to develop your subject all by yourself."

"Yes, I know. But when I first told you about it, Robert, you were interested. So if you told the story, you who know how to write a story, why wouldn't it interest readers?"

Exactly because it would be me, Robert reflected. A writer. Because I can't work up an interest except through Gerry, by a kind of trickery. Through Gerry's sincere interest and through his ignorance and lack of culture. Because in order to find a story marvelous and astounding that Gerry finds marvelous and astounding, I am obliged to stuff it with double meanings, with implications, must say that this story is not a story but a lot more or a lot less; because I know a lot less or a lot more about it, too much to be simple and straight-forward; because journalists are the ones who can still write stories that dumbfound and amaze their readers—

"Because I want to speak to those I love (since one doesn't write without loving) and I have forgotten the language to do so. My impotence is such that I can now write nothing but jingles like '*Ah, mon chou, mon loup, mon petit lapin-in-in.*' Onomatopoeias."

"It's better than nothing," said Gerry.

An ironic smile flickered on Catherine's face but was quickly suppressed.

"Yes," said Robert, speaking for himself and against the convictions of Catherine and his friends, against everybody, "it's better than nothing."

Catherine intervened, adopting the manner of "let's talk about serious things."

"Robert, I've been looking at your engagement book, and next week is almost free. You could take the opportunity of paying a visit down there."

"Down there? You mean the Cotentin?"

Catherine laughed aloud.

"Gerry, just look at him! You'd think I had suggested a trip to the North Pole!"

"My mother," said Robert, "had a friend who told her, 'I've never in my life gone beyond this fifteenth arrondisse-ment here in Paris—Oh, yes, I did once go to the seventeenth arrondissement on a vacation.'"

"Precisely!" Gerry exclaimed, stammering as he always did when seized with enthusiasm. "It's because you know Paris so well, the different arrondissements and so on, that you could help me on another idea. What's to prevent me from doing—me, too—an album of Paris scenes? I've already talked about it with Bernac—"

Robert immediately saw the connection this had with Gerry's current romance with Carol. And also what that "me, too" meant. It connected with Vaneck, another photographer and suitor of Carol, who said his photos had "texture."

"—and I've never before asked a favor of him. When I suggested a Paris album, he said, 'Okay, but your photos lack unity. Talk it over with Robert Guibal; get him to do the captions and a preface.' See, Robert, it would be a book about all the old neighborhoods of Paris, the crafts of olden times that still exist. I've actually found a blacksmith, an extraordinary old fellow, and a woman who keeps a cow right there in the Saint Antoine section. What do you say to that? And the furriers in the Temple district, I've some wonderful shots of them, and I've used no more than half of them in articles. Now, this is really in your line, isn't it? Of course, it's not a book for *Vogue*, but all the same it would make a good impression."

The photographer-suitor of Carol, Vaneck, whose photos had "texture," worked for *Vogue*. Mentally, Robert implored Dr. Coué to come to his aid and repeated to himself that all this did not in any way concern him. But in spite of himself, he was rather touched by Gerry's perseverance in his efforts to win Carol, who was so insignificant (except to Gerry) that she could be easily confused with the girls who had preceded her in Gerry's heart—with Daisy, Samantha, and Tweeny. His Lady, his Queen of Hearts. Robert sighed, thinking of Catherine, who had once been something like that to him. The dream that had appeared inaccessible, the thrill of dancing attendance on that Lady, the hope of doing big things for her sake, the determination to rival—no matter how redoubtable—an adversary.

"I'd be glad to," he said mechanically, "but do you really think such an album would please *her*?"

Gerry flushed bright red, embarrassed at having been seen through.

"Oh, there's a chance it would. She is very sensitive to— She loves art. And for you to collaborate with me, that would give me prestige in her eyes. Carol is very cultivated, you know. She's read your books, heard your broadcasts. And if she felt you were taking a real interest in what I'm doing—"

"But wouldn't it be enough just to tell her so?"

Robert and Catherine asked the question almost simultaneously. And Catherine added: "Robert really hasn't the time—"

"Oh, all right," muttered Gerry unhappily, "you could always tell her so, of course. But since she knows we are pals, it wouldn't have the same effect."

"You can still show me your little furriers."

Robert was weakening in his struggle against the new temptation, well knowing that if he wanted to write that book (but did he really?), he must cling to Dr. Coué and declare that writing a preface for Gerry's album was no concern of his. And yet it did concern him; any fight humble people waged against big enterprises, any effort they made to preserve the secrets of their craft, the pride in their handiwork, the pleasure taken in old-fashioned techniques did concern him. "It's handmade," they tell you proudly. But no one in the world cares a jot, my good woman, whether your buttonholes are made by hand and that you get up at dawn to go all the way to Rungis to buy your vegetables because you've vowed never to eat frozen foods. Who has time nowadays to make or tell the difference between a handmade buttonhole and a plastic welding? Or between a cabbage or artichoke grown with manure and one grown with chemicals? That was what must be pointed up, the prevalent derision of minutiae, that struggle of a minority worthy of medieval times, when heroic and absurd sects struggled over an article of the Credo. "Until I'm bankrupt or dead, I'll continue to do my cooking in butter." That is what the innkeeper of the Chien qui Fume said. A rather reactionary viewpoint, but the comic and pathetic side of it could be found in Gerry's photos.

"Yes, it's interesting, but you know I've already so much to do—"

Gerry's eyes were imploring. Catherine's silence was heavy with a forthcoming reproach.

"But I'll not say it's impossible; no, it's not impossible."

"Oh, how kind you are! What a good sport!" Gerry was electrified. "And if you could have dinner with her one of these evenings, and if Carol could see that we're working on it together—"

Catherine stood up and quietly left the room.

"Very well, Gerry, bring her to Reine's Tuesday or Wednesday, and we'll arrange something or other."

Gerry was suddenly embarrassed.

"Listen, I hate to say this to you, but—Reine—Couldn't we do something here, instead? Because Carol, you see, is— She's from a very good family."

CATHERINE NAKED

"That poor boy Gerry," said Robert, taking off his jacket, "it's pathetic to see how attached he is to that girl who is utterly devoid of interest."

Catherine made no reply as she crossed the room, naked, toward the bathroom.

Why was it that her movements were so out of harmony with her body? She had a pretty little body, every detail of it including her pretty little hands and feet, still with some baby fat noticeable in her slightly swollen ankles and wrists, but even this constituted a charm. Besides, there was so much of the infantile in her, more infantile than feminine. The way she put her feet down flat on the parquet, her complete lack of embarrassment at appearing naked before him. And then, all of a sudden, that stiff and ugly movement of the rounded hip, the plump arm, as she bent to retrieve the scandal that had slipped off. One felt like crying out, "Be careful, you're going to hurt yourself!" Because those movements of the arms and legs seemed so unnatural!

Nudity as a theme, a symbol. The sixteenth-century Adamites dashed out into the streets of Amsterdam naked, in frightfully cold weather, as a manifestation of something or other—desire for purity and truth, revolt against society? Those who did not die of pneumonia died in prison. Then, too, there were the Turlupins in France, about 1371 if I'm not mistaken. They were burnt at the stake on the Place de Grève for having wanted to live "like wolves"—and hence the name. People thought in vivid images at that time, and when they said, "I'll put my hand in the fire," the fire was there, ready for the hand.

Unconsciously, Catherine belongs to those epochs, Robert reflected. Her nudity was devoid of erotic intention. She is making a statement of the mutual confidence that should prevail between a man and wife, the truth in which she wants to live with her husband, and the impossibility of attaining this ambition. And so her nudity is both graceful and disgraceful, natural and constrained, troubling and stultifying.

Catherine returned, wearing a pajama top, and went to bed. Her silence was eloquent. (I'm not sulking, not at all; but talk to him I cannot, cannot. My throat goes dry; I want to vomit. Anyone, anyone at all can ask him to do no matter what and—Anyone, except me.)

As for him, he was wondering why she so fervently wanted him to write that book: Might this not be the cause of the mental paralysis that at times overcame him? At times? For seven years! It was almost a castration. She was all too typical of the ideal wife of a writer, who faultlessly "believes in him," who "encourages him in his work," and "shields him from tiresome people and demands." Articles on the subject frequently appeared in the magazines, interviews with the wife of a surgeon or of an orchestra conductor, "efficacious but effaced." Well, but supposing those men refuse to collaborate? Supposing they would prefer not to have that "obscure but indispensable collaborator" when she has become transformed into a statue of Reproach, accusingly pointing a finger at the scalpel or the baton?

He had not always felt like this, however. She had been, mind and body, infinitely precious to him. He had called her by sweet and silly names: Princess, my Little Clinging Vine —She had been an inspiration, a presence, a figure of flame brandishing a banner, an exaltation, an epic power. She had been his reward for triumphing over a difficult past, his hard years of study, the butt of the good-natured jests of his stepfather, his alcoholic mother, his acquaintances at the Café des Amis; she had been the very image of his prizewinning book, had been the crowning—

"Catherine?"

"What?"

Her teeth were set; her delicate jaw was taut with the effort to speak naturally.

"Aren't you feeling well?"

"Oh, no, I'm quite all right." (Must not lose self-control, must not scream, must not shed tears. And already her tears were welling up.) "Are you going to do that book for Gerry?"

"Oh, it's not a book! At the most, a few captions."

"A few captions and a preface. And you still have to finish that article on picturesque Auvergne."

"You exaggerate. The Auvergne thing is only fifty or so pages. And I can't let Gerry down. If I don't do that small amount of text for him, Bernac won't accept his album."

"So what?"

"You saw how set he is on doing it, for Carol."

"But," and now she was unable to keep her voice from rising, "what does it matter to you whether Carol is pleased or not? You're behaving like a matchmaker, yet you know perfectly well that Carol is a little idiot and a snob to boot and that if ever she decides to settle down with Gerry, their marriage will be a disaster for him. And you pretend to be his friend! Yet, you're steering him straight toward ruin!"

He knew very well that Gerry and Carol were completely beside the point.

"What can one know about the happiness of others?" He sighed, even while falling in with her argument. "To him, Carol is his dream come true. And he will be just as unhappy if he doesn't realize that dream."

"And you? What will happen if you don't write your book?"

Ah, now, here we go.

"Oh, as to my book—" Involuntarily, he exaggerated his detachment.

"So you've given the whole thing up? And only a fortnight ago, in front of Mamma and Vivi, you were pontificating"— the word slipped out, and she regretted it immediately— "about it!"

"By the way, hasn't Vivi telephoned?"

"Yes, she's telephoned. And so has Father Moinaud. And so have countless others that you can't let drop, people who consume your time and energies. It's easy to tell yourself you're kind because you lack the courage to say no. At this rate, you might as well set yourself up in the street with a desk and a placard Public Writer. At least you'd be paid for your services."

He had observed her as she got into bed, such a little thing in her rose-colored pajama top, her thick black hair in a braid, her clear, smooth skin freshly bathed. No one would guess she was thirty, with a complexion as fresh as that.

"I wish I could have given you a more interesting life," he said hypocritically, for he knew that wasn't what she wanted.

"But I don't care a fig for 'a more interesting life'!" she said in despair. "You've made money during the last few years. And with what!" (She paused, and they both recalled his most popular song, which Manuel liked so much: *"Ah, mon chou, mon loup. . . ."*) "But that," she went on, "doesn't prevent you from being a—" She stopped short, afraid of what she might say.

He hung his jacket on the back of a chair and sat down to take off his shoes.

"A failure," he said. "I know what you think."

But was it his fault that she was an anachronism, a survivor of an ancient Christian civilization, a woman made for love? Was it his fault that he was incapable of playing the role she wanted him to play, that of the self-confident male who would have given her life a meaning and would have explained the world to her? He knew she would forgive him everything if he could do that. Everything—his rather excessive drinking, his writing those nightclub songs, his making love to Reine. She might have adopted the traditional attitude of "men are like that," the attitude taken by her mother, and been confident that "essentially, he loves me." He had rejected the convention of monogamy, as he had rejected the convention of the novel. Instead of becoming the traditional husband (even an unfaithful one) and a respected writer of novels (even mediocre ones), he had left her free as air; he had turned his back on his early writings, had transformed himself into a journalist who wrote articles on any subject whatsoever and who kindly lent his aid to all those parasites. And in not divorcing her and having no intention of divorcing her to marry Reine, he had deprived his infidelity of any meaning.

"My dear," he said softly, in an effort to reconcile all these discrepancies in himself and in her, "if only you could accept me as I am!"

"But what exactly are you?" (Her voice was shrill, out of control. I'm behaving like a shrew, she reflected. Yet, I love him, and by nature I am sweet and gentle. All that's needed is for him to take me in his arms. Yet, she was doing everything in her power to prevent this.) "You're the one who's decided that you're incapable of doing what you should do! How can you know whether you can write that book if you don't even try? It was a good subject. In any case, it was original."

"That's not what you said when I discussed it with your mother and Vivi."

"Because I was sure you'd let it drop."

"If you were sure of it then, why are you reproaching me now?"

What childish disputes! He had never had such disputes with Reine, although he had less in common with her than with Catherine. But the absence of common interests did not bother either him or Reine. What a restful existence was Reine's! Now, if she had told him in her ponderous and slightly ridiculously sententious way, "I think you should write that book," he might have written it. But he knew he would never be able to make Reine understand why he wanted to write that book. He could not say to her, "That's an interesting subject," or "Such a book should make its way, don't you think?" It would have to be Gerry who could talk to Reine about the buried treasure. Maybe it would take a Gerry to love Reine, really. He himself could only love her, one might say, superficially. Yet, the one he would have chosen to love, if he could have chosen, was Reine. However, the one he had chosen and the one he loved, bitterly and badly, and the one he avoided out of love for her, was Catherine.

"Suppose we try to sleep? There's no end of things I must do tomorrow."

"Such as take the twins to the Jardin des Plantes?" she said acidly. "Or do the rewrite for Laffont?" (But why am I tautning him? By nature I'm gentle and sweet.)

As if he understood her thoughts better than her still-irritated tone, he took her hand under the sheet after she had turned off the bedside lamp. "It's better than nothing," as Gerry would say. "It's still better than nothing!"

"WE'RE NOT SAVAGES," SAID ADRIENNE

She had been that body and that face so intimately precious, that impulse and promise, that figure of a woman brandishing a banner, that figure of flame, that epic figure of exaltation. A fine marriage.

A fine marriage for a farm laborer. Monsieur and Madame Graff had practically guaranteed this marriage of young Pierre Sorel. They were proud of their good action in having practically raised this young man as their own child. "And he has given nothing but satisfaction," they said. They guaranteed him to his future father-in-law as they would have guaranteed a calf. Nothing derogatory in the comparison, for a calf is a serious matter. There was no mother-in-law; she had died. That was one advantage. And Pierre Sorel's life was a dream. With a beautiful creature for a wife, a flourishing business in her family, who owned a bistro and the only garage in Boissy, social status. Such things are not to be refused.

The astonishing thing, mind you, is the fact that all this had come about quite naturally. To be a bastard, the child of a servant girl, consigned as an infant to an orphanage—this places you in an undoubted position of inferiority with those peasants so established in a locality that they can show you where their great-grandfather, on his way back from the fields, had always halted for a while, a halting place that has become traditional, or can show you where their father, returning home from a drinking bout, was struck down by a heart attack in the corner of a field known as the Fosse aux Loups, although in the memory of man neiother pit nor wolves had ever been seen there. Yes, it's a position of inferiority to be a bastard in such a community. And also a mystery. "We'll never know where he comes from." He had overheard that remark, pronounced without spiteful intent. But taken literally, those words, "We'll never know where he comes from," provide a text on which to meditate.

But, returning to Pierre Sorel's marriage. In its modest

way and in its narrow frame, a village in the Cotentin where for a few more years there's a place for everything and everything in its place, that marriage represented a reparation, a *recognition*.

They had met in the Gué-des-Grues dance hall, where Adrienne had *recognized* him. As, in old-fashioned novels, the noble countess *recognizes*, by a certain sign, the foundling abandoned on the church steps. He would always remember her words when he had, very self-consciously, invited her to dance with him. You see, there are girls who will refuse to dance with a common farmhand.

"With pleasure," she had laughed. "I've always liked red-headed men!"

So his red hair, which was a joking matter in the Graff household (where little Jeanne Graff always shouted, "Fire! Call the fire department!", when she saw him coming), had been the sign of *recognition*. And Adrienne, a handsome girl, pink and plump, was the instrument of change in his destiny, a change he had vaguely expected on account of the mystery of his birth, his red hair, and his strange habit of reading books, not "to better himself," as Jean-Claude did, but merely for pleasure. Monsieur Graff considered it an inoffensive habit but a little foolish in a man.

An unequal marriage, this was the opinion of the Graffs, who still cherished ideas of former times; for Pierre it was a princely marriage but in a certain way not unexpected by him, for he had always thought something would happen to elevate him in the eyes of all, and then—It was this "and then" that he expected when he thought about it as he stood in front of the church in Flers, with Adrienne rose-crowned at his side, his shirt collar far too tight, as the photographer grouped the wedding party. But the "and then" had not come to pass. We no longer live in medieval times, people said, and they soon had the proof. You could not say that the father-in-law made Pierre "feel his position" and that when he had to do something to be worthy of his good fortune, he had to "prove himself" and show he deserved it. But the father-in-law's attitude was evident when he would say, for example, "Give me a hand, Pierre, with the bottles," or when Adrienne, ravishing in her nylon negligee, remarked, "We ought to buy a color television, don't you think?"

Well! Was it that easy, that natural?

He revolted against his good fortune. For nothing came to pass as he had expected. Should they enlarge the bistro? Buy an expensive car? Adrienne's father was a hard drinker; he would have a heart attack like old Guimard, like young Sainfouin, like everybody, and then Pierre would inherit.

Sometimes Adrienne said the word "Paris," and after all, the life people led down here was hard; perhaps they could ask Cousin Fernand to take care of the bistro during their absence, for the old man, Adrienne's father, couldn't be trusted any more. And so, the old king dethroned, off went Pierre and his dream girl Adrienne, she with her checkbook in her handbag, to explore from top to bottom that big department store in Paris, the Galeries Lafayette. And thus Pierre had shed his misfortune but had gained—what? The Galeries Lafayette! Ridiculous. There were, of course, the children, Frédéric and Génie. Born in the hospital and raised in an atmosphere of rosewood and beeswax. He was very fond of them, but, well, he was the one now who had the vague feeling of having married beneath him. They were respectable little people with respectable birth certificates.

In the long run, it was the fault of Monsieur Graff, of the isolation of the Graff farm. Pierre had been brought up to think that being a bastard was a great misfortune, that it classed him with the underworld. But once he ad got out into the world, where conditions were not as they were thought to be in the old-Christian mind of Monsieur Graff, he had seen that the curse was at the very most an inconvenience which money soon effaced; and he experienced the disenchantment of a person who had thought he was stricken with a fatal disease and acted accordingly, only to find that he has caught a bad case of the flu. He is ridiculous.

It disconcerted him to be addressed as "Monsieur Sorel"

—there was something gross about it—like Monsieur Guimard, or Monsieur Félix, his father-in-law. Without reproba-
tion, but also without particular esteem. Neither misfortune
nor miracle. No recognition, no peculiar sign marking the
forehead of the predestined. And if they still called him behind his back, "Sorel? Ah, yes, the redhead," it was because
the new butcher in town, who was from Lorraine, had the
name Saurel—to distinguish between them. It cramped his
style, even in bed with Adrienne, pink as a rose, with her
curly black hair, so pretty you'd think it was a permanent, in
her nylon lace and with the transistor music turned low; all
this was his dream in bygone times, the princess, the good
fairy to whom love lent an exceptional lucidity, a double
vision, allowing her to distinguish in the humble farmhand
the stranger, the unknown person, something that set him
apart and made him worthy of her. And in those first days
(her arms, her legs), lovemaking had been like a coronation.
He was the one, the unique and solitary man, he, Pierrot, that
she called for, whose kisses she wanted, the one she recognized. And now, in the main square of Boissy, when the
indifferent plumber tipped his cap ("Is that boiler working all
right, Monsieur Sorel?"), he told himself that had he not been
there, she'd have married Jean-Claude, the elder son of the
Graffs. And the love of Jean-Claude's putative wife was no
longer of interest. In the early days, he had sometimes said
to her, "Me, I never knew my parents," or "Me, without a
family." But Adrienne, thinking to solace him, always said,
"Whoever thinks about that, my Pierrot? We're not savages."

He would have liked to live among savages, endure
their tests, triumph over their enemies. He had no enemies.
Only Monsieur Graff was a savage who admonished his
wife: "You must not make him feel that he's not like the
others." Or when he, Pierre, committed a blunder: "It's not
surprising, when we consider his misfortune."

Yes, he would like to live among the savages.

Manuel was rather homely. Short and stocky, flat-nosed, with his big, dark, rolling eyes and thick lips, he made you think of a frog or the cliché Negro of advertisements or of a coffee planter. His ugliness gave him a mature aspect until he laughed; then you could see he was still a boy and suddenly good-looking. A serious boy. He was not brilliant in his studies but got passing grades, for he was something of a grind. He dressed with extreme care in well-cut suits, clean shirts; but his rather loud ties, usually a shiny mauve and brown, betrayed his mixed blood. It would surprise no one to see a diamond ring on his little finger and a pearl stickpin in his tie. (To get the picture, see Valéry Larbaud's description of Creoles in his *Fermina Marquez.*) He was lovable; you wanted to hug him. He was perhaps the only adolescent in France that could still be asked if it was true that Corneille depicts men as they should be, while Racine depicts them as they are.

Manuel expressed himself with distinction, as did his sister Marina—she, fair-haired, slender, and languid. Did they want to point up the fact, children as they were of a mother they adored but who was a little off her rocker, that they were obliged to act like adults?

"Excuse me for having pestered you," said Manuel, when barely seated in front of his glass of beer. "But my situation is rather delicate."

To mark the importance of the occasion, Manuel had added a pocket handkerchief to match his tie, which was of green moiré silk. His suit was brown corduroy.

"Béchir is my best friend," Manuel went on. "You know, he's the one who lent me his Mobylette, since Mamma disapproves."

The argument over that motorized bicycle was familiar to Robert, for it had lasted for two years.

"Well, since I couldn't go to the cinema with him, he

asked if he could take Marina, and I gave him permission."

As head of the family, Manuel liked to play the part of the protective male, and Marina accepted her role as protected female, not without some irony.

"And then, when they came home, Mamma and I were not there, and Béchir—Of course, Marina resisted him."

Marina, as beautiful as Manuel was ugly, looked sixteen, two years older than her real age, with the face of a madonna and incredible violet-blue eyes. But her fine, pale skin, the color of ivory, and her nervous temperament led to the fear that, like her mother, she might lose her good looks early. And sometimes she seemed to have a melancholy premonition of this.

"She resisted him, but the worst of it is that Béchir told all the boys at the lycée that he 'had made her.' "

Manuel pronounced the last three words within quotes, disgustedly. Manuel said "friend," not "pal," "cinema," not "movies," and "Mobylette," not "Mob." This had given him his reputation of being a sissy, which aggravated things.

"Because, you see, if I don't bash his face in, they will say I'm scared or that I'm a sissy or that I'm a pederast. And also, at the lycée, many of the boys will seize on any excuse to pounce on a North African, and if I fight Béchir, who is a North African, as you know, it will look as if I'm behaving like them."

This methodical account of his mental conflict, à la Corneille, was typical of Manuel. Through it could be seen the good pupil who made his plans and listed his tasks, carefully writing out his homework.

"What about Marina? What does she say?"

"She says to let it drop, that she's above such things. But in my class—"

"And what does your mother say?"

Vivi, violently opposed to violence, thought he should not worry about what people said.

"Now, mind you, I understand Mamma," said Manuel.

68

"She has a right to her own opinion. I don't set myself up as a judge. But she doesn't realize how very different the situation is for me. The boys at school see the whole thing in a very simplistic way. Either you are for or against the North Africans and the Jews. Marc—you know, he's the football player —told me, 'You must avenge your sister.' But Marc's father was in the OAS during the Algerian troubles. And in spite of everything, that has left its mark on him."

Manuel had had a pretty soprano voice, but it had broken a few months before this, and although the low notes had not yet come, his voice now ranged from a shrill tone to the hoarseness of an old boozer, much to his embarrassment. But this did not make his problem any the less urgent.

"You must find out," said Robert, "what Béchir himself thinks. That is, if you don't bash in his face, will he find that quite natural? What will he himself do?"

Manuel appreciated the question, for it proved that his uncle was really concerned with his problem and did not consider himself an incarnation of wisdom.

"Oh, he'll fight. You see, the North Africans have ideas like that. In spite of everything, they're different from us."

Manuel sipped his beer, his big eyes staring at the marble tabletop. Then he raised his frank gaze toward his uncle.

"No matter what happens," he said evenly, "our friendship is shattered."

It was rather painful to see Manuel so resigned.

"I believe," said Robert, "that you can't avoid fighting him. But after the fight, maybe you could show in some friendly way or other that you fought on principle, that you don't hold a grudge. Maybe you could invite him to the movies or treat him to a beer."

Manuel's face lit up.

"Oh, yes, that's a good idea. But I must win the fight. If I'm beaten, then I could not—"

"Obviously, that's indispensable. But if you tell yourself that you're fighting to preserve your friendship, you'll have fewer scruples and will fight all the harder."

Manuel chuckled, his boyish face wrinkled up with satisfaction.

"Do you know what I'm going to do? I've got a friend in the club who is good at judo. I've a notion to ask him for some instruction. And tomorrow, at recess, someone will get a surprise!"

"That's a very good idea," said Robert.

He was delighted with Manuel and was sorry to see him stand up to go.

"I think I'll see the judo expert right away. Since it's Thursday and no classes today. Do you happen to know judo?"

"No."

"Too bad. You see, we may all of us need to defend ourselves one day."

"There's little likelihood that I'll ever again have to fight," said Robert.

Manuel surveyed him appraisingly.

"Of course you're too old for a war, if we had one. But suppose someone assaulted your wife; then you'd be obliged to—"

"Oh, my goodness, that sort of thing doesn't ever happen in the literary world."

Next day Manuel telephoned. He was triumphant. Béchir had been vanquished and had taken his defeat nobly—along with two raspberry milk shakes as compensation. Marina had forgiven him. The three of them had gone to the movies together.

"That's the way Roland married the lovely Aude," said Robert, much relieved.

"Victor Hugo," said Manuel.

WRITERS AND RUFFIANS

Victor Hugo. Everyone knows him by heart. "Thus it was that Aymeri captured the town." Hernani, Waterloo, Cosette. Rewriting Hugo is not what is required, of course. But strong passions still exist, and good stories. Surely good writers must still exist, somewhere, writers different from all those gentlemen, professors or critics, intelligent and polite but a little too ostensibly the high priests of an obsolete religion, all the more rigorous in their judgments because the religion is obsolete. Those nice gentlemen who keep an eye on the promotion list, those theoreticians who are, granted, quite well informed, have decided that one *cannot* write any more on this or that subject; and those young cadres who have taken charge of everything—politics, economics, sociology, and psychiatry—they are quite intelligent and serious, often full of good intentions and sincerity, but, dear Lord, what a nuisance they are!

Sincere. They are often very sincere. With Jansenist austerity, they take account of their defects, their frustrations, their warts. With nothing of Tartuffe in them but with something of Vadius, Molière's pedant. And when they relax with open collar, hairy chest, a glass of liquor in hand, it is done with such affectation (granted, the effort is praiseworthy) that one feels sorry for them. There are some drunken bouts called "political actions" that are more meritorious than funny.

Essentially, writers and ruffians have always followed the same course. Good-bye to the Bonnot and Borsalino gangs with their submachine guns and fast cars! Mandrin* consults the public opinion polls. Villon is paying his social security and goes in for real estate. Nothing to be ashamed of in this, is there?

That's why I prefer jugglers, conjurers, and acrobats to

---

*Mandrin was a famous French bandit of the eighteenth century. He was executed in 1724 by being broken on the wheel.

the high priests' writers and the poets with their unnumbered sheets of glazed paper. The sideshow performers' work is more modest but more dangerous, more gratuitous. If the writer cheats or misses his aim, he can, if he knows the ropes, disssimulate, cover up his mistakes. But the acrobat or the juggler cannot; man or object crashes to the floor. It's either an accident or a miracle with him. For the writer, there are no longer accidents or miracles.

This is the moral Robert draws from this meditation. He lays down his pen with a sigh. He doesn't at all feel that he has the soul of a juggler.

A TREASURE

When Pierre Sorel was a child, the parish priest and the schoolmaster had charitably hoped to make him one of those great men of the democratic pantheon who, beginning with nothing, end up president of the republic or member of the Academy. Prestige of the foundling! Pierre responded very badly to their expectations. From year to year, "he could have done better" and did not seem to mind it.

"After all," said the priest with a sigh, "he's a good child."

"Alas!" said the schoolmaster, who had read Rimbaud.

Whether or not the Templars had ever sojourned in Boissy, whether or not Gilles de Rais, a century later, had searched for that famous treasure (this is questionable) has not been proven. This mattered very little to Pierre Sorel. For the moment, the hypothesis was enough, just as he had been satisfied at the age of ten with agate marbles, peacock feathers, a clump of rhododendron bushes. Those things had then played the part of a buried treasure.

Just as his grades at school had mattered little to him, now the money that Adrienne told him was "so easy to make" was of little importance. A treasure isn't money. It is luck, the unforeseen, the unexpected. Had Pierre Sorel thought about it, he would almost have said that treasure represented to him magic, poetry, and even, in the theological sense, grace. But he didn't think about it, and those words were not in his vocabulary. He merely thought, There must be a treasure buried under the château, and that one day he would excavate there to find out.

THE PASSIONS

A professor of French literature in the tenth grade at the lycée in Chartres is inevitably led to speak of the passions: *Phèdre, Le Cid*, etcetera. Catherine's pupils were fortunately headed toward careers in technology, and since literature was not given a very high place in their curriculum, they decently and courteously took little interest in Roxane and Bajazet. Catherine could not alter the programs, but her cool and clever analyses let her listeners understand that she did not require any effort of them beyond this polite half-attention. "Julien Gracq has written," she would say, "a very good preface to an edition of *Bajazet*, and in fact the taste for excesses among some surrealists explains. . . ."

They took notes. They didn't care a damn about Bajazet, all that bloodshed, or about Roxane's cruel love. "Come, see her expire" left them absolutely cold. And Catherine thought, So much the better. They would simply smile at "Yes, Prince, I long, I burn for Theseus," had not a precocious sense of social proprieties kept them from it. Even technologists respect the French classics. It's a ritual, like washing the hands before dinner, and it commits you to nothing at all. So much the better, thought Catherine, and tears welled in her eyes.

But she hated it when Manuel, who believed in books, said, "There's a lot of incredible exaggeration in *An-*

dromaque, isn't there, Aunt Catherine?"

"Oh, you think so?" she said wrathfully, and she left him to go off to her bedroom, her eyes still glittering.

"You shouldn't have said that," said Marina sagely. She considered herself an authority in matters concerning the heart.

Manuel was terribly sorry. Not that he was all that fond of Aunt Catherine, whom he considered "superior," but he was flattered to have for an aunt a Phèdre or a Bérénice.

MÉLUSINE II

"Oh, Monsieur Guibal! What an unforeseen encounter! You know, sometimes I am as if guided—"

From the terrace of the Petit Cluny, a quiet little café on the boulevard Saint-Michel, he had seen her coming across the street, draped in a loosely crocheted mauve and black shawl, teetering on her high-heeled buttoned shoes. Her slender silhouette seen at that distance could be mistaken for that of a young girl. Aside from the ridiculous shawl, she was dressed all in black (an attempt to be in fashion?), her hair in a loose bun, her fingers loaded with rings, her wrists jingling with bracelets; and once more he wondered, as he had when they had first met, just what it was about her that was so unsettling. Was it her evasive eyes? Or her voice? She appeared to be very troubled as she passed by, giving him a sidelong glance, on her way to the counter to buy a pack of cigarettes. And because she wanted to choose the picture on the matchbox, the counterboy grumbled audibly to another customer, "Crazy women, I see them every day. I'm only surprised when a sane one comes in!" Then Robert overcame his annoyance, and as she came toward him, self-conscious and touchingly coquettish, swinging her big tapestry hand-bag, he called out a greeting of forced cordiality.

"Mélusine! Will you have a cup of coffee with me?"

"Oh! I've already had a cup," she said with painful alacrity, "but I'll gladly take another one to keep you company."

She must have found out where he lived and hung around the neighborhood, hoping for this encounter. She sat down, luxuriously sniffed the aroma of the coffee that was brought to her (that long and mobile nose of hers gave her a foxy look), then dropped three lumps of sugar into the cup. Was she perishing of hunger? Or was it merely the gluttony of an old maid? Had she herself crocheted that shawl with heavy yarn, or did it come to her from a grandmother? Or did she buy it at the flea market? Or did she pick it off a pile of trash? Was she down and out, or daft, or merely a woman rather dessicated by solitude and who dressed in a style too young for her age? You can never tell in these times, when many young girls, with their fringes and their shawls and hems sweeping the ground, look as if they dressed out of trash cans.

"Are you working on your book?" he asked affably.

She pounced on his words as she had on the sugar.

"Oh, yes! Our interview was worth a great deal to me. As you made me realize, we writers still want to construct too much; we believe too much in logical reason; we must empty ourselves of all these established notions; we must learn to listen and register what we hear with untampered, virginal minds."

Her delicate hand trembled a little as she stirred her coffee with the spoon. He had noticed this trembling the other day in the office. She was wearing a ring that looked as if it might be Hindu. It must not have cost much, considering the popularity of that style of jewelry.

"You are looking at my ring—a gift from Annick, the ring of Mélusine. The design hadn't yet been copied and vulgarized then."

But it was certainly common now. Robert was far from being expert in fashions, but if that ring dated from before the war, it would certainly have been of a more precious material than that gilded copper, and the stone would not have been so cheap. She had probably purchased it the night

75

before, from some peddler's tray in the boulevard Saint-Michel, for three francs. But who knows.

"Tell me about Annick," he said gently.

He was suddenly interested in her and her story. The ring of Mélusine. That was as good as the Templars, wasn't it? The three-franc ring, the hole dug in the ground, the novel never begun—all this was worth something. These things are all alike; we search, and since we never find, we embroider, we invent, we buy a ring—

She seemed to be completely at a loss. Of course, "Tell me about Annick," must have given her a shock. At her age (forty-five? fifty-five?), she must be used to irony, rebuffs, indifference. The concierges, the storekeepers, the publishing house where no doubt she delivered translations or documentations paid at the lowest rate, represented just so many indifferent listeners, absentminded grunts, monosyllables pronounced without warmth. "Oh yes? . . . That's so. . . . We're all alike. . . . You're right. . . . After all, it's possible. . . ." This would be the sum total of the responses she would have garnered, instead of sympathy. "She's a lunatic, but harmless," people probably said of her or thought as they refused to listen. Let her embroider as much as she liked. Let her talk about jewelry, astral influences, rapes, and manor houses. No one would take the trouble to listen, reflect, check the facts, put a question, or utter a doubt. She was quite safe, in a manner of speaking. And he had said, "Tell me about Annick," as if speaking to a friend, a woman with whom he would normally have a quiet conversation. She was overwhelmed; she did not know where to begin. Like him when he, trying to begin writing something, sat staring at a blank sheet of paper. Or like him when starting to polish an article on the Etruscans, a preface for an Anglo-Saxon book, a broadcast on the love life of George Sand, or the scenic beauties of the Saintonge region while thinking how much he would rather launch out in a long narrative filled with happenings and characters. But was this really true?

"Well, you see, it was twenty years ago. And she is dead

—Oh! I lived with her, in spite of everything. I've always been sure there was a way to—Ever since I played the Ouija board. Yes, I tried it; you're familiar with it of course? There's an alphabet." (He was not familiar with it.) "An extraordinary clairvoyante, Madame Summa, called up the astral body of Annick for me—But I couldn't continue the séances because of—my very limited means."

"But before? Before her death?"

"Why, I've told you. She was a Breton. We were the same age, almost, and were in school together—Wait a minute."

She rummaged in her big tapestry bag, which she had set down beside her on the floor. It was the size of those shopping bags housewives take to market. She rummaged hurriedly, like an immigrant at the customs office or like a receiver of stolen goods at the police station, mixing up the yellowed envelopes, the old folders—there were at least three of them—rags that might be handkerchiefs, and finally brought forth some faded photographs, frayed at the edges, blurred, the treasures of the poor.

"Here we are. On vacation in the Ardennes, nineteen thirty-eight. We wanted to do a little rock climbing. That's Annick, to the right, with an alpenstock."

"And where are you?"

"That's me, there—a little in the distance."

He could only see her face, rather pretty, delicate, sensitive, where a shadow fell on it, foretokening her present wrinkles.

But the features were the same, the features of an oldish young girl, a little uppish and very much a dreamer, giving great importance to her good manners and her diploma. In her looks, there was something of the languishing beauty of 1900 and something of today's intellectual woman. The only difference was the network of wrinkles that had fallen on the pretty face, along with the hint of madness that had settled in her gray eyes. In another ten years, she would be the aged spinster in a tailored suit, maniacally clean, a member of the SPCA, subsisting with difficulty on a minuscule pension and the illusion of having been unappreciated. Or else she might be that vagrant woman in tatters, talking to herself at a street corner, unpitied by anyone.

"Do you realize," she suddenly began, with that vague look bordering on insanity that she had on occasion, "that until now I've never shown this photograph to anyone?"

He didn't know what to say. He was touched, yes, by the image of distress her remark created. Still more, he was touched by the idea of all those ordinary souvenirs, all those uninteresting snapshots carried in the pockets and the heads of all these unknown passersby who were not listened to.

"Only you," said the old spinster, former pupil at the École de Chartres, author of "Mélusine, the Breton Sprite." And he was overwhelmed with sadness, as if he had taken on the burden of memories and dreams, insignificant but unique, of this poor, skinny, and pitiful madwoman who could be just anybody.

"We were on the point of making a veritable discovery," said Mademoiselle Synge, now speaking with animation. "The origin of the Holy Grail—We would have made a name in the world of research—would have been distinguished by the National Center of Scientific Research, awarded, maybe, a grant—"

This did not seem more idiotic or insane than a lot of other projects. And Victor Hugo had also consulted the spirit world.

"Annick had intuition. . . . Our friendship was absolute. Oh, I know what they would say about us nowadays. I'm not the only one who has read Freud." She said this with a scornful sneer. "But our union—yes, I dare use that word—was pure. Had it not been pure, do you believe the communication from the Beyond would have been as clear today as it is? No!" Her voice, which had become shrill, now softened, became mysterious. "If you only knew the revelations she has made to me! And the music of the spheres—"

"Eh? What? The music?" (But after all, everyone has his own music.)

"Amazing!" she said with an air of triumph. "But you'll see, you'll see. You've encouraged me greatly in that sense. Perhaps your work is in that same direction?"

"Lord, no! Or not precisely. The Templars, alchemy. . . ."

(He began to tell her about his project. Why was it so much easier to recount a story to a listener than to write it? On account of the face opposite?)

"But that's terribly exciting!" she cried enthusiastically. "You see, I happen to know a great deal about the English Templars."

Her excitement was exaggerated, and he was a bit afraid, as he had been in his office when she was fiddling with the paper knife.

"And what a fine subject! That solitary man digging in the earth, seeing reality crumbling round him—What a fulfill-ment, both physical and spiritual!"

"No doubt, no doubt—"

"And what a magnificent critique of our modern world! Basely materialistic, fooled by appearances. What a wealth of symbolism! Oh, you have, in this book—It will be a mile-stone!"

He was embarrassed not only by her enthusiasm but by her vocabulary.

"Busy as you are with other things, Monsieur Buibal, what courage you have to embark—Well, now, have you thought of someone to do your research for you? It's very presumptu-ous on my part, but if you haven't anyone else—"

Of course. That was it. The poor creature was trying to make a few pennies.

"No, I hadn't thought of it," he said resignedly.

"Do you authorize me, then?"

"Why not?"

At least Pierre Sorel's endeavor would have given pleas-ure to someone. And who could say? Like Gerry, Mélusine would perhaps bring a spark of life to the magnificent subject he dared not tackle.

"Go ahead, Mélusine," he said cordially. "Leave your address with me, put together some pages. I might be able to use them."

"You need not worry," she said, getting up, with a touch of self-satisfaction. "You can count on me. I've caught your point of view. We will do this book, Monsieur Guibal!"

Her hands no longer trembled as she wrote down her address, and as she went away, it seemed to Robert that she held herself straighter, that everything about her was more assured. And he was glad. Of course, he also knew that once more he had a bad case on his hands.

He imagined the face Cathie would pull if he told her, "I've hired a researcher for the historical documentation of my novel, a woman—"

And she would say, "Oh yes? Who in the world?"

And he would reply, "Mélusine, a Breton sprite."

AT THE AGE OF ELEVEN

When they were both eleven years old, Robert and Anselme managed, on their way home from school, to stop in front of a café concert where, from six o'clock on, music could be heard. One might conclude that the charms of the lady violinist were what attracted them. No, it was really the music; the songs, *"Le Doux Caboulot"* and *"Le Petit Vin Blanc,"* filled them with dreams, made them smile. Oh, to write a song that could be heard nightly in such cafés!

At the age of fifteen, Robert and Anselme were anarchists or Communists; they weren't sure which. They attended lectures in the school playgrounds or in the smoke-filled back rooms of cafés. Oh, to make speeches that would fill the breasts of the weary and half-asleep crowd with hope and courage!

Robert's mother, with the warm generosity of an alcoholic, said: "There's no stopping this child in his studies! He's so gifted!" Robert's stepfather (good-hearted bully in blue apron, much given to boxing ears) said, "That's a sure thing! We're not savages."

Robert had received a good education. He had not written songs but had written some books.

Many books for children have titles such as *The Treasure of the Manor House* or *The Secret of the Incas.* Many popular novels have titles such as *The Rubies of Capa-Ichac* or *The Emeralds of Lady C.* There are many comic strips in which the hero, a hairy Tarzan or a spy in dinner jacket, searches for a fabulous diamond-studded idol buried in the jungle or the secret of a lethal gas, the formula for which is in the hands of a mad scientist.

After the discovery of the treasure, the idol, or the secret formula, the author writes, "The End."

But before the end, so many things happen! Doubts, suppositions, things to be done, miraculous pieces of luck: the retirement of the guard of the Boissy château ("too old to go on living in this humidity"); the first step to take in this venture, see the mayor and apply for a job (without displaying too much eagerness); objections to overcome ("But the garage is prospering!" laments Adrienne. "We can put a manager in charge of it." "Are you so fond of living way off in the country?"); and then the cooperation of friends, finding the tools and the timber, a few inspired hours of putting it all together—Even a man better educated than Pierre Sorel would have no time to think about that word "end," which also has an "after."

Was he going to write this book? Eager to help were Mélu-sine and Gerry, two very ambiguous guardian angels leading the way. Gerry, an intrepid and charming simpleton, a Gala-had in search of the Holy Grail; Mélusine, the pathetic old girl in need of hope and morning coffee, old maid, old sprite. Both of them so pleased to "collaborate" in this magic enter-prise (magic and trite), the writing of a book. For their sakes, he would like to manage this thing and be able to exclaim: "Here is what I've done, thanks to you and with your help; this will show what we are capable of doing."

"How's it going?" asks Gerry, radiant. "Are you making progress? If you like, I'll write to the parish priest down there or to the old fellow's ex-wife—she's left him, you know—or I could write to his old friend, the man who raised him."

Write, yes, write, imagine you are going to interest the whole world in those diggings; who knows, something may be found.

"So you're not working this morning?" says Mélusine, disappointed. "Have you drawn upon anything in the docu-ments I brought you Tuesday afternoon? If Gilles de Rais also lived for a time in that château, it doubles the interest."

He says yes. She is delighted and almost sprightly.

"This work is making me younger by twenty years," she says. "The work, and your understanding—Oh, don't misin-terpret me—"

She says, "We will bring off this thing. I'm going to consult the source, the Flers archives."

She said "we," and that word was very sweet to her, poor old fairy of the trash cans. And it brought him the assurance that he was doing the right thing, that it was not for nothing that he had asked Bernard to tell people that he was out of town, that it was not for nothing that he had told Father Moinaud that other preoccupations forbade him to study the possibilities of the manuscript the good priest had submitted; not for nothing that he had told Vivi he could not dine with her either this Thursday or the next. He wanted to believe Mélusine, believe "We're going to bring off this thing. We can do it." He wanted to do it for all those humble friends of his—the parish priest, the schoolmaster down there in the Landes, the proofreader at Flammarion, the old spinster, the ruined artisan—and wanted to prove to them that if their champion had not spent the usual time reading their manuscripts or having drinks with them or writing an insignificant article or listening to them with cordial if rather drowsy attention, it had been for a purpose: to bring all these disparate things together in a superior unity, a sudden harmony. To permit them to pronounce that all too frequently heard remark, "My life would make a book," and as others once cried, "We are all German Jews," to reply to them, "We are all writers."

Yes, he reflected, if I manage to write this book, it will be for that reason. So that Mélusine, Anselme, Jocelyn—and Catherine, too—along with me and through me can discover that puerile treasure of the fables. So that we can all discover —I only regret that in order to say "we," I must first of all be alone.

II

The Secret

ANSELME

At the age of twenty, Anselme, ungainly, fair-haired, pale, with face and countenance of a country bumpkin, introduced himself as Anselme, "Le Poète" (Anselme, "the poet"). Some people thus thought his family name was Le Poète. And why not? Others asked him, "Have you published some of your verse?" His answer to that question was, "No. I write popular songs. And at the dance halls, I invite the ugly girls to dance with me."

At the age of twenty-five, Anselme was a pederast and dealt in drugs and porno drawings. He was a militant advocate of Women's Lib. Kindhearted, lacking a taste for women, he was sorry for them. He would have liked to transform them into men and then welcome all humanity into his bed.

He was jailed several times for various traffickings. Father Moinaud, whose choirboy he had been, managed to get him released. He married a Polish girl who was a chemist and slightly mad; she had invented a process for tarnishing gold. Boris Vian took it into his head to talk about her at the Lepine competitive exams and published an article about her, sparkling with humor. To tarnish gold! Could any process be more democratic? After this, the poor girl believed she was famous and became a megalomaniac. She piled up debts while Anselme did the cooking and washed the dishes. And just as she was almost out of cigarettes, she died, spitting out her lungs.

For some reason not clear, Anselme went back to jail, where he manufactured mousetraps.

When he was liberated, he automatically sought out Robert, who offered him some coffee and some cast-off clothing, a coat and a pair of pants. Then he obligingly placed himself in the hands of Father Moinaud. The poor old priest was ready to tear out his hair over such obligingness.

Anselme became a traveling salesman, dealing in what he called "applied pieces"—leather patches to be sewn on the elbows of old jackets, "in the fashion of the English country gentleman," he said in an indescribable accent.

After this, he was for a short time chauffeur to an old lady, for whom he rendered other, more intimate services, on the Côte d'Azur. He sent postcards, depicting palm trees against a blue sky, to Robert and to Father Moinaud. His livery was flattering, but he was a poor driver; and the very, very rich old lady, tired of seeing her Bentley and Mercedes battered up, fired him, without ever having learned that he didn't have a driver's license.

Thumbing his way, he returned like a shot to Paris, picked up by a Jehovah's Witness driver; and by the time they reached the vicinity of Beaune, he was converted. "That's the limit!" Father Moinaud exclaimed when told of Anselme's transformation.

Anselme was now convinced that work was a kind of sin, indicating a loss of hope. He slept on the landing of the servants' floor, the top floor of a luxury apartment building, in front of the elevator, and subsisted on almost nothing. And now he preached to his former junkie customers, performed miraculous cures, quoted the Bible, which he knew by heart.

A native of Lorraine, Anselme had a drawling accent, a

long face, light blue eyes, and was of a naturally cheerful disposition.

"But now, really," said Father Moinaud, "what do you intend to do? What's to become of you?"

"What did I do before?" Anselme responded with dazzling logic. "I'm going to be saved."

That's not an occupation, thought the good old priest, but he had enough tact not to say it. He considered trying to find a spot for Anselme on the radio or in some back room of a publishing house through the intervention of Robert, who had rescued Anselme so many times before. But Robert seemed to be uncooperative. Wherever Anselme had previously been placed, difficulties had piled up. Employed as messenger boy for the publishing house of Larousse, Anselme, who at that time had been infatuated with a guard in the Luxembourg Gardens, had pitched a load of packages into the bushes in order to follow his idol. Stockkeeper for a pharmaceutical laboratory, he had filched solidified alcohol and drugs of the most varied kinds in order to try out some experiments. As a night watchman in an archbishopric (recommended by Father Moinaud), he had allowed vagrants to enter the place. At the *Geographical Magazine,* where he was employed as a cleaning man, he allowed drug addicts to spend the night. This ended up with a police raid.

"I know, I know," Father Moinaud sighed, "but since his conversion, he's made a great effort—"

"Then place him in a religious house. Anywhere else, his proselytism would make a bad impression."

Father Moinaud, having made two or three efforts in that direction, had to confess that in the ecclesiastical milieu, the religious fervor of his strange protégé had made an extremely bad impression. These setbacks in no way disturbed Anselme's equanimity. But his circle of acquaintances was visibly upset.

"Robert will surely find a job for me."

"Robert has done all he could! But I won't conceal from you that the last time I talked to him about you, he was discouraged by your recent follies."

"He said 'follies' to you?" Anselme asked with a good-natured chuckle. Then he exclaimed: "Mammon!"

"Mammon? What do you mean by that?"

"I mean Mammon. You cannot serve both God and Mammon. Remember? Well, Robert is ambitious. Mundane things have seduced him. He has already denied me once, and will deny me again."

"What do you mean, he denied you? He has just recommended you to—"

"Yes, but that fell through," said Anselme with admirable cheerfulness. "And when the chief of police telephoned him this morning, he hung up! Mammon! And the Son of man hasn't a stone whereon to lay his head."

"Stop quoting the Bible without rhyme or reason! And explain yourself clearly. What has that long-suffering Robert done to you?"

"Well, you see, yesterday I went to preach the word of Christ in the Bazar de l'Hôtel de Ville," said Anselme in a self-satisfied drawl.

"You went to that big department store to preach?"

"Yes! Remember, 'Go thou to the market place where the people are assembled in great number.' So where do you find more people than in a department store? You see, Father, one has to use a little method, which you lack, you Levites in a dead church. Very well, yes! I went to the Bazar de l'Hôtel de Ville to preach! And I saw a broken-down old man, poor, ignorant soul, who was buying a cane. I drew near and spoke to him softly, telling him he would not need a cane if he had true faith. 'Stand up and walk!' I said to him. Unfortunately, his ears were sealed by Satan. I had to raise my voice to make myself heard. 'Let the deaf hear; let the blind see!' I yelled. Then the salesman intervened. He wanted to get rid of his canes. Mammon! Always Mammon! Try as I would to explain the infamy of commerce, he dragged the old man toward the counter, while I dragged him away, intending to cure him by the laying on of hands, which would have cost him nothing—"

"In short?" the priest interrupted, tapping the floor with his foot impatiently.

"In short, he called the police, that salesman, that Pontius Pilate! And a policeman stopped me from curing that old man. I struggled; a crowd gathered. And who should I see, as they dragged me away? Robert Guibal and his Bethsaida, who were buying saucepans, I believe—this was in the basement—and Robert never said a word or made a move to bear witness for me—I spent the night at the station house, and he didn't once telephone. And in the morning, when the chief telephoned—a really good scout, that officer, who I believe is beginning to see the light—He telephoned Robert. And do you know what Robert said? He told the chief to leave him alone and that he didn't want to have anything more to do with me! What do you say to that?"

"It's only human."

"So I had to give them your name and address, explaining that you are my spiritual father, although evidently, with age, you are not as ardent as I am in bearing witness—"

"May God preserve me from it!" groaned the priest. "So what do you want me to do about it?"

"Why, bring Robert Guibal to see reason, to see the light! Convert him! That is what we're here for, isn't it? Deny me though he will, he was my boyhood friend, and I can't let him down now, can I?"

His long, pale face was wreathed in artless smiles. Father Moinaud contemplated his former choirboy and was overwhelmed. Ever since his tenth year, Anselme had always been impossible, exasperating. And yet now, for the love of God (and one might well wonder what God he visualized), he had stopped drinking, stopped taking drugs, lived chastely. Mad though he might be, he lived according to his beliefs— something not very frequent. But, oh, this language he employed! And this pretentiousness! This candid way he had of invading one's life, disturbing one, and without the least gratitude! Not at all surprising that Robert had suddenly decided that he could stand no more. Still, after so many years—

"I'll go see him after dinner," he promised Anselme. "But don't you bother him! And for heaven's sake, bear witness with less violence. If you don't look out, you'll get into serious trouble, and I'll not be able to do anything for you."

"The gates of hell shall not prevail," said Anselme joyously, filling up his coffee cup once more.

Speaking of hell, Father Moinaud reflected, this visit would give him an opportunity to speak to Robert about the Prix Vérité! Mammon!

THOSE LONG-AGO VACATIONS

Anselme presumes too much on the memories we have in common, Robert reflected. Our ball games, our school days, the church choir, and the church club. Of course, one's boyhood chum amounts to something. With him one argued over the existence of God and discovered the joys of chewing gum. But all the same—

"Anselme is becoming a nuisance, and he no longer amuses me," he said.

"He never amused me," said Catherine. "But after all, he was your close friend."

"Oh, not all that close!"

"Oh, yes! Remember those long-ago vacations in that little house called Olivette, with his wife Nadia doing the cooking, the dreadful things she cooked in the very same saucepan in which she made the coffee? Remember how awful her coffee tasted? And remember how Anselme was going from door to door trying to interest the peasants in a new and universal method of teaching reading? He always had a talent for being inopportune."

"It wasn't the same thing as now."

"Oh, yes! It was exactly the same thing. Those peasants were as upset as those customers in the Bazar to whom he wanted to bring the word of Christ. Imagine, he barges in just when they're sitting down to supper! It's exactly the same thing, only then you didn't mind."

"And you reproached me for it."

"Laughingly," she amended.

"Not all that much."

She had to admit to herself that this was so. She remembered those vacations in the Olivette, a small house with paper-thin partitions, smelling of mildew, the ants in the kitchen and the mosquitoes in the bedroom. Those were the days when they were stone-broke, and she remembered her distress at seeing Robert idling away his time doing no serious writing. And to cap all, there were Anselme and his Polish wife Nadia. Anselme in a greasy apron cooking terribly greasy messes of food, and Nadia smelling up the little house with her chemical experiments and in the evening singing songs of her native land in a little-girl voice slightly off-key. And all this so mean, so shabby, so very much a paid vacation. So much so that one day when the weather was too hot, the *cassoulet Toulousain* too Toulousain, Nadia too sententious (that girl had a superiority complex that was really crushing), Anselme too obliging (and especially Robert's tolerant smiling at all this, including Anselme's traveling-salesman jokes), the songs, and worse still, the so-called talents of Nadia (ill washed and mannish, that girl)—yes, suddenly it was all impossible to endure. She had *seen* the lamentable picture they made—No, it was not the lack of money; it was the lack of quality in all this that had turned her stomach, made her gag. She had packed her little suitcase in a kind of panic; she was afraid of being infected, of reaching a point where she would no longer even notice that mediocrity. She had arrived in Paris with 500 francs in her purse and had taken steps to apply for a teaching job. To consecrate herself entirely to the Robert of the Olivette vacations, to that handsome man who had already put on a little too much weight (but his brown throat in the open collar still terribly excited her)—No, it had become impossible.

He had rejoined her two days later, worried, not understanding. She had said, as if declaring war, "I've applied for a teaching job." And he had said, "Oh, fine, that will keep you busy." The worst of all this for her was his not understanding the meaning of her action, which was that she would no longer consecrate herself entirely to him. She had wanted to punish him, and essentially she was punishing herself, for she neither loved nor esteemed the teaching profession, which she exercised with cold precision. And were she to detach herself entirely from him, would she once more be the only one punished?

Robert was very proud of himself for having courageously stood fast against the combined assaults of Father Moinaud and Anselme.

"I sent them packing, categorically," he boasted to Catherine.

"We'll see for how long."

"Why—for as long as it takes me to finish this book, of course."

He seemed so very sure of himself. She wished she could hope that he would at last change and that she could allow herself to love him. But it took so little to distract him, to divert him from his work. And then, even if he persevered a little, what could he make of that subject? There had been so many years of articles written to oblige someone, of hackwork. Mightn't this have left its mark, and he would find himself writing in the popular style? *The Templars, in Three Lessons.* Or *Bluebeard, with Laughter.* One of those books that end up with luridly colored covers?

"Anyway, I'm through with Anselme!" Robert filled his pipe as he went on talking. "When he sold rabbits in cages, he was at least funny. But when he sets himself up to preach the end of the world, no thank you! I'm surprised that Father Moinaud doesn't try to make him see reason. He doesn't have the strength or the time; he's always been too lenient, however, with Anselme."

Catherine suppressed a smile.

"A priest can't exactly bawl out a convert," she observed. "Not even a Jehovah's Witness convert, not even when he's a semilunatic."

"Anselme isn't a lunatic," Robert protested. "At least, not till now."

"Well, I think he was crazier in the past. Now, at any rate, he knows where he's going."

True, it could be said that Anselme had always sought a form of renunciation—selling heroin at a loss to penniless junkies, washing dishes while Nadia floated in her algebraic Eden, maintaining his equanimity when his ingenious commercial transactions failed, recounting his prison experiences with gales of laughter.

"Come to think of it," said Catherine, "Anselme is something like your specimen of humanity—"

"What specimen?"

"That what's-his-name, Gerry's old fellow, the one who is digging a hole in the ground."

"Oh, not at all!" Robert protested indignantly. "Sorel, even if he doesn't discover the treasure, brings something to others, in a certain way, something of the fabulous, of poetry—"

"What Gerry calls 'childhood dreams'?" she said, not without irony.

"Well, why not? But now, as to Anselme, it's not that at all. The Bible. Judgment Day."

"Obviously, the theme is rather hackneyed."

For a moment they laughed together, as in bygone days.

"No," Robert concluded, "Anselme is unutilizable."

Unutilizable. That was a word he'd been fond of in days gone by. When he had been quite fond of Anselme.

95

UNUTILIZABLE

Had he ever really endured or liked the company of Anselme? And Nadia? And the company of so many others? Those evenings in the little house Olivette had been happy ones, he could not deny. The little house, pretty in a rustic fashion, had a certain grace in its proportions. The wavering, childlike voice of Nadia, issuing from that body lacking any grace—he was moved by it, as if by a revelation. Beyond that ugliness, that monumental pretentiousness, he seemed to glimpse what she had been, and perhaps still was at heart: a shy and awkward child, alone in a corner of the playground, humming a tune, not joining in the games of the others. And Anselme's devotion to Nadia, which made her participate in what was a kind of game (the supposed genius of Nadia, her Madame Curie airs), had moved him. Their incredible inventions—a new method of global reading, recipes for "instantaneous jam," rabbit cages that could be converted into cradles, heaven knows what else—amused him; being with them was like reading an episodic novel. "Obviously," he said of Anselme, "he is unutilizable; but whether or no, he amuses me."

To which Catherine retorted, "He is certainly unusable, and does not amuse me at all."

This was at a time when Robert and Catherine still had real conversations.

"But it is exactly because of his uselessness that I like him," said Robert as they took their customary stroll in the hills above the Olivette at the end of day, having managed to shake off the cumbersome couple for an hour. "Anselme, Nadia, Jocelyn, and that old geezer, you know, the one who came to the magazine the other day, who thinks he has managed to reconcile Marxism and Christianity by algebra—all of them give me the impression of being a collection of knickknacks where nothing, you might say, has any value, but only because no one knows how to utilize those objects, but which, if one did know how to use them—Take Picasso, for instance. He kept everything, used the empty can in a sculpture, used the handlebars of a bicycle in such a way that they became the forehead and horns of one of his sculptured goats. Suddenly you see the value of something you had thought could not be utilized. Because Picasso could easily have sculptured the head and horns of a goat—I believe it was a goat—without using the bicycle handlebars. And if he did use them, it was because, genius that he was, he liked and needed to collaborate with the bicycle handlebars. He rehabilitated them, he—"

"That's all very nice," said Catherine, "but I don't see the connection with Anselme. You're not Picasso, and you're not writing a novel about Anselme. Besides, you're not writing anything at the moment—"

"But I've never said I was going to write a novel about Anselme! I only mean to say that the bicycle handlebars (an example), even without Picasso, in essence contain the possibility of a goat's head and that Anselme, even if he is unutiliz-able, has, all the same, a value."

(This was not all that false, even today, with Anselme joyous, no longer drinking or smoking or trafficking in drugs, living on nothing, sleeping on the rug in front of his elevator, "for the Holy Spirit." It amounted to something, even if a little ridiculous and provoking, even if a little insane, even if he be judged by Father Moinaud as unutilizable. But Father Moinaud was likewise not a Picasso.)

"But of value in whose eyes?" asked Catherine, straightening up. (They were gathering pine cones for kindling the log fire.) "Do you mean of value to you as a novelist?"

"Not at all! I mean, of inherent value, in a category, how shall I say, in a category of absolute gratuitous values."

"You mean to say—God?" she asked in a hushed voice.

Night was falling; they were gathering pine cones; they were talking about God. They were in no hurry to return to the house that was too small but was full of the day's warmth and the acrid odors of a rabbit fricassee. They were still happy at that time.

LOVE AND LITERATURE

Robert loved Catherine, or at least he thought he did. And yet a combination of sexual hang-ups, of weak will, of a kind of absurd and misplaced generosity had always induced him to have affairs with other women. And try as he would to prevent it, Catherine always knew about those affairs. "Not a very brilliant conquest," she would mutter to herself, at sight of that schoolgirl with dirty hair and a briefcase full of tracts, or that aspiring young singer encountered in the back corridors of the radio broadcasting station, or those half-forsaken mistresses of colleagues, or those young women who were "wasting their youth on sheep ranches in the remote provinces" and whom he was inspiring to go in for literature, as if to go in for debauchery. She was not pleased that he showed so little discrimination in choosing his mistresses, since this lack seemed to diminish her own worth.

"I sometimes wonder," she meditated aloud, "if he didn't choose me by sheer chance." (At that time, she still thought aloud.) Yet, that is not the explanation. Not by chance. And perhaps that's why our marriage hasn't worked. (Reine, yes, he had chosen her by chance. Reine was the very image of unavoidable chance.) Nor had he chosen literature by chance; yet he had very soon betrayed it. Weakness of character, friendships, a kind of generosity, and something like modesty had made him accept work that, after all, he found as much worth while as writing novels: rewrites, articles, book reviews, prefaces—He discovered a forgotten monument, dipped into a variety of subjects: gastronomy, geology, botany; he discovered unknown, picturesque people: wine merchants who were specialists in prehistory, shoemakers who wrote popular songs, chimney sweeps who were poets. Granted, this might be a slight exaggeration—

But he, in that prehistoric period, he thought that it was literature he was engaged in, at least something like it, and thought this was love, at least something like it. Since then, he wasn't quite sure.

"How funny," Catherine said to herself, "I almost defended Anselme!" It was on account of the Sorel story, which interested her. Not the foraging in the earth, of course, that was not so much in her line, but the courage and tenacity of that solitary man. Nor did the treasure excite her beyond measure. One had to be Gerry for that. But who says that Pierre Sorel is searching for only one treasure? Do you live, like Anselme, on a stairway landing, do you burrow in the earth for twelve years, except with real belief in what you are doing? She felt a strange solidarity with those people who go straight ahead, straight to the goal. "Aiming at a star," Gerry would have said. But we are not all of us going to start writing like Gerry.

FROM MELUSINE'S POINT OF VIEW

Mélusine wandered down the rue de Rennes, plucking newspapers out of the trash cans as if plucking flowers in a meadow. She was wearing gloves so as not to soil her fingers. Her tapestry bag was stuffed with lucky finds. Over her heart, she was wearing her Bibliothèque Nationale card identifying her as a researcher. The weather was fine. She could therefore read her newspapers in Boucicaut Square. If it began to rain, she could take shelter in the Bon Marché basement, which was always crowded with women shoppers. There it was warm and commodious. You could settle down for hours, provided your respectability was evident—and Mélusine prided herself on looking respectable. At least, a certain leeway of doubt was permitted.

Mélusine knew of several such relay stations in Paris where she could spend the day without having to open her purse. There were the waiting rooms in the new Montparnasse railway station, all new and clean, and numerous little museums with trifling entrance fees, where you could sit among the crystal, the Louis Philippe furniture, the time-blackened paintings, provided you were on good terms with the guard. Thank heaven there was no lack of museum attendants who appreciated erudition even in a frayed coat, and Mélusine knew how to exploit this respect, visiting one after another of "her" museums with the feeling of conducting a kind of inspection: "Well, well! They've sent the little Lorrain landscape to the retrospective exhibition in London? That's not at all wise."

There were also the churches, but they were rarely well heated, and reading newspapers there is frowned upon. And the municipal libraries, but no smoking is allowed there. Some travel agencies with rather pleasant waiting rooms also provided emergency shelters. Some of the municipal buildings also had quite comfortable benches. Paris is full of such refuges. There was also the metro. But Mélusine dreaded the promiscuity of subways. Then, too, a number of down-and-outs took the subway to get some sleep.

Mélusine had the use of a bed every night from midnight on; to be exact, from half past twelve. She was not utterly without resources. The publishers Hachette and Larousse called upon her now and then to do some documentation, stingily paid, for there was competition in that field. Mélusine, however, knew how to live on very little. The main thing was to preserve appearances. Hence, the gloves. When your fingernails begin to blacken and split, nothing can be done about it. When your shoes begin to let in water, the coat to fray and lose its shape, the café waiters turn hostile, the floorwalkers in the big stores become suspicious, and even the museum guards—And that is why Mélusine had such a fear of the rain, for the rain is what gives your clothing a worn-out look and weakens shoe leather (quite good shoes can be bought from the Salvation Army for three or four francs, but you're lucky if you find your size) and turns an erudite person into a vagrant who evidently has to wear damp clothes until they dry out. But the weather was fine that day, and it was with a kind of comic grace (the two ideas are not incompatible) that she went down the rue de Rennes, plucking newspapers out of the trash cans as if plucking flowers in a meadow.

Today she gathered an *Observateur* almost up to date, and an issue of *Elle* from which only a few articles had been clipped but which remained attractive, and a *Figaro* of that very day's date. She had just spent three hours in the Bibliothèque Nationale, had had a cup of coffee and three croissants offered by Robert Guibal; and this had made her day, or almost. Life was good. She thought in a glancing way of the Cotentin. Would she ever go down there? "I'm sent here by the writer Robert Guibal, with whom I'm collaborating." For had she not discovered, that very morning, some precious information? In an old book about the Cotentin region, which contained some children's counting-out rhymes, one of which she believed contained some precious cryptic references to the Templars and to Gilles de Rais! She had copied it in her notebook. And as she sat down on a bench in Boucicaut Square, she mulled over these hidden meanings as she once more read the doggerel:

> On the wrong side and the right
> the horse of His Majesty the King
> our generous Royal Knight.
> Whenever he entered the church
> he entered by the head or tail end—
> no matter which end would do—

but going in by the tail end
of temples he had two!

Mélusine nibbled at a hunk of bread as she reflected on those lines. (She had three cigarettes but was saving them until later.)

Now, let's see. The wrong and the right side could refer to the Black Mass which the Templars were said to celebrate, the sacred mass recited backwards. Considering the pronunciation of the time, the word "royal" would sound like "roué" and thus refer to that noted roué Gilles de Rais. The word "church" could be a substitute for the word "temple" and would refer to the Templars. Again, in the next line, is a reference clear to me; it is again a cryptic account of the Black Mass. In the last line, the word "temples" makes no sense. The horse has two temples? Nonsense. The word should be capitalized: "Temples." There were two Temples. Who knows? The word here may be taken in its architectural sense? The Château de Boissy is perched on a hill, which has been thoroughly explored by the unfortunate Pierre Sorel, who has risked his life at every moment, digging into that hill. Who knows, he may eventually find the subterranean chapel, since there remains on the surface the ruins of another chapel appertaining to the château. That could be the infernal chapel of the Templars, the second temple, the secret temple, perhaps? At any rate, the hypothesis was exciting. Oh, what a theme! Those two chapels, the one infernal, the other celestial, superimposed one above the other!

The subject must be enlarged, elevated. The existence of Pierre Sorel, his wife Adrienne, and the village of Boissy was rather provoking. But would Robert Guibal be capable of elevating the subject to another plane? She had found him very distracted, his mind on other things. Whenever she had seen him at the Petit Cluny Café in company with someone or other, she said to the waiter who came forward to serve her, "I am with that gentleman over there," in a clear voice. And later on, as she pulled her notes out of her tapestry

102

handbag, along with some bread crumbs, she scolded him a little: "There's a great deal to do on this subject, Monsieur! A great deal!" She could never call him by his first name as he had told her to do. Never! She was not afraid of her employer, nor did she regard him as a friend, nor did she feel gratitude toward him, except very slightly. No. Mélusine serenely thought, What would he do without me!

Uncouth and frail creature, Mélusine, whose terrain is Paris. Her lodging is precarious; on account of the customers, the noise, the smells, she cannot return to it before midnight. On account of the woman employee who does the marketing early in the morning, returning from Les Halles at eight, which means that Mélusine must leave her bed before that, and she yields to the necessity as to a law of Nature. She escapes into the streets of Paris, striding along uncertainly, her bag slung over her shoulder, an unsocial, ungainly, pretentious, and timid person. She has no friends among those who huddle together for warmth. She does not beg for coffee or cigarettes. If she finds a cigarette butt, that's fine. She writes on a pad of paper placed on her knees or at a table in the Bibliothèque Nationale, her temple. She reveres Knowledge, that cruel god who does not feed his worshipers, her humble family having taught her from infancy to revere that god. She never dreams of better days, either past or future, or of the worst days. Her conscience is at peace when she has carefully examined some old documents; her stomach is satisfied with scanty nourishment; she wanders without anxiety and without aim, as if on a vast prairie, like a tall stiltbird, with globular and vacant eyes. Or a giraffe.

GRADE B

"I am the daughter of the satrap Artaxerxes, King of Sardis. Thank you, Goliath, for rescuing me from those miserable bandits."

"I only did my duty, Princess; that's normal."

"Alas, I have lost my father. I'm alone in the world, and I go now to rejoin Frederick the Great to place myself under his protection."

"I will escort you to his tents, for without an escort, you and your entourage will not arrive there alive."

"How can I ever show my gratitude?"

"You are the most beautiful woman I have ever seen. Grant me the pleasure of contemplating you one more minute. That is all I ask of you."

"You are the most loyal and generous of men."

Against a sunset background and with, at their right, a decorative rocky shore, Goliath and the Princess stand, holding hands for a long while. At their feet, the decapitated corpses of their assorted enemies. In the background, the Princess's ladies-in-waiting, beneath vaporous veils, their gowns cut agreeably low.

Manuel and Marina adore these Grade B films, but from beginning to end of the projection, they do not stop nudging each other and giggling. A few minutes afterward, Marina talks with some condescension about these films.

"Really, one has to see these films!"

Catherine, who has accompanied them, remains passive. Were they fooling themselves, ashamed of their enjoyment? Or was she the one who was still something of a child?

"So now, Aunt Catherine, I imagine you're contented?" said Marina sweetly.

"Why contented?"

"Because Uncle Robert is writing his book."

Catherine blushed faintly, surmising what had led up to this innocent question, the remarks overheard at numerous family councils. "Catherine so wants Robert to. . . . She has been so disappointed. . . . She, who has sacrificed her life for him. . . ." And she was briefly rather ashamed of that edifying and naïve role they obliged her to play, the role she obliged herself to play.

"Of course, I'm glad. Because I believe he is a born writer. If I thought his talents lay elsewhere—"

"But how can you know what he was born to do?" said Marina, smoothing her hair and peering at her reflection in a store window.

"But she feels it! And that's love!" said Manuel.

He spoke with warmth. He would always defend the rights of passion. Catherine was grateful to him but, all the same, was embarrassed.

"Well, so long as you are contented—" said Marina without too much conviction. "That's fine! *Ciao!*"

Marina couldn't see in what way that book could give pleasure to Aunt Catherine or what connection it could have with her famous grief, so often hinted at.

"Why, yes," said Manuel when they reached home. "She wants him to write a great book for her. Don't you understand? To prove his love for her."

"Like in *The First Love Affair of Michelangelo?*" asked Marina, bubbling with laughter. That technicolor film was one of their favorite subjects for joking.

"And in the meantime," she said with some bitterness, "she's the one who went to the movies with us, not Uncle Robert. And I'll bet he won't come to dinner with us tonight."

"Since he is working on his book," said Manuel, forever loyal.

Marina shrugged her thin shoulders.

"He with his book, and she with her grief—what a laugh!" she said, intentionally vulgar.

In the bosom of the family, they spoke of "Catherine's grief" in the same way that they spoke of "Vivi's situation," referring to her divorce. An established fact. Almost a property. All the family: Germaine; her sister Olympe, who appeared only at Christmas; Cousin Roger, of whom they were rather ashamed because he was a maître d'hôtel in a restaurant—a four-star restaurant, but still, the cousin of a Colonel!

They all said, "poor Catherine's grief," the way richer families speak of "Aunt Brigitte's rubies" or "her neck chain" or "the queen's necklace."

The family needed to think that someone in the tribe possessed a treasure. And if Catherine didn't have "her grief," why then—

Then they would feel robbed.

THE FAMILY

"Where's Catherine?"

"At the movies with the children," said Vivi, who was blocking out a fashion drawing.

Germaine, in the brown armchair, was knitting. The day was ending.

"And Robert? Still with that woman?"

"Oh, Mamma! Don't say 'that woman,' " Vivi exclaimed with a laugh.

"My dear child, what do you want me to say?"

"I don't know, but don't say that! It's so very prewar."

"That was my epoch," said Germaine with a tenderness directed, not at Vivi, but at the memory of the Colonel. Vivi put down her pencil and went over to hug and kiss her mother.

"Darling Mamma! Can't you leave your era for two minutes?"

"For what reason? To pay a visit to that—that young woman? Yes, I'll admit, I'm not yet modern enough for that."

"Why, no, not a visit. I just want you to open your eyes to what's going on."

"And what is going on?"

Vivi's smile vanished.

"Why do you think Cathie is at the movies with the children? And why go to see *Hercules Against Goliath?* Or *Ma-*

ciste and the Blue Men? And this on her day off from school, Thursday, when there are no classes and when she usually has more worthwhile things to do?"

"Why, I have no idea, dear. I suppose because Robert is too busy."

"Busy, yes. And doing what?"

Germaine let her knitting drop and raised her eyes.

"He's with that—that person?"

"No, you're way off the track. Busy working on that famous book!"

"Ah? But isn't that very good?" asked Germaine uncertainly.

"Well, no! It's not very good!" Vivi was ready to explode. "It's not at all good. Catherine drove him to write that book in order to separate him from his friends, from us. She would do anything, no matter what, to isolate him, to have him all to herself. Even to the point of making him look ridiculous."

"I don't see in what—"

"Mamma! You are so much outside things, so much—Oh, I adore you, but you can't account for the fact that in our time any novel that Robert could write would signify nothing. He's a man who, on that plane, has been completely left behind. Esthetically and politically. He hasn't the least idea what really counts in our time. He—"

"It must be said that sometimes it's hard to know where one stands," murmured Germaine, counting her stitches.

"For you, perhaps."

"Thank you."

"No, Mamma! I didn't mean to say—But for Robert to be writing a novel, a romance of chivalry, sort of, is absurd."

"More absurd than what he was doing before?"

"A hundred times more! Robert isn't made to—The whole affair about that pathetic illiterate who is wasting his time and throwing away his life in a ditch he has dug—It may be heartbreaking, agreed, but of what real interest? It's Zola or Maupassant with a touch of Féval—"

107

"Really? Are there still illiterates?" said Germaine uneasily, always ready for social action. "Shouldn't something be done about it?"

"You know, you're discouraging," said Vivi.

She had put aside her sketch pad and pencil and was now walking up and down in the room. She turned on a lamp, opened a book, then shut it. Germaine attentively regarded all these feverish gestures made by her daughter.

"You may be right, after all; I'm sure I don't know," she said, patiently obstinate. "But I don't see how this concerns you, Evelyn. Robert writes what he wants to write and does what he likes, it seems to me."

"Of course, he does what he likes!"

Vivi shrugged, then came to sit on the arm of her mother's chair. "But you know very well what Robert means to me, to us, to the children—"

"Yes. And it would perhaps be better if he meant a little less to you, better for him to be less indispensable to you— As you say, I really don't know anything about modern literature, but if writing brings him back to Catherine—"

"So they'll become alike, the two of them?" said Vivi, again petulant. "Egoists, shut off from the world, liking no one? Because you're not going to tell me that she loves him. She's become a veritable shrew to him, and he, since he wants to be left alone in peace, is writing that book, writing it solely to be left in peace by her, to be—" She stopped short, no longer able to go on, too tense, too close to tears.

"Vivi," said Germaine, taking up her green and rose-red knitting destined for Marina, "you ought to marry again."

34, RUE VANEAU

Mélusine's address. A vegetarian restaurant was on the ground floor at 34, rue Vaneau. Disconcerted, Robert stopped in front of it. He had reached this point in the course of his stroll almost without being conscious of where he was going. Here was where Mademoiselle Synge had her lodgings. Was it idle curiosity that had brought him here? For he had no intention of visiting her. She had given him to understand that her apartment, inhabited previously by one of her aunts, was for her a sanctuary, dedicated to the memory of Annick. Her "spirit" might be troubled by the irruption of Robert and abandon her familiar pedestal table. "The apartment is quite small but charming," Mélusine had said. "A little crowded, some good heirloom pieces that I've never had the heart to put into storage." He could imagine it now: a dusty cubbyhole in the style of Madame Suzy, his concierge.

But ever since he had tried to write this book, oddly enough, such things appealed more to him than formerly. Thus, idle curiosity impelled him to linger in front of the restaurant, a vaguely Breton place with the name O'braz. The menu posted in the window featured an entrée composed of rice; cost of the complete meal, 4.50 francs. O'braz. Strange, this presence of Brittany hovering round Mélusine. A big man, wearing a grease-stained apron, who was standing in the doorway, seemed to have all the time in the world at his disposal, and his benevolent aspect encouraged Robert to speak to him.

"Isn't there a concierge?"

"No, but tell me who you're looking for. I know everyone in the barracks," said the good-natured man.

"A Mademoiselle Synge," said Robert uncertainly, wondering what he would do if the man (obviously the restaurant's cook) told him "the third floor left."

"Mademoiselle Synge? You mean to say, Mademoiselle Vignes? She's on the fourth floor, but she's not there; she's at the salon."

"At the salon?"

"At her beauty salon. You're looking for a beauty parlor proprietor, aren't you?"

"No, no, not at all, she's a spinster, a rather odd person,

a little old-fashioned; you see what I mean?"

"I've got a half dozen of them at your service among my customers," said the man with a hearty laugh. "But living in this building, no. There are only young girls. Wouldn't you prefer that?"

Robert also laughed this time, along with the red-faced cook. It was a fine day, and he was in no hurry.

"It depends on what one wants to do."

The red-faced man roared with laughter. What a good joke!

"No, I'm looking for an oldish spinster who is a little odd, perhaps a little—"

"Deranged?" suggested the cook, understanding Robert's mimicry.

"That's it. And with a big tapestry handbag she slings over her shoulder, and she wears buttoned shoes."

"Oh, that one! Of course I know her! I'm paid to know her! But paid, that's a way of speaking. What did you call her?"

"Mademoiselle Synge, isn't that it?"

"Maybe that's the name she gave you," said the cook, who was obviously having a good time, "but for us, she's Mademoiselle Rebec, Yvonne Rebec. But if you want to give her another little family name—"

The good fellow's hilarity was getting on Robert's nerves.

"Rebec. A Breton name," he said to put an end to it.

"That, yes, a Breton name. If she wasn't from Brittany, I'd not give her the lodging she has. Consider how little it brings in! My kitchen is always crowded; in the evenings, my customers just miss crowding me out! And, say what you will, it's not very pleasant to sleep in the kitchen; there's the noise, the smells—But I've fixed it up nice for her. You can see for yourself; come in, yes, yes, since you know her—"

Drawn along by the huge, good-natured cook, Robert crossed a melancholy little room painted yellow and entered a dark kitchen, with one window overlooking a small courtyard, of ordinary uncleanliness. To the left, a red and yellow plastic curtain, which the huge man pulled open with a wide gesture.

"Just look. That's where she sleeps. Mademoiselle Yvonne. And you can see it's not very handy for me. I could use that space; it would just hold the sideboard I need. But, well, she's a compatriot. I'm from Quimper myself, and after all, I must give her credit; she's the one who gave me the idea of going vegetarian; before, I made crepes, and for a bachelor, a crepe restaurant, well, you see—"

Robert would never be able to make out the incompatibility of crepes and bachelors. Seized with an intolerable feeling that he had committed an indiscretion in standing there looking at the narrow cot, the two worn suitcases, the shoes on the cretonne coverlet like two derelicts, he fled and hurried down the rue Vaneau to its end, where he sighed with relief.

Oh, poor Mademoiselle Synge, or Rebec, or Mélusine! What would she do without that documentation with which she was overwhelming him? One more reason to go ahead with that book, which already, when he faced the prospect of writing it, numbed him with laziness. But Mélusine was evidently enthusiastic—or pretended to be, out of a sense of dignity. Oh, poor old maid, old sprite!

However, Bernard would say, "It's a good address, the rue Vaneau."

"Would you like—er—to move to another apartment?" Robert asked Mélusine, as he lowered his gaze to the papers covered with her fine, old-fashioned writing, which he would absentmindedly read later on.

"Why should I move?" said Mélusine curtly.

"Because I have a friend who happens to have, at present, a room which—"

He became entangled in his explanations, while she stared at him fixedly like a strict schoolmistress. Did she guess that he had seen through one of her secrets?

"No, Monsieur Guibal, I do not want to move," said Mélusine.

And when he tried to pursue the subject—

"Suppose we return to Gilles de Rais? He's much more interesting than I am."

He had the feeling that, basically, it was much the same thing. But he dared not justify himself. And since she desired it, he studied her notes on the rent-rolls of the Château de Boissy. After all, they had both moved and now inhabited a château.

Here I am, Robert told himself, again on the point of letting myself be sidetracked, in taking an interest in Mélusine. A guilty distraction? Anselme; Jocelyn; Alphonse, the charcoal dealer; Madame Suzy, the concierge—"Anyone, no matter who, can keep you from writing," Catherine complained. But if writing obliges me to reject these distractions? Catherine said, "If at least you drew something from those distractions." Catherine's hope was to see notebooks filled, novels full of characters. But as far as he was concerned, what pleased him most was exactly not to derive anything from them except that warmth, those futile chitchats, the fellow feeling of those wasted hours. He would almost go so far as to say that those hours, too, represented a creation. A treasure, why not? A treasure he had not managed to share with Catherine.

"It's nothing but glass," a little girl in a smock had once said to him when he showed her a marble he had called "a diamond."

A trifling remark like that can haunt you all your life.

CHATEAU

One day, Mélusine reflected, that fellow (she still used the word as she had in her school days: with mixed admiration and scorn), one day that fellow down there decided to go live in the château, to expropriate it. Abandon a garage that was making money? Abandon a busy little town? A reason must be found that *those people* could understand. And so he began to talk about the treasure. He invented the treasure.

Studying a yellowed manuscript that she was conscientiously deciphering, Mélusine had paused for a moment to think about that stranger, that solitary man for whom she had a fellow feeling. Yes, he must have invented the treasure. It couldn't be otherwise. Reassured, she returned to the work in hand, scrupulous work, enthralling, and totally useless.

THE CHILDREN

The twins were discussing with their uncle the subject of his projected book, which they found exciting.

"It's great," said Manuel, "that story of yours. But do you think your old chap is going to find the treasure, the treasure of the Templars?"

"I'm sure I don't know. It remains to be seen. The authorities, I believe, the local authorities will advocate a more systematic excavation."

The municipal authorities of Boissy did not interest Manuel and Marina. They were digging into the candy Robert had brought (classic excuse of guilty relatives), but this did not make them lay down their arms.

"And what about him; what proofs has he given?"

"He has found, at a depth of thirty meters, under the tower at the northeast corner of the château, some sculptured stones. At least, so he says."

"Couldn't he bring them to the surface?"

"Not with the tools he has. He only has some ropes, some old buckets, some sliding gear—"

"Couldn't someone go down with him to see?" said Marina.

"Someone bound by oath," Manuel specified.

"No one has as yet dared."

"So, after all, we have to take him at his word?"

"At his word. Like a writer."

BERNARD WRITES AN ARTICLE

Because Robert had let him down, Bernard himself had to write an article. On Brecht. It exasperated him; it obliged him to go home before dinner to work in that apartment which was both perfect and oppressive, obliged him to shut off his telephone and tell the servant not to let anyone disturb him. Obliged him to answer Geneviève's questions. And Geneviève did ask some maladroit questions. She was worried to see him return home so early, and besides, he had interrupted her yoga exercises, catastrophically.

"Would you like some coffee? Or tea?" she asked with nervous urgency. "I'll tell Nurse to take the children for an outing."

He felt diminished by this solicitude. He felt like the victim of an accident brought back home. He felt as though he had broken a bone or something and was unable to carry out normal movements.

"Is the lamp placed right? A cushion would help, wouldn't it?"

He was not in the habit of working at home and so had to settle down in the sitting room, where the distinguished colors (ocher, sepia, and brown) irritated him for the first time. Geneviève's "climate" was annoying. Baudelaire's *"Luxe, calme, et volupté"* was all very nice, but not conducive to work. And work he must, for this two-column article must be in by the next day. Up to this time, he had always counted on having Robert at his beck and call, was in the habit of asking him to render little services (very poorly paid) at the last minute. Brecht, the Alcazar, the Etruscans, gastronomy, literary and artistic conferences—No matter what the subject and time limit, Robert always managed to come through. Oh, without genius, but he always somehow managed. Bernard felt a virtuous indignation at suddenly being denied this commodity. The affectionate disdain he had always felt for his friend now turned against him; he had the feeling that Robert was revenging himself on the sly by dumping this article back upon him.

Of course, it was only a false impression, arising from the nuisance of having to write this article for lack of anyone else to write it. Bernard was sure that his friend had never experienced anything but affection for him, but as he settled himself in the too fragile armchair under the light shed too dimly by an ecru lampshade, facing a Ming Buddha drowsing in its niche, he was ready to send Robert to the devil. And he resolved that somehow he would whip this article into shape.

But he had a hard time getting started. These chairs were frightfully uncomfortable; the table was ridiculously small; and he had never thought of putting a desk in the apartment. He took time out to read through some articles written by others for his magazine and realized that he hadn't written one himself for ages. Another thing that kept him from getting started was the flabbergasting idea that Robert might obstinately go on maintaining his attitude of aloofness. Perhaps he wanted a raise? Perhaps I could manage that, he ruminated, but we've been friends for such a long time, and I never thought to revaluate the rates, since heaven knows when—And it's rather inelegant to discuss such a thing. After all, he could have told me if he wanted—And there's the symposium on Kafka to shape up for the next issue, and the retrospective exhibition of Léger—Can it be that Robert wanted to show how indispensable he is? But Robert and ambitions? The juxtaposition of the two words momentarily amused Bernard.

The fact of the matter was that to replace Robert, the magazine would have to find not one but two or three young writers, undergraduates perhaps; there was so much specialization these days. Robert, who could write on no matter what subject, was a cogwheel hard to replace in the magazine organization. An advantage to lack a personality, thought Bernard with revived bitterness. And as he recalled the article on the Etruscans (not bad, that article) and the survey of the young generation in 1968–1969 (which had so enthused Robert) and that article "Tracking Down the Ancient Volcanoes of Auvergne," Bernard told himself that if so many things interested Robert, it was because he had never mastered any one subject, really. But confronting the need to write this article on Brecht, a subject that did not interest Bernard at all, he asked himself, How in the world does Robert do it? How?, with a quite new curiosity.

THE IDEAL WRITER

"Hello, Catherine?"

"Yes, Jean-Francis?"

"I wonder if you'd like to go with me to the Grand Palais this afternoon. There's an exhibition of primitive jewelry."

"Yes, I know. But I'm booked; I promised to go somewhere with the children—"

There was a brief silence. Catherine perceived the surprise of Jean-Francis, and it irritated her. True, she rarely occupied herself with Vivi's children, and it was also true that she had given Jean-Francis reason to hope—But she had the right to change her mind!

"And tonight, could you come to the *cinémathèque* to see—"

"Robert is here," she said quickly.

"Oh! Very well, very well. I'll call you again."

He hung up. He sounded melancholy. Perhaps I've hurt him? But then, he's always melancholy. Robert calls him, ironically, "the ideal writer."

True, when she had first met Jean-Francis, Catherine had for a moment thought, he's the one I should have married. For he corresponded to everything she considered a writer should be. And what a man should be. He made no concessions; he didn't write silly songs. His job at the Larousse publishing house was obscure, badly paid, had no connection with literature. He reserved himself for his own writing. His collections of verse sold poorly but were esteemed. He read difficult texts printed on Japanese vellum. He ate little. More than once she had asked herself, Why not yield to Jean-Francis? Why remain a faithful wife?

THE WIFE OF PIERRE SOREL

She was called Adrienne. "A nice little woman," said Gerry, "devoted and brave. But she finally tired of her husband's always being away, always occupied at night and exhausted by day, without any visible accomplishment, and she began to drink and to take lovers." Gerry did not judge, did not blame Adrienne, nor did he blame Sorel. He merely recounted their story. It was a fatality, a logical fact. "It had to happen," as good people say.

And Catherine reflected, If I am unfaithful to Robert, will Gerry and the others think, "It had to happen"? No doubt, but for opposite reasons. Robert makes money, is often here; I reproach him for the very opposite of what Sorel's wife can reproach her husband for.

Lonely. She probably felt lonely. But does anyone feel lonely if loved? It was not Robert's absences that caused her complaints. Adrienne was a woman without intellectual resources and evidently without imagination, having only a simpleminded comprehension of what her husband was trying to do. He was trying to create something, something big in which she could have helped. If only by being loving and patient. But patience and faith were on Sorel's side. Maladroit and perhaps desperate as his attempt was, Catherine was on the side of Sorel. Therefore on the side of Jean-Francis. So why this fidelity that Robert didn't deserve?

STILL THINKING ABOUT ROBERT

Laboriously she memorized his faults, his defects, his infidelities, his laziness of mind and body. He had put on weight; he didn't read books any more. And his impossible friends and his dawdling. More than once, she had caught him having coffee with the concierge. Then, the kind of life he gave her. Not a life of deprivation, for she could have faced that with courage. No, the life he gave her was merely mediocre. For instance, his fondness for coarse peasant food. That might seem to be a trifling fault, but it represented a whole life-style, as when he came home after a day filled with nothings, with worthless articles, futile encounters. Were he to admit his faults and futilities, she would tolerate them, but he did not. Instead, he was smilingly self-satisfied as he ate his plate of Toulouse baked beans (and she had made that cassoulet for him, for what reason she really wondered), sitting there in his shirt sleeves, that meaningless, warmhearted look in his eyes, a tender smile on his lips—his greasy lips; and she had felt a surge of wrath, an impulse to shake him and say, "Wake up! Realize who you are, who I am!" Sometimes she even felt like blurting out, "I hate you!" But then she would go over to kiss that mouth shining with grease, giving him a deep kiss!

At night in bed she rejected him, digging her nails into the palms of her clenched fists, wanting to say, "Make love to your starlets, your nightclub singers—" All the same, she was not going to stand in line and take her turn! Yet she longed to take her turn. Why not? And now he was ashamed, dared not make approaches, so he kissed her chastely on the forehead. They said nothing, each detesting the silence of the other, full of love for each other. They were no longer happy at all.

Then why not Jean-Francis? Stop, executioner! Wait awhile! Leave off torturing me! I'll give Robert one more chance. Since he has begun to write that book—Not for the book's sake, I'm not such a schoolmarm as all that! But because if he can prove to me that he is capable of devoting himself completely to something—

But Jean-Francis has devoted his whole life to poetry, and I'm unable to take him as my lover. One day I must make an effort in that direction. But if there were a chance, no matter how small, of escaping it—Then, Sir Torturer, give me a little more time.

VIVI—GONE!

"Aunt Catherine?"

It was Marina on the telephone. Catherine rubbed her eyes. This time she was really awakened with a start.

"Really, Marina! Don't you realize it's not yet seven o'clock?"

"Uncle Robert," Marina murmured, "I want to speak to Uncle Robert."

She could at least say "please"! Catherine was all the more annoyed because Robert, as it sometimes happened, had slept out and was probably to be found at the apartment on the rue Saint-Séverin.

"What do you want with him?"

"Oh, quick!" Marina implored. "Quick, let me talk to Uncle Robert."

She was apparently close to hysteria.

"Tell me, at least—"

"Mamma!" Marina whimpered. "Mamma didn't come home last night. She isn't here; her bed isn't turned down! She must have been in an accident!"

"Dear Lord!"

Suddenly Catherine lost her head. Her sister! And Robert not at home!

"Robert—has just left," she articulated with difficulty. "I'll try to reach him. Where's Manuel?"

"He's gone down to the tobacco store to telephone Mamma's friends from there. And he gave me a list of other people to call."

"Well, go ahead and make those calls," said Catherine, trying to regain some calm. "I'll try to reach Robert. And I'll call you back in twenty minutes. Don't panic."

"Don't panic," she repeated to herself as she frenziedly opened the drawers of the desk to find Reine's number. Robert had given it to her one day "in case of an emergency," but where, oh, where had she put it? She had never used it. Was it in the address book? No. She had felt distaste at the idea of writing the name of "that woman" in her address book, along with the names of her friends. So it wasn't in the desk? She suddenly remembered an old account book in which she must have—a brown notebook, with an oilcloth cover, very ugly, had lain about on the night table; then, oddly enough, the very proximity of that name, Reine, in that book lying so close to her head, kept her from sleeping. And so she had—"Oh my God! Vivi!"—she had seized it, and, yes, she had flung it wrathfully into that old cardboard folder where year-old paid bills slumbered along with some rough drafts of Robert's writings.

She slipped into her dressing gown, only now aware that she was shuddering with cold, ran into the hall, broke a fingernail on the cupboard door. "Vivi!" she said aloud. "How many times have I told her she must not come home alone at night in that deserted neighborhood?" She imagined her sister murdered. No, more likely a banal traffic accident, maybe a broken leg; perhaps she fainted and was without identification papers—Call the hospitals? The morgue? Robert would tell her what to do. Oh, at last, the notebook! Under the old ski boots he hadn't worn since—But this was not the moment to go daydreaming. What a lot of dust! Even in her panic, Catherine felt disgust at plunging her well-kept hands into that dried-out mass of rustling old papers. Here it is! She seized it, blew off the dust, sneezed, riffled through it, hurry, hurry, and she read what she did not remember having written: "Robert's lady friend: ODE 43-09." She had simply been unable to write that name as one does with the names of acquaintances.

She returned to the telephone, notebook in hand. Then she sat down on the bed and consulted the clock. Only seven-twenty. "But Vivi!" she said aloud. It would be more tactful to wait until eight o'clock—Well, just too bad! If only Robert is the one to answer—which is unlikely. She had never heard Reine's voice, except singing on the radio or television. Would her speaking voice sound like that? It took all the force of her anxiety about Vivi, the need to reach Robert, but finally she dialed the number, realizing she was committing an insane act in penetrating like this the intimate life of Reine, a verity she had refused to face for three whole years. Now she would have the proof that Reine—a television image, sounds registered on tape or disc—was a woman who really existed.

"Hello?"

The voice was low and sleepy.

"I'm Catherine," said Cathie, maladroit, desperate. "Is Robert there?"

She hoped and prayed she would not have to say more. Robert's voice at the end of the line would put everything to rights.

"I'll go see," Reine's voice said. It betrayed only some astonishment.

There was the click of the receiver being put down, then

the more distant sound of a door being opened and shut. No voice calling.

"I'm terribly sorry—He left without—without notifying me," said Reine, more present now. (She had almost said, "without waking me up," Cathie very well realized.) "He had warned me that he would leave early—"

"Oh, my God!" said Catherine, now completely undone.

"Is there anything I can do?"

The shock of this offer restored Catherine's presence of mind.

"No, I don't believe so. Excuse me for having bothered you like this. I would not have done so except for a serious reason."

Reine responded to this in a voice more cordial and at the same time more solemn.

"A death?"

"No! Well—my sister—did not return home last night, and her children are in a panic. I don't know what to do."

"Oh, my God!" said Reine, exactly repeating Catherine's words. "And that—never happened before?"

"Never."

"My God! What to do? You could telephone the hospitals? The police station?"

"I doubt they would answer at this hour."

"Surely they must have a twenty-four-hour service. Shall I put through a call for you?"

"No," said Catherine regretfully. "I'll do it; I'll do it."

"In any case, don't hesitate to call back if—And if I see him, I'll send him to you immediately."

"Yes," said Catherine. "Thank you."

She remained sitting there on the bed for a moment, forgetting Vivi in the shock of having made this discovery: Reine was a woman like herself. She had said, "Oh, my God," and "What to do?" Reine was a woman like herself.

Then she collected her wits and telephoned Marina.

The entire morning was spent telephoning. Marina wept. Manuel clenched his fists. They had come to be with their Aunt Catherine, who managed somehow to preserve her composure. Then, at almost quarter to one, the doorbell rang. It was Vivi!

A pale and limp Vivi, but not at all conscious of the panic she had caused. All three flung themselves upon her, showering her with kisses and questions.

"But I have the right!" she said. And then she burst into tears and ran to shut herself into Catherine's little study.

Robert had worked all morning long at the Petit Cluny Library, and then, having no desire to return to the rue Saint-Séverin and still less to return home, he had offered himself as his right a lunch in a small restaurant behind Notre Dame where the woman who ran the place served up a marvelous *blanquette de veau*. One has to indulge oneself occasionally.

FROM ONE POINT OF VIEW

From one point of view, Robert reflected, it's very pleasant to write. He had forgone *the* weekly dinner at Evelyn's, had neglected to put the finishing touches to Reine's new tour, had forgotten the Prix Vérité and Father Moinaud. And nowadays, he lunched wherever he liked, without a feeling of remorse. Or almost.

But there are the imponderables. For example, late that afternoon, when he returned home and was surprised to see a light in Catherine's room, since normally at that hour she would still be at the lycée.

"What's going on here?" he called, his vague anxiety mixed with displeasure at the prospect of being disturbed.

She ran toward him, filling the study—so quiet a moment

before—with the clamor of excited words and badly garbled information.

"What's this, what's this? You say Gerry didn't come home as usual and Vivi's getting married?"

"Oh, you're just pretending not to understand! I'm telling you that Vivi didn't come home last night and that the children were in a panic and that I've tried all day long to reach you and couldn't find you anywhere—"

"Come, come, don't mix things up like this," he said with his exasperating equanimity. And he sat down in his armchair. Catherine, shaking with anger, expected him any minute to take up his pipe. And he did.

"First of all, where is Vivi now?" he asked.

"Why, at home! But what I want to say is that I telephoned you everywhere and—"

"But, in short, Vivi is all right; nothing happened to her?"

"Oh, oh, oh, yes! Yes."

"That's all that counts, surely. Cathie, I understand how anxious you must have been, but surely you know that I'm working now on my book and—"

"Yes, but I telephoned everywhere, to the magazine, where I got Bernard on the line—he was rather disagreeable, I must say—and I telephoned to . . . to your lady friend and to Gerry. It was then that he made the announcement."

"Announcement of what?"

"Why, that he's getting married! You don't listen to anything I say!"

"You tell me everything at once. I almost believed that Gerry was marrying Evelyn. But now everything is all right?"

"All right, all right! She slept out and didn't telephone the children to tell them she'd not come home. And Gerry is committing an irreparable folly. And Vivi—"

"Your sister was bound to meet, sooner or later, some man—"

"But to sleep out! And not warn the children!"

"Naturally, they were worried. But they're old enough to understand—" Robert muttered, feeling somehow to blame.

Catherine, who had gone toward the kitchen, turned back.

"The children blame you for everything! Because you've let Vivi down! Can you beat that?"

The Parthian shot struck Robert in the chest.

"Well! That's a little too much!"

Satisfied that she had finally had an effect on him, Catherine left the room, calling from the kitchen: "Would you like some beef tongue for supper?"

He ate some of the beef tongue without remarking that it was beef tongue which Catherine detested and which he had formerly been very fond of. His thoughts were elsewhere, and he could not keep himself from going on with the conversation.

"But I saw the children last Saturday night!"

"Yes, but you know how they are," said Catherine, ready to console him now that she had hurt him. It was her only way to love him these days. "They're so unjust!" Ah, her little air of triumph. "But it's Vivi who stirs them up. She is more of a child than they are. Even her staying out all night, if you want my opinion, is a childish reaction, the reaction of a spoiled child. She wanted to throw us all into a panic."

"Tell me why?"

"Because she thinks you are neglecting her. Because you are writing that book. Because she thinks she has rights over you."

"And she has. Not all rights, but she does have some," said Robert, making an effort to be courageous.

"And what about me?" asked Catherine.

Her face had paled, and her features were set in the hard lines of an exalted fanatic, the expression he had called her "Joan of Arc" face. Choose. He must choose between her and

Vivi, between her and Reine. (And only that morning she had told herself, Reine is a woman, like me, and she is perhaps the better of the two.)

He read her mind: he must choose between her and everybody else. But just suppose it's my right, my very modest vocation, not to choose?

JOCELYN

Jocelyn, his first love, a little fifteen-year-old whore, emerging from her hobbled adolescence and thrilled over so many discoveries, one of which happened to be her own beauty.

The beauty of Jocelyn, who was four years older than he —and the difference, at that age, was an abyss—was one of his discoveries in a year of discoveries; she was like a first voyage abroad, the first love story devoured at night, the first poet, the first drunken bout with comrades; she was everything, in short. And fifteen, no, twenty years later, he had been ashamed of Jocelyn in front of Catherine.

That was their first disaccord. But was it the first? No. There had been a remark made by Anselme one day: "I wanted to talk about it to your mother, but, you see, it was two o'clock in the afternoon, and she was sozzled." And Catherine had tactfully averted her eyes. He would have preferred less tact, less ostensible pity, but already had lacked the strength to laugh it off, to declare that having an alcoholic mother was funny, was quaint, and not at all shameful.

But to return to Jocelyn.

Jocelyn, twenty years later, was a great big incorrigible has-been, emaciated, clicking with cultured pearls, really lamentable with her talk about Prévert, the Liberation, surrealism, black magic, for she lacked the mentality to bring herself up to date and get in touch with current tastes; she still hummed forgotten tunes, wore her hair shoulder-length, wrapped herself in trench coats, thought of herself as a vamp with a distraught look in her eyes. All this in an incredibly shabby and crumpled version. Oh, my God! Have your clothes pressed, my poor dear Jocelyn, too disinterested, too taken up with things of the mind; she knew by heart all those beautiful poems of hers that had defied so heroically the efforts of so many agents in the marketplace and had finally offered themselves free of charge to those bearded poets who laughed at her behind her back. A martyr to Culture, was Jocelyn, and was all the more deserving of praise, since she had within her a touch of the concierge that surfaced in her predilection for quilted satin eiderdowns, lampshades that screened the light, a profusion of green plants, cozies, and so on. But her room on the sixth floor, the floor reserved for servants in the days when there were servants, was a filthy walk-up with noodles simmering on a hot plate. That was poetry, that was duty, and the minute she had any spare change, she treated her pals to drinks, while her shoes let in the rain. The tragic thing was that her pals were in their twenties, all her contemporaries having dropped her, busy with their successful careers in radio or journalism, public relations, or what have you. She accused them of "compromising" with the established order, so she had been obliged to renew her stock of friends in her frantic effort to cover the distance between *lettristes* and *structuralistes*—but, panting and breathless, worn out, body and soul, still not quite sure in the depths of her carefully studied derangement, not quite sure of being really abreast of the times. Poor Jocelyn!

She had sat there, in the Colonel's blue armchair, her legs crossed far too high, her mauve pullover far too tight over her torso (what courage!), saying that she had never known how to save money but had lived from day to day, after us the deluge, had always lived in the intensity of the moment. This noble discourse had worried Catherine, who had given him a sidelong glance that he interpreted as asking, "Should we lend her some money?" At that time they themselves were barely scraping through, he had not written a book for the past four years, did not yet have a spot on the radio. Catherine's anxiety was quite justifiable, for at that time it was she, with her classes, who shouldered the main burden of their expenses. Thanks to Germaine, who had ceded the apartment to them, they were well lodged, even luxuriously in appearance. (And, oh, the condescending look of indulgence Jocelyn bestowed upon the furnishings!) Even so, the expenses swallowed up everything. Catherine, mind you, was always impeccably well turned out; that day she was wearing a dazzling white shirtwaist, black velvet slacks, a red cardigan of some synthetic material but smart, everything as usual simple but irreproachable, with her hair glossily clean, her hands well kept, her complexion like porcelain, making her intensely dark eyes even darker. As neat as an architect's blueprint, yet mysterious all the same. At that time, she wore her hair long in a thick braid over her shoulder, this giving her a subtly sensual look. He liked her looks; he loved her; he feared her a little; and yet that day, he had felt the first wave of hatred—No, no, a feeling of opposition to her. Because, through her reactions, which he felt, he saw the millimeter of black dirt under Jocelyn's fingernails (bright pink, the nails), saw the bad taste of the mauve and green shoes that were aristocratically dusty, saw the ripped hem of the daringly short skirt, saw the sagging breasts under the too-youthful sweater. And the fact that Catherine could not see beneath these things and through Jocelyn's stale words, the beret and cheap accessories (American surplus, the elegance of the years 1945 to 1947) and through the breath heavy with hurried delicatessen meals gulped down and ill digested, could not see the emphatic innocence, the original purity of Jocelyn.

But now, let's be just. It was his own weakness that was at fault. He had made no attempt to convince her. He had let her be condescending, patient, full of tact. He had let her behave like her mother: a saint, caring for lepers. "Why, of course, we shall always be glad to see you again—And, of course, one of these evenings, we shall be glad to go up to your place for a drink." She, Catherine, had said "for a drink" like a missionary speaking to respectful African Negroes: "Chocolate him good? You content with pretty necklace?"

When Jocelyn had gone, he made a weak attempt to do something about it.

"Essentially, mind you, she's a fine girl."

"Why, I'm sure of it, dear."

(He had felt like saying to her, "as fine a girl as you." But if that were so, why had he married Catherine instead of Jocelyn? Why did he prefer clean fingernails, tactfulness, and a well-ordered home?) With an effort, he made one more plea.

"You should see the milieu she comes from."

"Of course, dear," she had murmured, like an incantation. Always in that tone of the missionary to whom all men are equal provided they know how to keep their place.

"You're so good, dear, so good," she had said. "But you must take care not to let your time be consumed so much by others. Think of your work, your writing—"

She kissed his eyes. He had beautiful eyes, feminine eyes, with long, curled lashes. "Think of your work, your writing." Maybe reason was on her side. He was ashamed of having introduced Jocelyn, who said "authentic" and "valid," whose nails were bordered in black, who wore her beret over one ear. Forget all that, and tomorrow write some really good pages. With a well-manicured hand.

"Oh, my sweet, my dear little missionary!" (His animosity had evaporated. He desired her.)

"Why missionary?" she murmured, her eyes half closed, a little perverse.

He lifted her up and carried her toward the bed, her body light but plump, and he thought of the pitiful bones of Jocelyn.

He had made love to the missionary. They had fallen asleep, believing they were still happy.

She had told herself, next morning, "I should not have yielded myself to him." As if he had been her lover.

GERRY THINKS ABOUT SOREL'S FRIENDS

Gerry liked to think about Pierre Sorel's friends, in whom the idea of a buried treasure had first crystallized: the old priest who had surrounded the child Pierre with lifelong kindness from his infancy; Monsieur Graff, his foster father, who had remained his friend; and also Guimard, the agent, who had taken a tremendous interest in the diggings. Devoted friends. Gerry could understand them. He, too, liked to devote himself to something without personal gain, without ambition. He thought up ideas, which he handed out to the right and left, just as he distributed his photographs among his girl friends. He was much moved by the noble conspiracy of silence among those friends of Sorel as to what was happening at the château. He rather regretted that they had felt obliged to keep Adrienne in the dark about her husband's venture. If she had been informed of it from the start, mightn't she too have taken an interest in it? To exclude her was a sign of mistrust, which alas was justified by the events. But suppose they had acted otherwise? Very regretfully, Gerry decided that Sorel had not behaved as a good husband should. He ought to have shared the idea of the buried treasure with Adrienne. But suppose she had been unable to understand? Surely, though, everybody would be capable of understanding. And if the friends had gradually lost heart, it was because Sorel had stopped talking and explaining.

It's easy to explain a treasure, thought Gerry, who had his friends and liked to share everything with them; for instance, he told them about Robert's novel, about his own photos of the Saint Antoine neighborhood, and about his love for Carol. Only a week ago, he had asked her, without any hope, "Will you marry me?", and she had replied, as she smoothed her hair, "Yes, maybe I will." He would have found it hard to explain the feeling he had then! As if he had found a treasure, not by struggling and digging for it, but just by chance. Later on he thought, Perhaps Sorel has found the treasure and doesn't want to tell about it?

PORTRAIT OF CAROL

Carol's real name was Danièle, a first name that suited her better, being evanescent, for everything about her slid, fell, disappeared. Her necklaces broke and fell to pieces, her rings forsook her, and even her clothes floated; her shawls snagged on her fingers and on doorknobs. Her voice was plaintive, almost whimpering. She suffered from a thousand ill-defined maladies and from a becoming lassitude, which did not keep her from posing for six hours in the rain but made it impossible for her to carry a package, climb stairs, or read a newspaper. As to her physique, it is hard to describe. Very slender and not very tall is about all that can be said about her figure. The rest was only accessory, even the feminine face she painted with prodigious talent on her naturally pale and childlike visage.

Carol was always on the point of having a migraine or a nervous breakdown or a common cold or about to commit suicide. Her equilibrium was precarious. On the edge of a roof. Graceful, desolate somnambulist, travestied as a hippie or an astronaut, she wore her disguises with a resignation that seemed to convey the idea that essentially she was only an eternally romantic young girl, a pale, lithe creature that only a Hercules could defend and console. The question she posed to men without uttering a word was: Are you Hercules?

From her melancholy narcissism, her regal incapacity in all domains, from her laziness and lack of culture (the most apparent result of a "good education"), Carol derived a feeling of superiority so strong that it rendered her almost human. Thus, she endured Gerry's adoration with easy detachment. Since Gerry was the most zealous of her admirers—and the one who photographed her best—she granted him a corresponding part of her time, her thoughts, her absentminded kindnesses. Not without making him feel that her gracious gift in any way gave him any rights.

Carol was attractive, fascinating. But as Catherine sometimes said, "Deprive her of her fine clothes and her makeup, what is there to her?" (Everyone called Gerry and Carol "a handsome couple.") And Catherine answered her own question with, "Exactly nothing!"

Carol was an allegory. Death or Nothingness, beneath the graceful and vapid exterior of a rich young girl (her family's apartment was in the wealthy sixteenth arrondissement). As a fashion model, she rubbed elbows with bohemians and squandered other people's time as irresponsibly as she would pluck the petals from a flower.

Carol and Gerry had waited a long time in the Blue Bar for Robert, and he did not come.

"It's not like him," said Gerry, nervous and disconcerted. He was wearing a necktie.

"What *is* like him?" murmured Carol. She had violet eyelids and blue lips. She looked at her reflection in the mirror opposite her and was utterly satisfied. Her eyes reflected the mirror that reflected her eyes. If she shut her eyes, if the mirror were taken away, what would remain? Nothing. The nothing that Gerry passionately loves.

Perhaps, Gerry ruminated, still thinking about Sorel, perhaps he has found the treasure and doesn't want to talk about it because it's not money and it's not jewels. Perhaps it's a very beautiful fresco at the end of a gallery, which he discovered little by little, with the aid of a flashlight; and perhaps when exposed to the light of day, it will suddenly disintegrate (he had read this in a story about the mummies brought out of the pyramids and how they dissolved into dust). A beautiful fresco that only Pierre Sorel knows about. That must be a wonderful, agonizing, almost terrible joy. (The joy Gerry experienced when he looked at Carol, who was so beautiful and who, when he asked her, "Will you marry me?", had replied in her flat voice, "Yes, maybe. . . .")

A TERRIBLE JOY

A terrible joy it had been, confronting those sculptured stones where fragments of a fresco appeared; it was a meeting there, underground, with other men who had been there—

"What? What?"

Pierre did not reply, but stubbornly fell silent.

"In any case, men had once gone there," said Guimard, full of good will. "Because Pierre, here, discovered some—"

"But," objected Monsieur Graff, "did they go down there to hide a treasure? That's the whole question."

"Why did they go there?"

Pierre Sorel watched them as they argued. They were sitting close to him but were a thousand leagues distant. And what about himself, Sorel; why had he gone down there?

"I don't know, and I don't care to know. If they went down there to kill little girls—"

"Gilles de Rais killed little boys," said Guimard, proud of his newly acquired erudition.

"Boys or girls, it comes to the same thing," said Monsieur Graff, blushing under his tan. "They were children. He went down there to kill them. Or for a Black Mass? Or I don't know what. It doesn't matter, and anyway, it's not proved."

"Come now! Gilles de Rais wouldn't murder children on the public square, would he?" Guimard exclaimed, rather offended that anyone would cast doubt on Gilles de Rais, a folkloric treasure.

"He didn't live in this part of the country. And he could have needed to take a rest, that man."

133

"But the ancient chronicle says—"

"The ancient chronicle? Bits of gossip, maybe! As soon as he was arrested, you see, whenever a little boy drowned in a pond or even ran away, they pinned such things on Gilles de Rais. Look what they're saying about Monsieur Chanzy-Lenoir, just because his factory smells bad."

"Monsieur Chanzy-Lenoir! Why drag him in?"

Both men were excited and enjoying it along with their anger. They asked for another round of Calvados, and Madame Bâton, who had followed the argument from her station behind the door, now appeared.

"Would you like me to lay out the tarot cards and tell your fortune?" she asked, forgetting to pretend total ignorance of their conversation. And she laid out the pretty cards: The Hermit, a secret vocation; the High Priestess, the occult powers of nature; the Wheel of Fortune, a happy change—

"You see, you old doubters?" said Guimard. "We're to have a happy change, a secret. Pierre is sure to make another discovery. See? We must be patient for a while longer."

Guimard, good soul, was earnestly desirous of establishing peace, of preserving the warmth of their friendship, of continuing these evenings talking and drinking Calvados together, of having the tarot cards laid out. This affected Monsieur Graff, who yielded once more.

"Perhaps if he dug a little more to the east," he said, "something of interest may be found under the ancient chapel."

Something interesting from Monsieur Graff's viewpoint could only be gold, the sole mystery in his lexicon.

"All these stories," he concluded, making ready to go, "all these stories about little boys, Black Masses—Well, all I can say is, they turn my stomach."

"Why, yes, yes indeed," said Guimard placatingly. And to Pierre Sorel, when Graff had departed: "Pay no attention; just keep on. You've struck on something very encouraging in those stones, the what-you-may-call-it stones. As to Monsieur Graff, you know how he is; he's apt to flare up; he lacks education, but he'll come round, don't worry."

But Pierre Sorel must already have realized that Monsieur Graff and the warm companionship that had endured many years, the boyish pleasure of doing things together, of sharing enterprises, would not always be theirs. Perhaps he had already begun to foresee that the day would come when they would no longer be even two, that he would be alone. Perhaps this was what he wanted?

THE EPOCH OF HAND-SEWN SEQUINS

You can shake off your wife or your mistress, but you can't shake off your concierge. Whether Robert left the house early or late, he couldn't avoid being seen by Madame Suzy, who was always on the lookout for him, behind her glassed door.

Madame Suzy was a round little woman, as lively as a fox terrier, and as snappish, but without animosity. Like all concierges, Madame Suzy had known better days. She had been, first of all, a chorus girl, then a dresser at the Lido, then a milliner, then head saleswoman in a department store. She had posed for some painters, had made dolls. Madame Suzy prided herself on having engaged only in "artistic professions." This, she felt, gave her reason to treat Robert Guibal as an equal and a comrade whom she could invite to have a cup of coffee in her loge—an invitation he accepted now and then. On those occasions, she seized the opportunity to give him her opinion on his songs, his radio broadcasts, and to have him inscribe his books to her (she had an ample supply of them on a shelf above her cozy). She also took occasion to pass along to him various pieces of gossip concerning the show-business world, of which she considered they were both a part.

"Last night, I again heard *L'Accordéon* on the radio, Monsieur Guibal," she said as she busied herself in the kitchen.

"Oh, what a lovely song, the kind they used to write in by-gone times. But what a funny idea to have it sung by a woman. You need a Chevalier, poor devil, or a woman who has some class, like Miss Ethel, who sang it at the Lido when I was working there."

With time, Madame Suzy's memories of the Lido had been considerably magnified. But on the walls, various photographs proved she was not an inveterate liar. For there she was, young and already plump, emerging, half naked, from a giant cardboard pineapple; and there she was, dressed as a Roman soldier; and in that other one, she is enfolded in the embrace of an artificial python.

"In those times, they called upon talented people, like you, Monsieur Guibal, for variety shows! Songs—that's all very fine. But when you have a chorus of fifteen beauties all in sequins—and sequins of real gilt, sequins sewed by hand, not the plastic sequins they glue on nowadays—that's another matter, isn't it! And with a set like the one in 'The Virgin Forest,' she pointed to a framed yellowed newspaper clipping that showed trees turning into Greek pillars, "well, after all, that's certainly another thing, isn't it?"

Robert agreed as he sipped the coffee that was always rather bitter. He liked to imagine himself writing revues for dozens of beauties crowned with bananas or travestied as Renaissance pages in the epoch of hand-sewn sequins.

These stopovers in Madame Suzy's loge, surrounded by her souvenir photos, were a ritual. There were the pictures of her in Zouave uniform, in First Communion dress, as a naked baby and one of himself, shaking hands with an American actress on an opening night; and besides the photographs, there was the alcove with ruffled hangings, and the tasseled lampshades, the braid-trimmed window curtains—in short, a resolutely 1925 decor that the antique dealer on the corner declared was "absolutely fascinating." And as Madame Suzy poured another cup of coffee for him and resumed her recital, a hundred times interrupted and taken up again, the story of her life, Robert lingered on, his energy ebbing slowly, insidiously, like a flow of blood.

Madame Suzy would be well over sixty, but with boldly dyed red hair, and she dusted the seven flights of stairs every morning, singing to herself in a voice that an occasional nip of Scotch had only made a little hoarser. She knew all about the grandeurs and miseries of this world, was both cantankerous and good-hearted, taking milk and bread up to the top floor every morning to the old man there but sourly making him use the service stairway. Caustic, curious, obliging, Madame Suzy was a show that ingenuously amused Robert as much as it amused her to put it on.

Despite the Zouaves and the communicants on the wall, the doll on the divan, and the mail to sort out, Madame Suzy's loge was a theater loge. She was always ready to play a grotesque dramatic part, holding forth on the misfortunes of France and of the butcher's daughter, imitating the lady on the third floor—the "so-called" lady—and demonstrating to Robert how his songs ought to be sung. In short, despite her red hair and her fortune-teller's shawl, her tobacco-jar figure, Madame Suzy managed to give the impression that she was still twenty and could still, if she cared to, appear on the Lido stage emerging, half naked, from a giant cardboard pineapple.

"And what about that novel, Monsieur Guibal? Are you getting on with it?"

The typical question. But when it was Madame Suzy who asked it, Robert did not have the usual feeling of embarrassment and guilt. His novel, for Madame Suzy, was on the same plane as the misfortunes of the butcher's daughter (who deserved them) and her memories of the Lido or the hat factory she had tried to set up in the Ardennes, which went bankrupt. Were Robert to fail, she wouldn't hold it against him. "It's like that beautiful Aurora, whose career was ruined by a ripped pair of tights," she was fond of saying. After all these years, Robert had not yet asked to hear the story of the beautiful Aurora. And he thought, That's the way the story of Pierre Sorel should be told. He lingered on, half suffocated by the smell of onions cooking and the warmth of the coal stove, still lit, although April was now ending. Yes: It's like that poor fellow Pierre Sorel, who failed in his attempt—But why decide that he would fail? He might succeed, appear on television, become a familiar figure for all the Madame Suzys. Does one ever know? And he himself might perhaps succeed in writing his novel and "make a comeback," as Bernard put it. Sloth overwhelmed him at the thought, and at last he could not refrain, after all these years, from asking the question.

"Tell me, Madame Suzy, who exactly was this beautiful Aurora?"

Madame Suzy, who had been going to and fro, at last sat down, to create an effect, her round face wrinkled up with malicious pleasure.

"The beautiful Aurora, Monsieur Guibal, was a contortionist who first appeared at the Elysées-Montmartre in the thirties, doing a cobra number."

Trumpery, flashy trumpery not worth three sous, part false, part true, always referring back to the *Belle Époque* forever gone. Stories that activated puppets without a background, a shadow play, graceful and unreal. But it was a trumpery that enchanted them both, making them momentarily coconspirators in a childish but very secret game.

There would perhaps come a time when Robert would be sufficiently humble to content himself with recounting his memories to a naïve audience in a bar or the back room of a shop, tell of his encounters with Sartre, his meeting with Brigitte Bardot. In the meantime, he was only humble enough to listen and ask the necessary questions.

"Tell me, Madame Suzy, what exactly is a cobra number?"

"A music-hall turn where the contortionist is brought on stage coiled up in a big, round basket and. . . ."

And there Robert was, listening as if bewitched, stifling his remorse (Catherine, upstairs, thought he was working on the novel), and deciding that obviously there was no need to hurry away, since his morning was already ruined.

GEORGES GUIMARD

Had Pierre Sorel ever known such temptations? At the moment of going out into the cold night, was he ever tempted to remain in bed with Adrienne of the black, curly locks and the clean smell of soap? Or at the moment of leaving his friends, was he sometimes tempted by the perspective of a cheerful drinking bout and a game of cards lasting into the night? And as to the Templars, well, too bad, but that affair could wait for the next day. At the moment of leaving on the bus for the town of Valognes to consult the books in the library, was he ever tempted to linger with the old parish priest, whose mind wandered a bit but who knew the properties of herbs and the best recipe for an omelette flavored with sorrel? Or to remain with the schoolmaster, that "lay saint" who in the past had engaged in political combats and one day had shaken hands with Léon Blum—which was surely on a par, in the realm of souvenirs, with memories of Mistinguette and the Blue-Bell Girls, wasn't it? We hope so. At least, Robert hoped so, for he needed to feel sympathy for the main character in his novel. Had Sorel never wasted time?

These are some of the questions Robert asked himself during spells of discouragement.

True, if no treasure was found, if there had never been a treasure, then Sorel would have wasted his life. But that wasn't quite the same thing.

Guimard must also have had these same thoughts, more or less, that day when he decided he'd had enough of it and backed down, scared. Who knows whether he had ever believed very much in the treasure, even in the beginning? Or in the importance of the treasure? And with his meridional gift of speech—more sedate than usual, however, savoring each word, without haste—he had wanted to talk about it. But to whom could he talk without risk? For, mind you, there would have been the risk of having it stolen. He could talk to no one about it except Madame Bâton, who always listened from behind the door, anyway. But who, more than Madame Bâton, stranded at this rainy crossroads like a milepost, without family, without diversions, had more need of a treasure?

Naturally, Guimard must have doubted and wondered if Sorel, after all his labors, would ever bring back anything more important than the shards the parish priest brought back from his Sunday strolls, a few broken bits of crockery, some chipped flints, that he proclaimed were of "inestimable value," without ever risking showing them to anyone but ignoramuses. Bah! If a treasure were not found, they would at least have had, for a certain time, a secret.

Guimard was essentially a likable man, with his reasonable doubts, his unreasonable enthusiasms—and he was wasting his time. His conversations with Madame Bâton and the dog Mirza, his rather disillusioned reveries—disillusioned, but with that foolish little hope at the end of the evenings, under the stars. But why, if he had any hope, no matter how little, why did he leave the digging to Sorel? Not once had he lent a hand; not once had he gone down into the great subterranean realm of galleries and tunnels. Was it from laziness or fear?

As Robert left his building, he happened to think about Guimard with sympathy because Madame Suzy had some points in common with the stout Madame Bâton, who was, however, more malicious. But it was the first time that the hypothesis had come to his mind: that laziness could well be a form of fear.

Fear of wasting one's time is one of those fears. He, for whom time had always passed smoothly, like a landscape slipping by the traveler, all of a sudden felt responsible for each hour and minute. Time was cut up in slices that he must consume, must not let go to waste. Otherwise, insidious remorse destroyed his luxurious indolence.

"I'd forgotten that writing is such a bore."

"Oh, Robert! How can you say such a thing?"

That, of course, was Catherine.

OPTICAL ILLUSIONS

But to some extent, she was really only pretending to be indignant.

"Well now, Cathie, aren't you delighted?" Germaine asked, as usual beaming with kindness.

"Yes, Cathie, aren't you delighted?" Vivi demanded with a touch of acrimony. (She hadn't slept out again but was nervous, flighty, and dressed even more wildly than ever— that canary-yellow poncho, for instance!)

"Yes, I'm delighted," said Catherine.

Delighted. Why, then, did she have the feeling that Robert, because of the book he was writing, was drifting farther away from her instead of drawing closer? On account of those stories of tunnels, excavations, subterranean places? An optical illusion.

GUIMARD II

And there Guimard was, taking on more interest, more substance. He was taking over page after page. Well, at least he was a fine man, a great guy. Of course, it would be Guimard, for Madame Bâton was not a subject, she was by nature a grocerywoman, eager for profit, a particularly ugly woman and as a rule disagreeable. Especially in summer, when she revenged herself for her ugliness and loneliness by taking it out on the summer tourists, who were all rather out of pocket, since they didn't own a car and thus had to choose carefully when buying their provisions from her at hair-raising prices or else pedal nine kilometers on their bicycles.

But Guimard was an agent for a commercial house, was a character really without interest, in no way picturesque, a jovial man who loved life, a bit alcoholic, but a fine man, well-spoken. And when he sank down on a bench in the grocery and wineshop, he seemed to have settled there for eternity. In the mean and narrow life of Madame Bâton, that Medusa, the presence of Georges Guimard was the only thing that revived in her a spark of humanity. And that is not a subject for a novel. Nor even for a short story. Scarcely more than a chord, three notes lightly touched on a keyboard in an empty house. Scarcely heard.

And now Georges Guimard was getting into his little car, a rather banged-up car, quite unaware that he had created the only harmony in this big, slack silence. "Women," he was fond of saying, "are like cows. They need only a friendly word to let down their milk. After all, Madame Bâton has some good in her." But if he were asked what exactly that good was, he'd be hard put to answer. Well, she was a human being, living and breathing like his cows, his dogs, which he treated better than is usual in the country; and besides that, she was a part of her setting, polished with beeswax in the boulevard Michel—No, that's wrong. She was a fixture on the corner of the Flers highway in Boissy-la-Forêt, like a familiar hill, a turn in the road, the form of which is no longer questioned, because it is like an old acquaintance whom one salutes in passing.

To be acquainted, for Georges Guimard, meant, in a jovial and trivial way, liking someone. And thus he must have been the only person in the countryside—one might say, in the world—to show this kind of sympathy to Madame Bâton; and this had left her, for ten years now, in a state of quiet stupefaction.

142

Yes, a fine man, Guimard. Why he became interested in Sorel's idiotic enterprise remains a mystery.

Robert stared for a moment at the words he had written on the white page, words that seemed to have escaped from him, in a fit, no doubt, of ill humor.

THE VERB "TO BE"

"Basically," he said to Gerry, "I'm beginning to feel that I was mistaken in thinking that Sorel's digging under the Château de Boissy was a subject for a novel. I'm wondering if it's not merely a news item."

"What do you mean?"

"Well, I'm wondering if it isn't Sorel himself who is the interesting element in the whole affair, and if we shouldn't try to help him. I'm not sure how. Perhaps with an appeal to the Ministry of Culture, in the style of 'Endangered Masterpieces'? Since the subject in itself is not really interesting."

"Because he hasn't yet accomplished much—Is that what you mean?"

"No, that's not it," said Robert patiently. "It's because— You know, what initially drew me to the subject, the thing that gave it strength and beauty, was this unavoidable abundance of the verb 'to be.' For Sorel, the treasure *was*. Grammatically speaking, without an object. It existed in the ruins. For Adrienne, Sorel *was* insane. For Gilles de Rais, the devil *was* quite near and at the mercy of a ritual set of words. Graff *was* loyal; Guimard *was* jovial; Mirza *was* a dog.

"Each of the characters in this affair appeared to me with the vividness of a crudely colored woodcut, easy to reproduce. Blue pantaloons, brown jacket, pink face—and if the color bleeds a little, it doesn't matter. Sorel's dream (or Sorel's life, which is the same thing) presented itself to me with the admirable simplicity of a comic strip, or of childhood dreams (he, Gerry?), or of hallucinations. Simple, schematic gestures. Sorel goes to the château; Sorel digs a hole. A treasure is hidden in the earth. (Shades of La Fontaine!) The simplicity of a comic strip or of hallucinations. Madame Sorel is neglected and takes to drink, is unfaithful to her husband. The Sorel children fail their end-of-term exams. Captions, you might say, for a series of colored woodcuts, the short phrases of a book destined (almost) to be read by small children. The verb and its subject, the present indicative, the verbs 'to be,' 'to go,' 'to do.'

"And the thing that has repelled me in this subject is the unavoidable abundance of the verb 'to be.' The reader of today is well aware that this verb is a booby trap, like the pinup girl, the dwarf, the chevalier, who are in reality only the trademark of a soap or a line of canned foods. All this backs up Freud. No longer do we *exist;* we *represent*. And what we represent is not very much anymore. Saint George was not a saint; he was Courage; the dragon was Sin, the rose was Courtly Love. And even the Marquise of the serial story, who exclaims, 'I *am* a virtuous woman,' and, likewise, the grotesque bully, preceding a duel in the Bois de Boulogne, who exclaims, 'I *am* a man of honor.'

"They belong to a religious or social mythology that has finally worn out. Today, whoever says, 'I *am*,' is suffering from a complex or is garnering clandestine publicity."

And, Robert reflected, Gerry says, "I am," of course, and Catherine says, "I love." But they are talking to themselves in some dark hole or corner. And as for me, I don't want to talk to myself.

A MAN WHO DRINKS

Reine, the offspring of Polish working-class parents (as was Adrienne, the country girl), knew what a man is like when he drinks to excess. At first, he is jollier, more communicative than usual; the world has apparently taken on bright colors; once more pieces of good luck are possible, along with happy encounters. He is rejuvenated, laughs at fatigue, and banishes money worries. After this, he becomes more taciturn; the world no longer obeys the magic formula. The condition known as lucidity returns in spite of everything. He is weightless, while things continue to be heavy. He is in color, while the world is in black and white. He floats in a stable world; people can't help but notice him; he feels betrayed. He feels open and vacant; he is sure he has discovered a truth, a secret, and he wants to share it. The world wants none of it; he is rejected; he glowers.

"Your grandfather," Reine's mother Rozena had told her, "was a gentleman; he wore a bowler and striped pants, was very proper, with a silver watch chain on his stomach. He was tight with money, almost stingy. Well, believe it or not, when he'd had a drop too many, he took out his stuffed wallet—he always had a lot of money on him to take care of the marketing—and he ran down into the street wanting to give paper money to everyone. Your poor, dear grandmother would run after him to try to get back the money. 'Excuse me, sir,' she would say, 'my man is dead drunk. Give me back those notes; it's my housekeeping money!' And just think, the people were so nice—but it was in a small town; they all knew each other—they gave back the money! Maybe they were afraid of trouble if they didn't. But it was always like that. And next day he woke up with a hangover. 'Is some money, paper money, gone from my wallet?' he would ask. Rarely was one single bill missing but she, to teach him a lesson, would say, 'Yes, two notes are missing.' And she managed to economize a little to be able to buy some sugar or tea—miserable economies—for he refused to give her what she needed."

Yes, there are men like that who lose their heads and want to share everything. "Let's have some music!" (In Poland, that would be violins. But after all, Reine knew nothing of this, for she was born in Paris, in the Saint Antoine district of Paris; and if she sometimes sang Polish songs, it was to please her impresario.) And then, that man, in a panic the next day, asking, "Is some of the money gone from my wallet?" But there are also men who drink to get everyone else to drink and who drink again, persistently, in order to make the world move, to make things change.

There always comes a moment when that kind of man sees that the world doesn't change, that he's the one who changes. He may become taciturn and scowling, or he may go all the way, become a tramp, a vagabond who leaves his family—like the endings of certain movies, like the songs one sings about sad clowns, emigrants, lonely people—all of them lonely people, thought Reine, armed with an ancestral experience of men who "take to drink." She, on the contrary, yearned to put down roots, to stay put, and she surrounded herself with objects, carefully arranged her apartment (yet with a naïve taste or lack of taste that rendered her more human, the Reine that Robert cherished), and although perpetually on tour, traveling, attending galas, she preserved an intense immobility. But then, what about her singing? That amplitude, that simplicity (which never exists without a certain degree of bad taste) when she sang, her hands clasped and the blue spots focused on her, that song "Vitrail d'Amour," it was a flight from mundane things, a gratuitous gift she was bestowing on her audience (yes, gratuitous, despite her practical character and her reverence for money); was this not her grandfather all over again? When, in Bar-le-Duc, she held out her beautiful arms and sang the noble and ridiculous words her "librettists" had composed for her, tears flowed down her face (simplified by her makeup, which emphasized only the eyes and mouth); wasn't there in this something of her grandfather? "Take, take, I beg of you, take!" And when, afterward in her dressing room (always too cold), she mopped her face with a towel, she was overwhelmed with anxiety; wasn't this her grandfather asking, "Is something missing?"

Reine was, however, saved from the urge to sacrifice herself by her feeling for the sacred. With grandiloquent simplicity, she had convinced herself that in singing she played a part that she was almost tempted to call her "mission." The words "idol of the public," so often applied, did not suit her, but she could almost think of herself as a priestess. The Reine who sang and who put all of herself into her singing was not the Reine who loved Robert. Song and love manifested themselves through her, and she, passive and queenly, had only at certain times to let them transpierce her.

This preserved her serenity. At home, Reine dusted her bibelots, added up her accounts, simmered a goulash, followed slimming diets, pasted her press clippings in an album. She adored her mother and wanted to own a little dog and would have had one if she could have found someone to take care of it.

And she had recently begun to wonder why Robert, who did not drink excessively, was now behaving like a man who must be drinking.

"Is it going ahead?" Reine asked him obligingly and self-consciously.

"No, it's backtracking."

"Funny how irritable you are ever since you began to write that book," she said placidly.

And since she had little experience with writers, she supposed that it was always like this with them. However, she felt the need to consult a specialist: Bernard. Reine had a childlike faith in specialists.

"Bernard, is his behavior normal?"

"Alas!" said he, with an irony that left Reine perplexed. But he spoke about it to Geneviève, much irritated.

"Robert is behaving abominably with Reine!"

"You mean to say, with the magazine," said Geneviève with gentle irony. She always glimpsed his real meanings.

"It's the same thing! Here it is the end of April; she goes on tour at the end of June, and she's still waiting for the songs he promised her!"

"You don't usually worry like this about Reine."

"It's Robert I'm worried about."

"Because he's writing that book?"

"Because he's changed."

It would be a mistake to ascribe Bernard's irritation to self-interest. Doubtless Robert's repeated derelictions had obliged him to call upon outside help. But if Robert had abandoned the magazine because of illness, there would have been the same problem. Bernard's irritation was similar to that of someone witnessing the demolition of a house perhaps devoid of charm but where the witness had spent a happy childhood, a banal neighborhood but full of irreplaceable memories of life there for something like fifteen years. The destruction is an attack on a personal life, habits, attachments that go deeper than esthetic matters. And after all, was the old neighborhood all that banal? One never really looked at it closely. It was a place for a stroll, a place where you felt at ease, nothing more. Today, in memory, it takes on a mysterious aspect you had never noticed because you had never visited such and such a garden or dusty little museum, nor taken that picturesque side road. I should have done that one day or another, you tell yourself.

"I should have—"

"What?"

Should have spoken to him in a friendly way, perhaps, should have listened to him, accepted as an office employee that boyhood friend he recommended, should have read that very strange manuscript written by a stonecutter, should have entered that small and disparate universe. Robert had asked no more than that.

"Oh, it's too late—He's washed up."

"You're the one who is rather washed up, it seems to me," said Geneviève softly.

Even so, Robert was worried about Pierre Sorel.

"We ought to do something—write to the ministry or go down to see him, perhaps."

"Aren't you afraid that might sterilize you?" asked Mélusine with a circumspect pout. "His viewpoint might lead you astray."

Astray from what? But out of laziness or fear, he postponed writing to Sorel or making him talk.

He let Mélusine ramble on and on about Gilles de Rais.

"After all, Monsieur Guibal, you and I agree that the point in common between Gilles de Rais and the Templars is alchemy. And you see quite well the metaphysical importance of this. 'The philosopher's stone is the Christ of metals,' said old Paracelsus. Gilles de Rais invoked the devil. Evidently that was to relieve his conscience of a too-heavy burden. Possessed by the devil, he was no longer guilty."

But was Sorel ever really interested in the Templars or in Gilles de Rais? And what could a man of his limited education make of them?

Gilles de Rais was a historical figure. Sorel was no doubt ill acquainted with the story. But after all, it wasn't hard to imagine that Gilles de Rais was rich and well dressed, with the money troubles common to the rich (poor people don't have money troubles; they simply don't have money). Gilles de Rais also had interesting connections (Joan of Arc, for instance) and enemies at court (oh, the banners, the great, damp halls lit with candelabra!) and obligations (farm rents to collect). But Sorel could have only the faintest notion of all this, and it would certainly not fire his imagination.

There was also the other life of Gilles de Rais, those caves, those grottoes, his beastiality, his lechery. He raped, he murdered, he tortured, and no doubt all this was frightful. But country people are well acquainted with violence and lechery. No doubt they blamed Gilles de Rais, but without surprise. The walls, the woods, the silence of the countryside foster the slow unfolding and growth of a dream that the noisy town soon cuts down, whether the dream be bestial or contemplative. Facing a wide and empty horizon, could not the dream include God? Or why not that little girl down there, riding her bicycle?

But Gilles de Rais went in more for little boys. And he killed them. Such things really happen. But news items hold no mystery. What about that school inspector who last year fathered a child on the little Ferrero girl, twelve years old; yes, and what about the small-town mayor who presumably goes off to the horsefair and is seen at the only striptease show in the region? We all carry within us the seeds of this banal duality. However, in Gilles de Rais we are not dealing with the apparently respectable man who in private becomes a beast. Between honors and debauchery, the opposition is merely apparent. But crime as a *calling*, a vocation, takes us into another domain.

Madame Bâton, concentrating on the enigmatic tarot cards, shuts her eyes, and says she will now "convoke" (call up, summon) an astral body. Gilles de Rais does not stop with the still-warm and -quivering body that satisfies his senses; he calls up, summons by means of and through that body, through an act not restricted to himself, an inexpressible revelation.

Through crime, he is still close to humanity, to the men who wage war and eat meat. But crime as a *calling*, a vocation, condemns him irremediably to solitude. Solitude. Yes, Pierre Sorel must be beginning to understand this. But why is it that we always come back to this point?

"I'm a bit afraid for Vivi," Germaine confided to Catherine. "Just imagine, she's—she's having an affair with a young fellow, a German, I believe, that she picked up on the street."

"What? On the street?" Catherine exclaimed, horrified.

"Well, I mean to say, on a sidewalk where he was selling jewelry on a kind of trestle table set up in front of the Saint Marcel Church."

"A peddler?"

Germaine sighed. She wasn't sure. She'd find out.

"Deplorable!" Catherine exclaimed.

"Well, what can you expect? She doesn't know how to live alone; she doesn't know where to turn—Oh, she never complains. But—"

She sighed again and mechanically took up the knitting she was about to finish.

"How ugly it is! Heavens, how ugly those colors!"

Catherine was referring to the green and raspberry-red shawl.

"With a little blue and brown added," she suggested, "it wouldn't be so ugly."

"Marina's the one that chose the colors. All the young girls dress like this now, gaudy as parrots! But I'm not going to make any objections just now."

Catherine perceived an implied reproach and rebelled.

"Listen, Mamma. I've taken the children out three times. I've telephoned Vivi. I can't spend my life—It's not my fault if she behaves like an idiot!"

"It's not your fault, but you could—Oh, no matter! So long as you're happy!"

Germaine didn't seem to be any too sure of that happiness, and to tell the truth, Catherine wasn't at all happy any more.

"Does Robert have his dinner with you?" her mother

asked above the clicking of needles. The connection with what had gone before was evident.

"Yes," Catherine replied grudgingly, "Robert has dinner with me."

And since Robert dined with her, she had no reason to complain, did she?

MERRY CHRISTMAS, DARLING

Germaine piously kept, among her treasures, a postcard received during her betrothal to the late Colonel. It pictured a swallow carrying in its beak a message surrounded with lace. On the reverse of the card, her fiancé had written, in a careful, old-fashioned hand, "Merry Christmas, my darling. Faithfully yours, Jean."

For hundreds of years (centuries of good bread, evenings spent by the fireside, fair-haired daughters who were decked out in bride's veils for their First Communion), those words had been written hundreds of times. Not surprising, then, if Catherine had believed happiness in marriage was so easy! So easy that she only had to take the pen fallen from the hands of an ancestress, and the swallow with its innocent and banal message surrounded by lace would remain faithfully hers. A snare. Raised with love as though love were the rule of the world, along with fidelity and honor, which weren't even virtues. They were quite natural, and anyone who didn't possess them was as unfortunate as an invalid.

Germaine spread her balm. "Essentially, they are very attached to each other," she would say of a couple who were tearing themselves asunder. Or of a spiteful or envious person, "At least she's good at heart." Thus the maternal goddess handed down her decrees. Her magnificent wavy black hair symbolized the vitality that radiated from her, the magic power that her daughters thought could conquer and exorcise all evil. Goddess of bouquets and fruit preserves, of music and white sheets, great, benevolent pythoness, who, in the wedding picture, stood slightly in the background but with her hand on the bridegroom's shoulder to transmit her power to the god with epaulets, the blue-eyed god who in 1904 still wore the sword. Why be surprised; what was there astonishing in Catherine's childish faith (no, conviction) that happiness was her due?

The gods, even the benevolent ones, are dangerous. There, in the statuettes in the Saint Sulpice Church, where she had once seen flat simplicity, she now saw faces of stone, shut upon their mystery, enigmas prepared to lead mankind astray; and revolt surged in her when she looked at her mother's big handbag full of mint pastilles, useful addresses, calorie-counting cards, recipes clipped from periodicals—all the paraphernalia of an inoffensive housewife, that mask of a benevolent woman, that odd creature, a woman who had given and received love as if it were the simplest thing in the world.

And that woman had been unable to provide happiness for her daughters.

She had thought it was her due; this was what now revolted Catherine. They had made her believe that happiness was her legitimate portion, her heritage. When she had met Robert, Germaine had at once been delighted ("I am confident that. . . ."); she had been delighted that her daughter had encountered love and that, in Robert, she would now have a son. Everything was as it should be, as she had always hoped and prayed, and she had never doubted for a second that it would come to pass. And since Germaine had always won her wagers, she and Robert at the end of fifteen years were still on the best of terms. He had consoled her widowhood to a certain extent; she had comforted him at the death of his mother (who had died of cirrhosis of the liver, advanced alcoholism) with such tact. Their perfect understanding was one of the things that most deeply hurt Catherine.

And yet, she told herself, it wasn't a perfect understanding that I wanted with him. What I wanted was love. It is easy to come to a perfect understanding with Robert. I imagine he has a perfect understanding with Reine. I can just visualize it. While Mamma and Vivi imagine God knows what—love-philters, dances of the seven veils—I'm quite sure there's none of that. He writes songs for her. She cooks meals for him. They're a couple. And that isn't what I wanted, either. At least, I think not. But then, what was it that I wanted?

Why doesn't he love me? she muses, and sometimes the question becomes a rather sweet melody, poignantly sweet, accompanying a melancholy remembrance of childhood, of certain privileged moments when love appeared a possibility, as if quite near—in that landscape, that concert, that silence. And sometimes nauseating memories, when she felt as though she were rejecting a viscous bundle of entrails, impossible to swallow; she gagged at some recollections of mean actions, stupid hopes stupidly renounced, tasteless and at the same time ferocious sentimentalities of unrequited love.

Then there had been all those stupid efforts. The illustrated magazines, those pictures of Queen Soraya, those articles on clairvoyants, on gynecology; that book on sexuality she had consulted many times; those shameful attempts to beautify herself, visits to the hairdresser, the masseuse, and the slimming diets; everything that could let her hope against hope, miracle medals, antiwrinkle masks, and so on. A vertigo seized her as she reviewed that foolishness. Then there had been all those attempts to be a model wife, saying he was right when he was running someone down, saying he was right when he was wrong, ready to descend with him into the abyss—but no abyss awaited him. Oh, if only he had a vice!

Then there had come her sudden revolt at all this. Her curls were plastered down; her makeup was left off or just slapped on anyhow; all the trained-dog tricks were rejected with horror. Her bared forehead and her purchases of canned foods marked one woman's liberation. "Let him take me as I am." But after a brief period of consolation, she caught herself with a cigarette dangling from her lower lip, talking about her "job" with an affected vulgarity that filled her with disgust. "As I am. But what am I?" Her head swam when her mother or sister, in the course of conversation, pronounced the words, quite naturally, "a woman like you. . . . You remember, that girl who resembled you a little. . . ." She couldn't understand what those words meant any more. Love transforms, but the absence of love also transforms. "Cathie" or "Catherine"—those words no longer meant anything.

"I am the woman who is unloved," she said, echoing a line of Claudel. Germaine was touched.

"There was a saint who said, 'I am the saint who is not.' "

"If you think that is any consolation!"

But she no longer had any reason "to get things into her head," as her mother put it, for Robert now came home to dinner. And the wife whose husband comes home to dinner ought to thank the Lord and not ask for more, isn't that so?

"So, Mamma, since Robert comes home to dinner and doesn't sleep out, what more could I want out of life? Is that your viewpoint?"

"But, my dear girl," said Germaine bovinely, "life is no more than that."

"You say that, Mamma, because you're thinking of Papa. But you and Papa—It's not the same thing as Robert and me. You were a perfect couple; you shared so many memories—"

"And you have no shared memories?" asked Germaine almost roughly.

"I'm not sure—" Catherine murmured, brought up short.

"Then search your mind!"

You thought of Germaine as harmless, even a little naïve; and all of a sudden, without spite, she hurt you. Being in contact with Germaine was like, for a poor person, to be in contact with a millionaire. No matter how tactful the millionaire, there always comes a moment when the abysmal difference is felt. She always seemed to think that it only depended upon you to be happy, that if you didn't have her ease and vitality, it was your own fault, your lack of wanting to play your part. She was so upset by the unhappiness of others, Catherine reflected, that she denied its existence. Or am I being unjust? Catherine asked herself. And she was almost glad that Vivi, Germaine's favorite child, was also going in for the weakness of being unhappy.

"If Vivi persists in being unhappy," she said, "then neither one of us will have followed your example."

"Yes, but Vivi's not doing it on purpose," said Germaine with her implacable good nature.

MELUSINE NOTES THE STAGNATION OF THE BOOK

"I see you're not getting on at all with your novel, Monsieur Guibal. Is my documentation at fault?"

"Your research is perfect, Mademoiselle *Rebec.*"

He gave her a sidelong glance. How would she react? Her fine hands trembled, but her expression remained unaltered, was neither more nor less distraught. He felt the shame of a little boy who has said a bad word.

"But the book isn't advancing," she said guardedly.

"What about *your* book? How's it going?"

His hackles were up, and he spoke with a cantankerousness that was new to him. But he was in for a surprise. A smile of complicity was on her face as she answered him.

"After all," she said, "we're not in a hurry, either of us, are we?"

YOU THOUGHT YOU WERE DREAMING

In the beginning, Sorel must have said to himself, When I finally discover something, a grotto, a vault, a fresco, what a day of triumph that will be! And then, that day had come, and no one dared to go down with him to see what he had found, and no one completely believed him. Perhaps he did not even try to make them believe him. Perhaps when the faithful friend had exclaimed, *Victory*, he was thinking, they will have to believe in it now; they'll feel cornered, the mayor and the others! Then, astonished at his feeling of something like disappointment, he had postponed his triumph to a later day. Perhaps he had said to himself, It would be better to wait awhile, for a more categorical proof, something more definite, and had said to Guimard, "No, Georges, promise me not to talk about it yet; it's too premature; you don't want to throw all my work out of gear, do you? So promise. Let me have still another year, or not even a year, say, six months."

Guimard must have been amazed. Why didn't Pierre feel triumphant? Why was he in a panic; why did he act uneasy, almost guilty? "Now, Pierre," Georges probably said, "of course I'll not say a word if you want to keep the secret a few more months. But, you see, they might help you then, and you'd get ahead a lot faster. There are machines for excavating."

"I'm not in a hurry to get ahead."

Yes, he had said that. Georges Guimard had heard correctly. Pierre Sorel had said, "I'm not in a hurry to get ahead." You thought that you must be dreaming.

VIVI IN THE EVENING

For some time now, Vivi had no desire to go home in the evening. The worst of it was that she also had no desire to linger on at that cocktail party or to accept the dinner invitation or go to that film preview or that first night at the theater or that lecture which would have tempted her only a month or two ago. Only a short time ago, life had been an Ali Baba cavern where you had to seize quickly, quickly the glittering treasures scattered here and there, without pausing to distinguish what you were seizing, which was surely desirable. Life's colors now had a strangely altered aspect, were drained of vibrancy.

In the evenings of the past, Vivi had sometimes not gone home because she was afraid of missing something. And now, on the contrary, right in the middle of this thrilling concert of modern music or standing at the "country buffet" garnished with ivy and whole hams or in the obscurity of the *cinémathèque* where "for one single time" (what a pang at Vivi's heart was given by those words "one single time"!) a rare Marx Brothers film was being projected, right in the midst of her enchantment, Vivi couldn't help but regret that the twins weren't with her, and she visualized them lying in front of the television, eating ham and potato chips, or she thought of them in a panic, visualizing them in some unexpected danger—a fire, and Marina on the big ladder! Or a burglary, with Manuel struggling with a masked bandit! Then, suddenly, she simply had to be with her children, had to be at home enjoying the odd peace and relaxation of being a little ugly, with uncombed hair, wearing an old sweater and her gym tights. But how to resist those words "one single time"? True, one evening she had found Marina making a cream tart in a kitchen filled with eggshells and flour while Manuel had decided to tinker with his Solex motor, ruining his pants and getting oil stains on the moquette. She visualized again Marina's face, once more childlike, with a smudge of flour on her nose, and Manuel's brows gathered in serious concentration. And so, Vivi sometimes left Pierre Henry's concert of percussive instruments between two clappings of the cymbals, or left the private showing of the Marx Brothers film between two thrown custard pies, and ran toward the rue de l'Université to be with the twins, who were not at all embarrassed to be discovered nibbling sausages and sipping crème de menthe with their friends Béchir, Marc, Jeanine, and Sylvie, the record player going full blast and the telephone unhooked to cut off possible complaints from neighbors. She objected, laughed, then rushed away, seized with the conviction that something not to be missed was happening elsewhere, slapping on any old hat atop her undone chignon as she left. "I'll come back; I'll be back in an hour!" she cried; and the twins chorused, "Yes, yes, don't worry about us," which meant they didn't worry about her.

"Your mother, who is never at home," Catherine had said to Marina one day when she had quarreled with Vivi; and Marina had opened wide her violet eyes and said, "Mamma not at home? Why, she's here all the time!" And she believed it.

Vivi was, indeed, at home all the time; she came home fifteen times a day, for about five minutes. And when she wasn't there, she was telephoning, either because she had forgotten her engagement book or her evening bag or had forgotten to leave certain instructions or to leave money for their dinner, so would they arrange to have dinner at Béchir's or Nathalie's, or else they could buy some pizzas on credit at the Italian's shop—In any case, she wouldn't be out very long, not longer than ten o'-clock, so there would still be time for them to eat something together; she would stop off to buy something on her way home in a taxi—

"She's always at home," said Marina.

And so Vivi did not think it urgently necessary for her to be there in the flesh. Did it matter whether she was at home, sketching, or at a fashion collection, again sketching? The feeling that a revelation was always possible, the revelation of a secret that would suddenly reveal itself, this feeling had left her one evening.

Since then, she remained at home more and yet was less there, really.

"Mamma is going through some crisis or other," said Manuel with a worried look.

And Marina, who had hoped to witness some romantic episode following that night when her mother had slept out, was disappointed when no man of genius—an Andalusian sculptor. a Polish count, a persecuted hippie—put in an appearance. And she began to feel uneasy.

In the evenings, Vivi remained at home, a little too calm. Or she went to see a film, staying to the end. Before this change in her behavior, she had seen only fragments of any film, a puzzle, bright-colored morsels of a big fresco that another fragment would explain some day or other; her attention had always been fleeting but alert at night, when she felt that cheerful revulsion at the very idea of going to bed. Because Marina was about to say something definitive, or because the rose-orange lampshade she had bought at the flea market required more thought (perhaps the violet-colored one would have been a better choice), or because somewhere someone was speaking and what he said would raise a corner of the veil (as a child she had been so fond of the transfer pictures, the decalcomanias that Germaine bought for her), and now all this was finished. She now went to bed at night, turned off the light, *renounced the secret.* All this in moderation, because she had little talent for tragedy, having been immunized by Catherine's example, immunized against big words and excessive sentiments. She merely said to herself, "I wonder what's wrong?"

"Because Robert is too busy just now to see his friends is no reason why you should let yourself go like this," said Germaine.

"Oh, it's not on account of Robert—It's a combination of things. Robert, after all—I'm quite fond of him, but I've never understood how Catherine—" Vivi paused, then went on with sudden animosity, "Robert, after all, is just anybody!"

"Not everyone can be somebody," said Germaine.

She didn't even want to see him. And when she ran into Gerry, who was rather disconsolate, for those captions weren't shaping up, or when Anselme came to tell her he wanted Robert to recommend him for a job at the Baron biscuit factory, where they could use men of his abilities, and she had to say, "I'm sorry, but I don't see Robert very often at present," it was annoying.

But when, one evening, he blew in for a moment, she had burst into tears, absurdly, resting her head on his shoulder; well, the imbecile must have thought God knows what and had taken her in his arms, then abruptly had stepped back, as if—For goodness' sake! She was certainly not in love with him! No, it was something more serious.

THE WORLD UPSIDE DOWN

"I quite agree with you that you shouldn't waste your time with him," said Catherine in a voice she tried to moderate. "I've always told you so. But this doesn't justify your refusing all help to that poor Anselme!"

"That poor Anselme! You've always detested him!"

Robert was pacing the floor.

"I detested him when he was wasting your time. But—"

"You don't know your own mind! I'm the one, now, that wants to stop wasting my time with him. And you reproach me for it. This is the world turned upside down!"

It was a mean, vulgar quarrel. She tried to alter its course.

"But one can lose a little time to render a service without wasting all one's time—"

"A little time!" he shouted. "Tell me how much? A quarter of an hour? Seventeen and a half minutes? Set an alarm clock? Hire a secretary or a bodyguard? 'The interview is ended, Monsieur; will you please leave'? What twaddle! The only thing to do is liquidate him! I waste my time and energy for nothing! For nothing!"

Her nerves were stretched to the breaking point; her patience had drained away, and she was unable to hold herself in check. That he could say such a thing, shout such a thing at her! For she had always encouraged him, had so wanted to throw out the time wasters, to free him of all those obligations he himself had created out of kindness—or weakness. And now it was because of his weakness that he was yelling at her and had rebuffed Father Moinaud with such brutality that she had been unable to refrain from making him realize what he had done. She had been wrong. He had taken it as an allusion to her having had a more refined upbringing than he and had made her admit (speaking rather coarsely) that she contradicted herself (which was partly true, but only partly, for she had never advocated rudeness). And now he was shouting and gesticulating, something he had not done for many years, and had even kicked the Colonel's desk!

"And what about me?" she asked in a trembling voice bordering on a shriek. "Have you ever asked if I waste my time and energies for nothing? You have never asked, have you, whether my energy could be put to more viable use, have you?"

"Being the inspiration of Jean-Francis, for instance?" he said with heavy irony. "Why, yes, that's it. And when you have thoroughly inspired him, you'll see which one of us has obtained the best result. And you'll set up a prize? What á good idea! Vivi is right; you are a Stakhanovite. Write a book, write another book, you say, write book after book; how much time did it take you to write this one or that one? Faster, work faster! And so on. And you're also a Stakhanovite when it comes to lovemaking! Love me, you say, love me more, still more; how much do you love me? And so on!"

He began to laugh, and so excessively that she suddenly noted that he had been drinking. In a certain way, this consoled her. Yet, he hadn't drunk to excess for many years, or, anyway, for a long time. He must be in a very troubled state.

"Come, Robert," she said, recovering her self-control, "come to bed."

"Me, go to bed? But that's still more time wasted! Me, go to bed? I've got an appointment, and with Jean-Francis as a matter of fact. We're going to league together to give you satisfaction! Or maybe we need three men or four to satisfy you? A whole team! Mountains of books and mountains of lovemaking! And in record time!"

Several times in the past, he had alluded to Jean-Francis and his sentiments, but rather in a tone of harmless jest. Now she flushed with anger, ready to give him a straight reply. But he had already left the room and was in the entrance hall, fumbling with the zipper of his raincoat.

"At least, don't take the car," she went to tell him, overwhelmed with anguish at the sight of his maladroit movements and lack of coordination. The door banged behind him.

She had to sit down for a time in the brown armchair to control her breathing and recover some calm. Tomorrow morning, she told herself, he'll regret it; you'll see, he'll be very nice tomorrow morning. And it was true. Robert was incapable of holding a grudge against anyone for more than an hour at a time; she had noted this many times (regretting it when someone else was involved). But to what extent had he expressed his real thoughts? Stakhanovite! What an ugly word! Of course, Vivi had to butt in! I'll tell that girl what I think! But Robert usually doesn't care a hoot what Vivi thinks! Oh, if only he doesn't have an accident! Oh, if only he hasn't taken the car! Did he mean what he said? And she wondered if he really detested her; and if he detested her, wasn't that better than indifferent affection? Or worse? After a scene like that, wasn't she morally obliged to be unfaithful to him?

Provided he didn't take the car!

And what had she said to him? In sum, she had said, "I've

wasted my time with you!" But perhaps he won't remember. In the old days, when he had been drinking, he never remembered. Not even the words of love he had spoken. But she would remember. Robert was right; she did contradict herself. She didn't want him to waste his time, and she herself had wasted her life.

Oh, provided he didn't take the car!

Her useless fidelity. Her small attentions, her big reproaches, her silences, so praiseworthy—and so useless. Then why reproach his parasites, his billiards games? I've played at being a wife as if it were a game of billiards.

Perhaps she should forewarn Jean-Francis by telephone as to the state Robert would be in. Oh, let them work it out between them. She needed a hot drink. Should she make a cup of cocoa? Or bouillon? She chose cocoa. Then she would go tranquilly to bed. She had a nine o'clock class next day, on Lamartine. Fine. A very good biography of Lamartine had just been published; she had been sent a copy. She would glance at it as she drank her cocoa. A peaceful evening. Nothing had happened. A husband drinks, from time to time, one drink too many. Everyone knows that. Even the Colonel —"A little tipsy," Germaine said indulgently when that happened. Those ridiculous, outmoded expressions! Germaine also said, "We had a little set-to." A military man, what could you expect?

With complete dignity, Catherine went to the kitchen, turned on the gas, put a small saucepan of water on to heat.

From now on, she would live for herself, without bothering herself with what Robert thought. I will open out, she told herself; I will spread my wings, as Vivi says. (Stakhanovite, forsooth! Just wait till I get hold of you!) But Vivi is right. I live only for Robert, think through him; I am not a complete woman.

She turned off the gas, hurried down the corridor, put on her raincoat, and went down to the garage to see if the car was there. It was. Oof! What a relief. She ran back upstairs, saw herself in the entrance hall mirror, shrugged. Incorrigible!

Not without some trouble, Robert managed to reach the Saint-Claude Café on the boulevard Saint-Germain, where Jean-Francis was waiting for him, sitting at a table, reading *Le Monde*. Robert gave him a big surprise by slipping up behind him and snatching the newspaper away.

"What's this you're reading? A poet shouldn't read *Le Monde*."

"And what, in your opinion, should a poet read?" Jean-Francis asked rather angrily, for Robert not only had kept him waiting but had arrived obviously drunk. Very annoying.

"Here, take this," said Robert, sinking down on the banquette. "*Détective*. My only reading nowadays. It's prodigious."

He spread out the magazine, opened to page seven, with a caption running across a double-page spread, and read aloud: " 'The Satyr of Moulins Was Only a Timid Man.' "

"Here, you can read it for yourself." But he continued to read aloud:

It is the hour of the siesta in Moulins-sur-Sierre (Var.). The quaint little town drowses in sweltering heat. Only Madame B., a lively sixty-year-old, takes advantage of the respite to hoe her strawberry patch. Suddenly, on the freshly plastered wall, a disturbing shadow appears—

"You see? It's all there, in a very few lines. The climate, the place, the leading character. Try as you might, you'd not manage to express better the case of the brave old lady who, while everyone sleeps, hoes her strawberry bed. 'There is life, simple and tranquil.' No, try as you might, you'd not manage to be more right, more concise, more direct and accessible to everyone; you'd not find words better than 'lively sixty-year-old' and 'quaint little town.' "

"But neither of us is going to write it," said Jean-Francis rather uneasily.

"Oh, but I am! I'm going to write like that!"

"You'll never be able to."

"Tell me why not? And if what you say is true, then what remains for us to write? Shall we rewrite *Ulysses?*"

"But, my dear fellow, it's quite simple. At fifty, you're up against an evident fact: It's no longer possible to write novels."

"Then what to write? *The Reversed Eye?*" (The title of Jean-Francis's latest collection of poems.) "I prefer my Templars, my Bluebeard. What do you suppose Gerry could make of your *Reversed Eye?*"

Robert ordered another drink to maintain his inspiration. Jean-Francis, who was holding an antinicotine cigarette holder in his too-well-manicured fingers, regarded him pensively.

"You worry me, Robert."

"Because I drink?"

"Not at all! But because you have plunged into a subject without realizing how impossible it is. To find a common language, what you called in your radio broadcast 'a cultural patrimony,' is impossible. But there is no middle course, my friend. Either you write serial stories for grocers and concierges, or you write literature, which is read by only literary people. I'm ready to agree with you that it's not ideal, but— It's a problem of civilization, don't you see?"

Jean-Francis tossed back his abundant hair and tapped his cigarette case. He had delivered this discourse—a rare effort with him—in a slightly English accent. He was never more affected than when he was sincere.

"Then, we are robots?" protested Robert, more and more gloomy. No one, he reflected, simply because he had had an English nanny, should write *The Reversed Eye* and nothing else. Aloud, he said, "You're not interested in buried treasure, passwords, secrets, and childhood dreams?"

He thought of Gerry and laughed too loud and long.

"I'm no longer fifteen," said Jean-Francis, slightly embarrassed. He stretched his long legs and arms. This endless conversation was unpleasant. "And our civilization is no longer fifteen. One must espouse one's epoch if one wishes to—"

"Espouse! Yes, that's it! We must marry!" said Robert in an outburst of energy that at once subsided. "It was thus that Roland espoused—the beautiful Aude—"

"Pardon?"

"Victor Hugo," muttered Robert, who wanted to order another drink but was incapable.

Jean-Francis looked round him searching for someone, an acquaintance, who could take Robert home.

A TRAP

The question about buried treasure was a trap, and Jean-Francis was bound to fall into it. Robert laughed to himself at the thought. Jean-Francis, so obviously in love with Catherine (even though unhappily in love), rather aggravated him. Still more aggravating was his conviction that Jean-Francis, like Bernard, considered him a member, still active (though fallen from grace), of the same aristocracy of the pen, of the arts. But he reproached himself for his aggravation. What a demagogue! For hadn't he, Robert, also fallen into the trap of the treasure, the château? If you believed in it, he told himself, you'd have written something quite different from those few melancholy pages on Guimard—a dreamer, no doubt, but a man who would not go down into the hole. For after all, that was the question. To go down into the hole, into the underground darkness, *without knowing.*

A LETTER TO ROBERT GUIBAL

Sir,

May I be allowed to interrupt you in your multiple occupations by writing to tell you what pleasure it has given me to read your writings, particularly your short book on the Agriculture of our locality? Indeed, I was enthralled. As I was to hear you on television defend the cause of popular art, of the artisan, and of so many causes and values that are dear to me. Many of the ideas you have expressed, either in your writings or orally, have found a great resonance in me, and I have ended up by thinking, audaciously, that perhaps you would listen to my request.

Since 1949 I have been the principal of a Technical Instruction school (formerly a school of apprenticeship) and thus have had the occasion to deal with many children and young people whose social situations were lamentable and whose lives would constitute a veritable book. My belief is that to reveal to the world the importance of such beginnings in life would be a useful work. I would have liked one day to write such a book, but I am incapable of carrying out the task. Would you consider putting your talent to the service of working-class youth? If you could do this, my colleagues and I are ready to supply you with a rich harvest of data, a harvest that would earn you a profit, along with the admiration of the world. As far as I know, this subject has never been treated in a serious book or novel.

I am completely at your service for an appointment to discuss this matter, and on which occasion I could give you any information you may require. I believe that the sensibility and human warmth of the author of *Café of the Friends* and of the book on our local Agriculture to which I earlier referred would sensitize opinion in this noble cause.

No matter what your decision may be in this matter, I want to thank you again and tell you how grateful I am for your writings, unfortunately all too rare, which have often comforted and sustained me in my difficult task. Please accept the best wishes of your humble servant,

André Renard.

This letter put Robert into a very bad humor. I'm expected to do everything! he fumed to himself. Impossible! Another Georges Guimard! All these people are doing their best to distract me and entice me away from my book!

Very little was needed to distract him. And he realized he wasn't all that fond of Guimard. In a temper, he sent Mélusine packing. "I can't fiddle around with your documents just now," he told her, "for I've promised to write an article." Of course, that wasn't true, for he had more or less fallen out with everyone who had formerly asked him for articles. And Sorel was menacingly waiting for him in his hole in the ground.

He decided to think of something else and settled down to write a sad song for Carol. (She had told him the other night that she wanted to sing.) Why for Carol? Well, why not for Carol? She, too, had her rights, like all unhappy teenagers—and like Mélusine, who had gone away staggering a little but holding her back very straight. "Yes, why not Carol?" he muttered, without quite knowing whom he was challenging.

MÉLUSINE OBEYS HER SACRED DUTY

That is how she expressed herself almost immediately to Bernard. She said she was obeying a sacred duty.

"Yes, yes?" said Bernard in a daze. He needed all his savoir faire to stay there in his office talking with this strange visitor.

She said she was "collaborating" with Robert Guibal and that she saw how preoccupied he was with Bernard's magazine, which he had momentarily abandoned. She said that

Bernard must realize the primordial importance of the work in which Robert was engaged. It tied him down. The Templars! Gilles de Rais! She said that as far as she was concerned, she was close to believing (this in a more mundane tone) that the Templars, far from being vulgar diabolists, had discovered the "intermediary world," that neutral world of the spirits floating eternally between heaven and earth, whose force could be tapped and put to forgotten uses.

"Do you follow what I am saying?" she asked.

And he, too bewildered to utter a word, nodded his head.

She said that all of Robert's friends should back up his enterprise, for he was hesitating on the verge of the Invisible.

"Ah, yes?" he said hesitantly.

"Yes, indeed—"

Her tone was suddenly more assured. Now she knew what she must do. She must persuade this publisher of the *Magazine des Arts* not to burden Monsieur Guibal with requests and reproaches. Instead, he must encourage and console him, for he lacked self-confidence. And a work such as that book required the complete abandonment of every other activity. She was sure of this.

Bernard gradually pulled himself together. There, sitting on a chair facing him, was this old maid, her fine hand firmly grasping the handle of her bag, and she was talking to him with frenzied conviction. Poor Robert! Into what a trap had he fallen! This was what demagoguery and egalitarianism led to! All these semitramps and provincial amateurs that Robert drew in his wake! One would have thought that by plunging into the writing of a novel, he would have been freed of these parasites—and the contrary had happened. Bernard surveyed the dilapidated buttoned shoes and the resolute but twitching features of Mélusine as he thought, Oh, good Lord, poor Robert!

"One would have thought that his writing a real book—" Bernard began, as he handed a glass of whiskey to Jean-Francis, and he repeated what he had been thinking since the visit of Mélusine. They were in the small beige sitting room, under the fixed gaze of the Buddha.

"What do you call a real book?" asked Geneviève as she arrived and stood smoothing her hair in front of the Venetian mirror.

"Why—a book that responds to a profound need," Jean-Francis said almost mechanically.

"Which seems to have led him to drop all other diversions," Bernard added with a sigh.

"In any case," said Geneviève, sitting down near them, "he's dropped you. On that plane, you have no reason to register a complaint.

"Bernard is right; Robert should also have dropped those hangers-on of his—Robert must have a fundamental need for the admiration those spinsters and erudite priests can supply. They make up his public."

"Which is not a real one?" Geneviève asked softly.

"Oh, come now! You must know that a writer's public—I'm speaking of a veritable writer—is very restricted in our time. The masses are completely conditioned by audiovisual modes and by—"

"You're always saying 'true' and 'real' and 'veritable,' but after all, what right have you to set yourself up as a judge? Granted, the judgment of that spinster is not the same as yours, but why should I take your judgment rather than hers? Because you're armed with a diploma?"

"Geneviève!" Bernard exclaimed.

Jean-Francis had flushed slightly. Beneath his disillusioned exterior, he was painfully sensitive.

"Robert has apparently won you to his cause," he said with uncertain irony. "The other day he was talking enthusiastically to me about a magazine called, I believe, *Dètective. Détective!* Evidently there is no written proof that *Détective* has less quality than a poem by Éluard or a novel by —by—"

"By Robbe-Grillet?" Geneviève obligingly proposed.

"But you wouldn't dare to support your argument, even

on the days when you try to hurt me," Jean-Francis went on nervously.

"Hurt you! Why, for goodness' sake, I was joking! Obviously, between you and an old maid—What is she, Bernard? An archivist or something like that?"

Bernard barely had time to say "a graduate of the cole de Chartres," for Geneviève was wound up and went on with what she had to say.

"Between you and her, of course, there's not the least rapport. She must write incredible stuff! In any case, it will never be published; there's no chance of her ever reaching a public—True, a veritable writer, according to you, has no need of reaching a public—Then what criteria do you suggest?"

"Geneviève!" Bernard exclaimed again, having recovered his self-command. "You're being very aggressive!"

"Not at all! I'm discussing 'a problem of civilization,' as Jean-Francis puts it. What valid criteria do you suggest for defining a veritable writer, since it isn't the public?"

"Why, a writer that we read, a writer who shares our taste, our critical sense—"

"Who can say if your taste is the only one? Besides, I don't want to be unjust. You have read the old maid's book, I assume, and you found it bad. All right. Now, tell me why?"

"No, of course we didn't read it. We didn't feel it was worth the trouble."

"We can immediately see whether—"

Both men had spoken in unison, then stopped.

"I'll wager that Robert read it," said Geneviève.

With this said, she resolutely poured a glass of whiskey for herself, although as a rule she didn't drink hard liquor.

A silence fell.

When Jean-Francis had left, they went into their bedroom to dress for dinner, since they were dining out.

"Whenever Robert is the topic of conversation," said Bernard cautiously, "I notice you are really unjust. I'm afraid you've hurt Jean-Francis's feelings."

"He's aggravating. Shall I wear my tailored pantsuit? He's so pretentious."

"He—pretentious? Why, he's modesty incarnate! He stays in the background, writing; he doesn't pretend to anything!"

"Modest, and proud of being so," said Geneviève, quoting her daughter Valérie.

"Your draped green dress, preferably. It's going to be rather formal. I can never understand you—so discriminating, yet you prefer Robert to Jean-Francis."

"I don't prefer him," said Geneviève seriously. "I esteem him more, that's all."

"Esteem Robert?"

"Robert. With his Reine and his cabaret ditties, with his traveling-salesman's jokes, and even with his tippling. I find him—courageous. Or if you prefer, honest."

She took out her dress and removed her pullover.

Bernard thought over her words. He was upset.

"Courageous?"

"Yes. And you, too," she said, turning her back to him. "And probably you don't know it any more than he does."

She pulled the green dress on over her head and went on talking in a muffled voice with it still covering her face.

"That's why I love you."

He blushed like a young man, a blush she didn't see, fortunately.

"Ready? Once more we're late."

In the dark entrance hall, he took her in his arms, with touching awkwardness, and kissed her. That confounded Robert! They signaled for the elevator and avoided meeting each other's eyes as they waited. They both wanted to laugh.

Hurt? Oh, that's too strong a word. He didn't give that much importance to Geneviève's opinions. Geneviève, Robert—Besides, she never read anything. He had a feeling that she hadn't even opened his last collection, *The Reversed Eye*. She merely repeated Bernard's words or the remarks she heard at the dinner parties she attended, and she was cold, was a snob. No personality whatsoever. The thing that hurt him—No, that's too strong a word—What ruffled his feelings was that she had attacked him, as a result of a criticism Bernard had let slip, about Robert. A lifelong friend! True, Bernard was not a creative writer, absolutely not. An animator, a promoter. And yet, in the most vulgar sense of the word, he evidently saw himself as a patron of the arts, a Maecenas, an Adrienne Lemonnier, a Jacques Copeau. Bernard made him think of "the gentlemen organizers" of the Club Méditerranée.

But, Jean-Francis told himself, his ambassadorial distinction doesn't impress me. After all, a maître d'hôtel has that same distinction! And to think I had expected to have a conversation with them that would relax me and make it possible for me to take up my work again—

But how unjust that statement she made about a writer's public! How she misunderstood the courage it takes for a writer to work alone, without encouragement, without making any concessions. Like that spinster what's-her-name. The difference between him and that old maid, for example (and why 'for example'?), is the culture, the quality—And that question she asked: "Did you read her manuscript?" Just to hurt me—No, that's too strong a word, certainly. Because there are people you only need to glance at to know they'll never do anything worth while. Unjust? But life is unjust. Those would-be writers Robert collects aren't writers at all, they are merely characters. What Robert wants to do is to give them a voice—a desperate undertaking. It would take a genius to do that. And we haven't any geniuses; this epoch lacks geniuses. And how to set oneself up against one's epoch? One is alone, one writes well, but even so, to imagine that one is a—

He sat down at his desk to write. His Left Bank studio apartment was tastefully furnished. The desk was a Louis XIII sideboard, well polished by his cleaning woman. He had a first-rate record player. There were bouquets of cut flowers in the room, and on the walls were some lithographs (first-pulled proofs)—in short, a background for the evolution of a refined, thoughtful, harmonious oeuvre. "Then," Geneviève would say, "is being a writer a question of interior decoration?" And Robert—but then, he was drunk—had said, "Are we robots?" To hurt him—No, the word is too weak. To humiliate him. He surveyed his setting. It had not one false note, yet he was secretly humiliated. He would write; he could write. And from this decor, his culture, his modest but adequate fortune, even from his social connections, mathematically there should logically be created a refined and thoughtful oeuvre, appreciated by connoisseurs. What then? Then, it was this very evidence that suddenly humiliated him.

CRAZED; OR, "THE RAPTURE OF THE DEEP"

From this time on, people began to say that Sorel was crazed. For years, nothing really strange had been noticed. Merely, "He seems to be in a bad way," because he lost weight, became taciturn, had dark rings around his eyes. "It's not his work that's killing him," they also said. For tourists came only in the summer, and his work on the northwest wall he had promised the municipality to rebuild was advancing very slowly. Was his malady cancer? Or diseased lungs? A mortal illness was the only explanation to justify his having left a cheerful little town and a thriving business to go bury himself in the country, living in a damp, old, tumbledown place. Had he perhaps taken to drink? A solitary drinker, that's bad. Then these comments were no longer made, and no one would have been surprised to learn that he was in the hospital or even dead. Why not? And then Adrienne began to talk; and after her, Georges Guimard, just a little, to defend his friend and explain. Because after five years—or was it six?—Guimard had given up all hope of any treasure except for a confused vision he had gathered from talk with Sorel of an epoch when men struggled by a kind of mental tinkering to attain a dimension in which they lived a life of laughter and dreams, and he had wanted to share with others his own amused perplexity. He talked about it first of all with Madame Bâton in the late afternoons. Georges Guimard was a good talker. Madame Bâton grumbled some ominous predictions. Monsieur Graff said nothing, but perhaps he was the only one who felt that Sorel's case was more serious than it seemed.

They joked a little about it, but in a friendly way, Georges Guimard in the lead. They always ended up by saying, "Who knows? After all—" And really, they were rather grateful to Sorel for providing them with this diversion from routine. Already some were saying, "He's crazed." But they said it kindly. For who is without some crotchet or other? The mayor, that corpulent man with the fluty voice, said, "Sooner or later, he's bound to talk it over with me." He could not account for the work done by Sorel—no one could. He envisaged some scattered digs, a few trenches, some fragments of clay pots that didn't amount to much, like those of the parish priest, who bragged (and one never knows) that he had been the one to inspire Pierre Sorel, or as he put it, "set Pierre's foot in the stirrup."

But having a mania, as everyone knows, keeps a man healthy and happy. You had only to look at the parish priest when he returned from one of his "archaeological expeditions" proudly exhibiting to his choirboys his latest finds: a cracked old jug, a tarnished medal, "of in-estimable value, my boys, in-es-ti-ma-ble!" He was a happy and healthy man. And he was quite unaware of the nickname the little rascals had bestowed upon him: Old Crackpot.

Pierre Sorel might also have earned such a nickname had it not been for his tragic aspect. When people addressed him jokingly, his response was to stare at his teasers as if he would like to devour them. Adrienne, after waking up many times in an empty bed, had found out what was going on and for a time artlessly took pride in it; the words "my husband's excavations" were often on her lips. Two years earlier, perhaps, he would have been flattered, and that paltry flattery would have sufficed; he would have had admiration, notoriety, even if derisive. He would have tried, perhaps, to bring to the surface those sculptured stones he had unearthed at a depth of twenty-four meters. But now it was too late. A treasure spoken of in a back room smelling of coffee, with the little window overlooking the too-well-known roads—that is one thing. A secret imbibed along with sips of wine among friends, with Madame Bâton listening behind the door; and the suppressed laughter, the seemingly practical musings ("How do you suppose they managed?" and "How many were they?" and "Did no one ever notice?"); and Guimard, who had some education, talking about the secret rooms of the Egyptians and passwords, magic words; and Monsieur Graff, whose devotion to money was stern and, you might say, disinterested, saying, "You'll not make me believe there's no gold down there"—all this was one thing and a good thing. The treasure, the secret told to Adrienne in a whisper as the bed warmed up little by little, and she becoming excited little by little, exclaiming (for a moment again like the passionate girl of yore, dazzled by the first "I love you"), "Why didn't you tell me from the beginning?"—all this is something and a good thing. But at thirty or thirty-five meters underground, with the lantern swaying and the stifling weight of the earth above you and threatening to cave in and bury you at any minute, those good things no longer have any meaning to speak of.

177

Who could gauge or understand his effort? Not Guimard, so warmhearted and jovial; not Monsieur Graff, with his loyalty and outdated morals; nor Adrienne (the thought of her dark curls no longer affects him). They are not down with him, deep underground. No, he is confronting, alone, an absurd and desperate endeavor. They would be unable to judge what the greatest treasure in the world would mean to this man, half naked and panting, doubting that he will ever be able to return to the surface again: that treasure is nothing to him. A kind of pride, even, makes him tell himself that it is not a treasure—a vulgar bait—that has made him thus expose himself, within and without, for he now realizes (in the fifth or sixth year) that he will be called a fool, a buffoon, a town half-wit, and he is ready to admit that he could have avoided this with some good-natured talk—which would have betrayed his blind and obstinate labor of the night. But he, Sorel, can no longer either amuse or hold out the fabulous hope of unearthing a buried treasure. Like the deep-sea divers or the miners working deep mines, he is experiencing the strange affliction known as the "rapture of the deep." Naked to the waist, sometimes trembling so terribly that he must stop, squatting in a tunnel so low that his head painfully grazes the tunnel's roof, groping his way, forced to turn back by a granite wall or a damp softening of the earth, along with a weakening of his limbs, exhausted and (for a long time) without apparently having found anything—all the same, it is when he returns to the surface, covered with dirt, his limbs limp, that he feels strangely out of his element.

"How far have you got, Uncle Robert?" asks Manuel.
"To where his wife leaves him."
"Oh! And does that upset him?"
"I don't know. I've not yet written the scene."
"Why not?" asks Marina, who is polishing her nails.
"Because it upsets me," sighs Robert.

However, the facts cannot be denied. Adrienne has actually left for Toulon, taking their children with her.

TOULON

"I just can't understand how you can still excuse him," said Madeleine Graff with an emphasis unusual for her. "He's quarreled with the parish priest; he's quarreled with the mayor; he's quarreled with you—" Monsieur Graff tried in vain to interrupt her flow of words. "He's quarreled with you!" Madame Graff repeated more emphatically. "And now he's driven Adrienne off to Toulon!"

"Now, now! He didn't drive her away; she's the one who—"

"You'll never convince me," said Madame Graff, her hands thrust into the stomach pocket of her apron and trying for once to speak ironically, "you'll never convince me that it's for her own pleasure that a woman who has everything she needs right here in Boissy will leave it all to open a café in Toulon!"

Sure enough, it was hard to believe. Monsieur Graff searched his mind for arguments.

"She had taken to drink," he suggested.

"And whose fault was it? Besides, she could drink at home! She didn't have to go to Toulon to drink! There's plenty right here, it seems to me."

"She was sleeping with the postman."

"One more reason to stay here, where he is," replied Madame Graff with a logic that left Monsieur Graff speechless. Obviously, Adrienne could be blamed for drinking to excess, for sleeping with the postman, but that didn't explain Toulon.

"Do you want me to tell you something?" Madame Graff went on with bitter satisfaction. "She realized that Sorel was

179

going crazy, and she was afraid of being *assassinated!* Because when you dig graves, you end up by putting someone in them!"

Monsieur Graff gave up trying to explain why he, a steady and reasonable man, had quarreled with Sorel, had got into a temper, instead of having pity on the poor fool, if fool he was. It was inexplicable. As inexplicable as this scene in the Graffs' home, where the hard but humble Madeleine had never before raised her voice. As inexplicable as Toulon.

BERNARD LOSES PATIENCE

"You must realize," said Bernard, speaking with a kind of acerbity, "that under these conditions, I cannot keep you on as contributing editor to the magazine. Either you decamp, or you buckle down to work."

Robert started to protest, but Bernard would not be interrupted.

"Yes, yes, I know what I'm doing. I may not have your facility to go from one subject to another, but I know my business. Your article on the witches of Berry was a flop. Your essay on dreams and fanaticisms is very nice but quite irrelevant to the subject. You were given a precise documentation, and you didn't even use it."

"Oh, as to the documentation—You know very well—"

"I know. And I know better than you think I do."

Bernard's ill temper was inexplicably gathering force as he continued.

"I had a visitor two weeks ago—a lady who said she was your collaborator!" (Bernard himself was wondering why he was so angry. At the time, that visit had seemed more hilariously funny than anything else.)

"Who? What?" said Robert, unable to believe that Mélusine had dared.

"A spinster, a Mademoiselle Rebec."

(So she had given that name! Then was it her true name? Robert was bewildered as he distractedly recalled the vegetarian—formerly crepe—restaurant on the rue Vaneau. Then, coming to himself, he guffawed.)

"Mélusine! She actually came to see you?"

"There's nothing funny about it. She came to expound to me the importance of your oeuvre, which nothing should disturb, and to demonstrate how wrong we were to take up your time with writing articles. I needn't tell you that I sent her packing. She went so far as to tell me she was accomplishing 'a sacred duty' in paying me that visit. And even though I'm almost sure that she came of her own initiative, it reflects your basic thought—"

"Why, no! Not at all!"

"And it leaves me free to find a replacement for you here."

Robert was stunned, not so much by what Bernard was saying as by the way he was saying it. That aggressive manner, that mask of editor in chief he had assumed, that cutting irony. (Of course, there had always been a touch of irony in Bernard's friendship, but the friendship had existed.)

"See here, Bernard, I've never asked for—"

"We've always had good teamwork on this magazine," Bernard continued, as inflexible as Justice, "a spirit of solidarity, of—of belief in the esthetics which, at least so I believe, compensated for our readership, which you judge to be too limited in number."

"Me? But I—"

"But when that spirit no longer exists—I see clearly that you have lost interest in an endeavor of this kind. The only thing I reproach you for is not to have spoken frankly to me about this state of things—"

"But really, Bernard!"

"Let me finish. I repeat that I quite understand. You have devoted your time and energy to work for us, and I'm aware that your pay—"

"For heaven's sake, there's no question of that!"

181

"I stick to what I said. You devotedly worked for the magazine while you believed in it. You no longer believe in it, and that being so, it is entirely normal for you to give up, at least partly, work that is absorbing but ill paid. Of course, you are free to send us occasional articles."

Robert was about to become furious.

"Really, Bernard, you exaggerate. What's got into you? Only three days ago, Geneviève telephoned to Reine to invite us to dinner, along with Bérenger."

"I've postponed that dinner; in fact, I called Reine personally to tell her this. I'm not angry with you, but sometimes one feels the need of keeping a distance."

"Very well, keep your distance!" said Robert, now absolutely furious. "And as much of a distance as you like! But you could have sent me a letter telling me you were reducing your staff!"

"Well, you see, I happen to possess a sense of the ridiculous," said Bernard, unperturbed.

GENEVIÈVE

Bernard was sure that Geneviève would not wholeheartedly approve of his brutal treatment of Robert.

And thus, since he needed her approval, he had to tell her that Robert had resigned, at least temporarily. She, of course, had loyally pretended to believe it, concealing from him the fact that Robert had come to see her that very afternoon and had recounted the whole affair.

"Bernard should have understood," Robert had complained.

"What else could you expect? That magazine is his cherished creation," said Geneviève noncommittally.

"But what fanaticism! From my point of view—"

"If you set yourself to understand the viewpoint of others, you'll never get anything done," said Geneviève dryly. She was sure that if she tried to understand Robert's point of view, to doubt that the magazine and Bernard deserved so much abnegation, effort, and discipline, she would never get anything done. And yet she had sympathy, almost tenderness, for Robert. She wanted to help him, to get him out of the mess he'd got himself into. For a moment, she let this impulse prevail.

"A point of view, Robert, is never more than a working hypothesis."

Robert looked up at her, and a faint current of understanding passed between them.

"You really believe that?"

"It's a problem of esthetics," said Geneviève crisply, already regretting her weakness and adopting Bernard's vocabulary, like a soldier taking up his arms again after a respite. The current of understanding dwindled. Robert began to take his leave. When he had gone, Geneviève, relieved, allowed herself one lump of sugar in her tea.

How simplistic it would be to imagine that Geneviève, while being a faithful wife, was sexually attracted to Robert! A psychoanalyst might affirm it, but Geneviève would retort that Freud was out, as out as rococo or as Louis II of Bavaria. As for Robert, the idea of falling in love with Geneviève would appear to him as absurd as the idea of entering the French Academy—and in the same order of things.

A SILENCE

Was I perhaps foolish to plunge into this thing?" Robert was worriedly asking himself. Bernard had a grudge against him; Jean-Francis was annoyed; Anselme and Vivi were remaining aloof—But for heaven's sake, am I going to take a referendum to determine whether I have or haven't the right to write a book if I want to?

But suppose the book never gets written? And suppose there isn't any treasure?

Money—that's something that can be shared; it has warmth and variety, is amusing. A secret—that communicates, speaks, changes shape, swells, collapses. It's alive. But already Sorel was heading toward something else when, having explored the fourth gallery and, as with the others, finding that it led nowhere, he turned back and began once more to tunnel in the direction of the tower, the northeast tower, of course. No question but that he'd begin again, for when, turning round, his back bowed from working for such a long time in a cramped position, he looked at what he had accomplished and saw those crooked arches, those exposed stones, he stood still for a moment, his pickax at his feet, and muttered softly, filled with wonder, "I'm the one who did all that—and maybe for nothing."

THE MIRROR

To call up, to convoke—these were expressions unknown to Gerry. He did not go in for clairvoyants and fortune-tellers. Madame Bâton held no mystery for him. He had questioned her; she had responded very pleasantly and with prolixity— a prime mystery of which he was unconscious. If she had talked about tarot cards, crystal balls, dark ladies, mysterious letters, this would merely be "a part of the Sorel affair." An affair is an affair; words are words; happiness is happiness. All this was clear, precise, glitteringly immaculate in his mind, like well-polished sideboards. Perhaps too clear?

In the mirror above the counter in Bobby's Bar, the mahogany stalls were reflected; and sitting in one of them could be seen the reflection of a young couple, good-looking, well dressed: Gerry and Carol. He wanted to kiss her but was checked by all those mirrors, by the perfection of the decor, of quiet luxury, the small bouquet on the table, the goblets filled with cool, translucent liquids of different colors, theirs green and rose (he was drinking Green Dragon; she was drinking Hawaiian Moon), and their own beauty. Gerry was wearing a white T-shirt, and his suntan showed up to advantage his white teeth and wide-open, light blue eyes. Carol was wearing a kind of honey-colored East Indian chemise, and her makeup was perfect: eyelids, mother-of-pearl; lips delineated with a brown pencil. He imagined vividly the perfect photograph that could easily be taken in this bar which stimulated one to order exotic beverages, to wear new fabrics, softer than soft—The image of happiness promotes sales. But exactly what is the image created by happiness? He felt a familiar anguish (perhaps the word is too strong for such a vague feeling), a kind of emptiness. It was a sensation he knew well; he always had it in Carol's presence. Perhaps that was what he loved in her? Perhaps that emptiness was happiness?

"I wish," he said, trying to conquer the impalpable sensation, "I wish I could carve everywhere, like we did when we were fifteen, 'Gerry loves Carol.' "

"Oh, that would be lovely," she said, smiling at the mirror. He took her hand. The hand in the mirror abandoned itself.

"Tell me if you love me?" he asked with a kind of despair.

"Why, yes, I love you," she replied sweetly, with a smile.

No falsehood was in her eyes. Why should she lie? She wouldn't go to the trouble. She quite evidently loved the handsome, tanned young man in the mirror. And Gerry continued to look at the image of happiness there. Did he as yet know (surely not) the role played by mirrors and reflected images in magic? No, but all the same, he summoned their image to betray, to liberate its secret. He called up; he convoked. The young mirror-girl leaned toward him, her sweet lips inviting a kiss. A fresh kiss, with the metallic taste of cherries. Gerry felt close to tears.

He had so ardently dreamed of marrying Carol after he should have performed gigantic exploits. And now he discovered that he had only to pluck the golden apple, had only to reach out his hand. That was the exploit: to hold in hand the golden fruit of the Hesperides and to perceive that one had only to pluck it. Gerry was too frank and high-minded to be disappointed. He would confront happiness and silence with courage, as he would have confronted a dragon. The dragon figures in the romances of chivalry—and yet, isn't it the monster we all flee?

ALONE

Let us take up where we left off earlier.

He is alone. Adrienne and the children are sleeping. He loves them most at that moment when he has left them sleeping and when he, the solitary man, crosses the three-hundred-meter distance which separates him from the hole, the entrance to his kingdom, like an arm of the sea or a continent. The pain he feels at the moment of tearing himself away from the sleeping Adrienne, the only woman he has ever known, and from his children, Frédéric and Génie, that boy who is such a hard worker, so serious, a real little merchant, like his grandfather; and Génie, so adorable, so complaisant, 'a real little woman,' as people say (he carries their image with him as if he were leaving them forever). It hurts and yet does him good. He is alone.

And now, here he is. To risk your life is something; it is still more of a feat to risk it in darkness. Every night, every night for many years, he has had to conquer fear—No, not fear, it is a repulsion he feels at the moment of burying himself down there. More than forty meters down, the lantern threatening to go out at any moment. Then the corridor he had dug, along which he crawls, a part of it ill buttressed, the other part still not shored up at all. By the glimmer of the lantern, he had twice, at the end of a tunnel, come across flat stones, laid down horizontally and sculptured. In a filthy notebook, with the stub of a pencil, he had copied the designs. At forty meters underground, at the end of a tunnel twelve meters long, he had encountered the traces of men. Men who had been there. Men who were not satisfied with the earth's crust, with the crust of things, who could not be satisfied with surface things. For a moment, he had forgotten danger and repulsion; he had run his hand caressingly over the sculptured stones. Would he speak of it to Guimard, his last faithful friend? He imagined Guimard's noisy jubilation, his exaggerated cries. "Oh, this is fantastic! Oh, this proves they went there!"

Yes. But the important thing, Pierre Sorel ruminated, was, not that "they" had gone there, but that they had felt the *need*—like him—to go there.

Alone and not alone. Because the depth in which he was buried separated him from those who, up there, came and went, had goals to attain. Because the depth became the only goal of the man who delves and forages. And the sole temptation now, of this man who had wanted to regain the surface with full hands, is never to remount again at all.

ROBINSON CRUSOE

"Then who is Sorel, when you come down to it?" the children were finally to ask.

"A question easy to answer," says Manuel, and he proceeds to give a dissertation for the benefit of Marina.

Sorel, why, he must be the man confronted by the problem of Creation, the meaning of life, that man-mannequin the teachers trail from one dusty classroom to another, the flayed man of the natural sciences (it can be taken apart, and there is always one item missing, a tibia or the liver), that man dissected and analyzed along with *Madame Bovary* and *Le Malade Imaginaire,* the auricles and ventricles, and later on, Freud, Camus, and conditioned reflexes. Manuel possesses all this knowledge in his impeccably kept cardboard folders of different colors, with subdivisions and bracketed words, examples, and quotations.

"You're wrong," said Robert. "No matter what Sorel is, he is not that. Rather, he is Robinson Crusoe on his island, trying to reconstruct with trunks of palm trees, dried leaves, and rusty nails an ideal model of English civilization. In his cabin built on stilts, sheltered from wild beasts, he reads his Bible, carves a kind of calendar in wood, drinks his tea made of mangrove leaves, as a matter of principle. Valiant Robinson! Absurd hero of Anglicanism and five o'clock tea! But Robinson was rescued; he returned to England, found again real tea and the boredom of Sunday. Then Robinson became Friday, his double, his complement. And that heroic struggle he had made to remain the perfect gentleman, wearing breeches of tree bark, abiding by the city routine, was worthless, now that everyone drank real tea and went to work at eight every morning. When everyone wears striped trousers, heroism lies perhaps in eating with one's fingers and exhibiting one's behind, doesn't it?"

"Oh, Uncle Robert!" Marina remonstrated.

"It's only a manner of speaking. I mean to say that in order to remain a common man, a civilized man, Robinson had to become a hero. And once returned to civilization, he remained a hero; the imprint was ineradicable. And consequently, he is not just a common man. Robinson had made a superhuman effort—"

"No, not superhuman, merely human," said Manuel, a little depressed. (Easy to understand why his professors adored him, for just this kind of remark.)

"Yes, I agree, human. After all, he had expended his maximum physical and moral effort; he had hardened his muscles and character. And afterward, alone in London, with his muscular arms, the very effort he had made to remain an

English gentleman will prevent him from remaining so."

"His new energies would find an outlet," Manuel commented.

"Exactly. And he would no longer communicate with his fellowmen. Because they could not understand the effort he had gone to in trying to remain like them. Suddenly, he is no longer like them."

"The theme is interesting," Manuel granted. "I almost feel like taking notes." Then, reflectively, "I always wondered what would have happened if Friday had been a woman."

Robert said nothing.

"But goodness me," exclaimed Marina, superior, "Friday is a substitute for a woman. As everyone knows, all Englishmen are pederasts."

THE USE AND LIMITS OF POETRY

As she arrived at the rue Vavin, not far from where Jean-Francis lived, Catherine wondered if it was really her duty to have an affair with him.

Naturally, she had the *right* to sleep with him; indeed, she had so much right that it had come to seem almost a duty to make use of it. "After all, if I don't really want to, though?" she murmured to herself. And answered: Very well, then, continue to spend your nights with a man so indifferent to you that he's not even bored. If only he hated me! But he doesn't. He feels as comfortable in his own home as at Reine's or anywhere else. Then why shouldn't I? Why shouldn't I prove to him that Jean-Francis is as good as he is, that I, too, can be happy anywhere and with anyone?

Prove to him—prove my indifference as I have wanted to prove my love—No, that's not what I want. I want to be really indifferent! Oh, Robert—

She paused to blow her nose.

On the affective plane, she mused, I must be a little retarded. I earn my living; I have an interesting job; I can do very well without him. Can he do without me? Perhaps not. He's quarreling with his friends, is bogged down in that book; perhaps he needs me?

For a moment, she felt intense relief and a little hope. She was on the point of turning back. Then, brusquely, she was ashamed of her weakness. Had she descended so low that she could hope? No, no! Book or no book, he did not understand her; he did not love her. There was only one thing she could do, only one person to whom she could turn: Jean-Francis.

Again she blew her nose.

A head cold, perhaps? And could one properly go, with a head cold, to give oneself to a man who had been waiting three or four years for you? She tried to sneeze but could not. And she scolded herself: That's enough of these pretexts. Resolutely, she continued to walk down the street. Her feet hurt. She must have chosen subconsciously to wear these uncomfortable shoes. For no reason at all, she began to remember certain trifling details she disliked about Jean-Francis. That seal ring he wore on his left hand—not very authentic, at that. Then, his rather thin lips. And the distinguished way he had of speaking with a clipped accent. Didn't it remind one of the English accent adopted by snobs? Yes, it did, she suddenly decided. She halted again. She was now on the rue Delambre, in front of the health-food store; and looking at the window display, she tried to revive her irritation at Robert's passion for *cassoulet Toulousain,* the baked-bean concoction he was always asking for. But this had rather an opposite effect. It called to mind the image of Robert, calm and confident, ready to put his arms around her; it made her want to go home and wait for him.

Should she reflect a little more? After all, she had told herself that if he got down to writing again—But that hadn't brought them together. She had been wrong, perhaps, to treat his subject ironically. But, oh dear, those Templars, that treasure—The subject *was* puerile! Of course, the subject isn't everything. That she hadn't believed in his subject, wasn't it because she had lost faith in him? And this had made him suffer?

She felt a stab of pain in the region of the stomach. Oh, had he suffered? Her eyes were still fixed on the display of health foods: soya crackers, Vitaflor for diabetics, natural bilberry juice—that mightn't be too bad—whole wheat bread, carrot juice, cracked wheat—You'd never get Robert to eat soy bean crackers. He might be suffering, but it hadn't killed his appetite. There was a roll of fat at the back of his neck. No, she must not think about that, for her legitimate indignation was tinged with a secret fascination.

She was still fond of him. But she found Jean-Francis attractive for otherwise valid reasons. His writings, to begin with. *The Reversed Eye* was a first-class collection. Louis Aragon had boosted it and so had Maurice Nadeau in *La Quinzaine.*

Leaving the health-food window, she resumed her walk, this time condemned to her doom, for the building where Jean-Francis lived was at the far end of the rue Delambre. Aragon, yes. Besides, Jean-Francis had a good physique, was even handsome. "There's nothing of a Don Juan in Robert," he had said one day. What does he know about it? He is a little too conscious of his romantic good looks. And that gets on one's nerves. Still, Robert, too, had been good-looking and conscious of it in the old days. But in a nicer way, with more warmth. It's not the moment to think of this! Think of Aragon, Aragon. He had written, *"The Reversed Eye* makes Jean-Francis Roy the equal of a Reverdy or a René Char." That, after all, really counts.

She now walked resolutely toward the end of the rue Delambre, disregarding two dress shops and a bookstore. To begin with, she couldn't go on living alone forever; it was "unhealthy," according to Vivi, who preached by example. "Can one feel alone when one really loves?" said Germaine, rolling up her eyes stupidly like the Saint Theresa depicted by Bernini. Yes, one could. All the lonelier. Robert, who loved no one (you can't tell me he loves that Polish woman), is never lonely. Whereas I live in an empty world, a desert, without anybody.

She had only two more street numbers to go before reaching the respectable-looking apartment house, period 1900, where Jean-Francis must be waiting for her, on the fifth floor. There was an elevator and a view over the rooftops. Is he perhaps a pederast? she asked herself. For goodness sake, if he were, it would be known. Let's not lull ourselves with false hopes. He is waiting. Perhaps he is brushing his teeth. Will there be a glass of port, as always in the novels Aunt Olympe let lie around, and which I read when I was a little girl? If I'd had other lovers, I would know, and I'd not make such a tragedy of it.

As she passed the concierge's loge, she repeated to herself, reproachfully, shuddering a little, No lovers as yet, and thirty-five years old. It's grotesque!

The tiny elevator looked like a cage.

I told him if he would devote himself to one single thing, as I have devoted myself to him, he would understand. Understand what?

The elevator was going up too fast for her to find an answer. Shouldn't I have worn a hat, perhaps? The brown one, so becoming. No, decidedly, that would be too much in the period of Paul Bourget. Impossible to stop this elevator. I hope he'll offer me a drink of something. On one floor, she had a fleeting glimpse of her dentist's smiling face, Dr. Vatenel. Then the elevator stopped. I leave the elevator; I ring the doorbell, quite naturally, quite at ease, smiling; he's not going to fling himself upon me; that's not his style. In a way, that would be better. This is something! He doesn't hear the bell! Exasperated, she pressed it hard a second time and held it. No doubt he's playing the flute. Long and thin like himself. Do I really like him? Shall I leave? No, there's his footstep in the hall; it's too late for second thoughts; I can't—

"Hello, Jean-Francis?"

He looked bewildered, a little stupid. Or moved?

192

"My darling—"
(Naturally. Aragon, Aragon, Aragon!)

MY HUMBLE ARCHAEOLOGICAL FINDS

Somewhat later, the parish priest was bound to call on his former pupil.

"See here, Pierre, this can't go on! You are losing interest in the world around you. You snub even the tourists I send to you—I completely understand that your poor wife's departure—But after all, everything in its time! You will end up by losing your museum job! Me, too, I've got my humble archaeological finds, but does that keep me from saying mass?"

Even with a very great deal of imagination, one can have no idea of what Sorel may have replied.

THE JANSENISM OF THE TUNNEL

Because archaeological digs, a hole in the ground or a tunnel, are things hard to defend, aren't they? This absolute austerity leaves far behind a work such as that of the factor Cheval, who builds and elaborates, who aspires to beauty and joyful expansion, who erects, before the eyes of all, a palace, a château; and even if you deny its beauty, you cannot deny its existence. It took so many sacks of concrete, so many meters of scaffolding, so many years of work; that's something you can see. But others, such as Sorel, do not build; they dig. On the surface, nothing shows. A tunnel is not a work of art. A tunnel lacks beauty. It gives no satisfaction in itself to the one who made it. A creator, even a solitary creator, even an unknown one, can behold his work and find it good. A tunnel is not a work. The underground galleries and corridors differ in no way from those burrowed by moles and beavers and other instinctively burrowing animals. If there is no treasure, no secret, the tunnel has no existence. It is concave, has no volume. The tunnel is the extreme hazard, the Pascalian wager, an extreme of Jansenism; it scares you. Let us turn back before we are overtaken by total darkness—or light.

CAROL SINGS

Carol riffled through the sheet music, absorbed in what she was doing. Reine surveyed her, sizing her up with ruthless honesty. Gerry, sitting in the Mexican armchair, worshiped in silence.

"In my opinion," said Reine, "you had better work on your high notes."

"Oh, no—no high notes," murmured Carol, as if refusing a helping of cake. She was wearing an olive-green tunic that just reached the crotch and was less pretty than usual. A fairy trying to become human, which effort gave her a pinched look.

"And I find your middle notes rather nasal."

"I'm more comfortable with the low notes."

Gerry and Robert were embarrassed, like men in a women's dress shop.

"Well now, Robert, don't you agree with me?"

"Oh, as for me, you know—"

He wondered if he had any opinion. And why Carol wanted to sing.

"The song Robert gave me is for a low voice."

"What song?" asked Reine with the serenity of a proprietor. She wanted to be nice to Carol but was persuaded the girl would never sing anything anywhere.

"You don't know it," said Robert, more and more embarrassed. "It's a song I wrote several weeks ago and found in a desk drawer."

194

A song he had written on a sudden impulse, in revolt against the work on the book that was isolating him from everyone—he now remembered this. He had said, "Why not Carol? Why not just anyone?" So disgusted was he with himself.

"But you wrote it for Carol, didn't you?" Gerry said delightedly.

Reine said nothing.

"Would you like to hear it?"

"I'm not sure I could accompany it without the score."

"Oh, I have the score," said Carol.

Reine said nothing but went to the piano, where she played a few measures.

Carol stood very straight, threw back her head. In that posture, all her bad features showed up: the unusual largeness of her nostrils, the skinniness of the throat, the prominence of the canine teeth. She half closed her eyes and wrung her little monkey hands. She was almost ugly, almost human—a miracle.

She sang:

> À la petite semaine
> J'ai marchandé le bonheur—

She "haggled over happiness" in the throaty, almost hoarse voice of a boy whose voice is breaking; and by its very gaucheness and affectation, it moved you. She tore the song out of her throat with a superhuman effort that revealed a wizened and deformed childhood, and it had the painful beauty of a birth. For a moment, she gasped for breath, stopped, glanced at them with the look of a madwoman who suddenly perceives that she is naked. She hesitated, glanced at Gerry, and went on with the song, breathing with effort, reckless of her profound shame at showing something of herself without a mask, without adornment, expressionless. She exaggerated her gestures, placed her hand over her heart, held out her arms, then drew them back at once, in despair at not being able to convey or even to feel what she was singing, then, arms folded, withdrawn into herself, renouncing everything, all effort, except emptying her lungs of air, and she finished on a strangled sound that deeply stirred Robert. For a moment, he understood Gerry, who loved something in Carol beneath that beauty and youth and insignificance, the secret torment that was another kind of beauty.

Then Reine said, "If I were you, I'd pitch my voice a tone higher."

And he was almost horrified.

PROFESSIONALLY

"She'll never amount to anything, that little friend of yours," said Reine when the door had shut. "I'm willing to give her some advice, but really—No, she'll never do anything, professionally."

There was nothing spiteful in what she said; she condemned, but without rancor or regret. She had the right to pronounce judgment after ten years of work, of calm obstinacy, of poverty disguised as unconcern. She had the right to. Professionally. After all, she had not *seen* the human being who had been there, pathetically naked in spite of her tinted eyelids, her bleached hair, the armor of costume jewelry; she had not even seen her. She had not bothered to see her. It was none of her business to see her, she would have said if she had been conscious of this. Professionally.

"How hard you are!" he could not help but say.

"Me, hard? When I think how I've been waiting months for you to write some songs for me and you find time to write for that child who has no future—"

Exactly, because he had wanted for an hour or a day to escape the book, the edifying book, escape from a love that was proving itself, from a future that was constructing itself. Because he had wanted to return to a freedom whose meaning he could not discern, which was perhaps idiotic, and in any case would serve no purpose. And that freedom had momentarily assumed the insignificant visage of Carol.

Reine said he had never loved her. Like Catherine, who said the same thing. He was so hurt that he could find nothing to say in reply. Had she said, "You have always loved me," it would have been equally true. And had she said, "You have always loved Carol," would that have been false?

He said nothing.

She wept.

LIKE A QUEEN IN TEARS

Reine wept. With all the accessories you could think of, all the adjectives and prepositions. She did not cry by halves; she cried wholeheartedly, with deep sobs, like a child, her nose red and swollen, rubbing her eyes with her fists; she cried with the puffy face of a baby, her shoulders hunched as if bent from hard work, no doubt like her poor old scrubwoman of a mother, her voice attaining the shrill tones of any woman no longer in possession of herself.

(Oh, Reine, your low notes, your low notes so full, so perfected.)

She wept without art or tact or moderation. Suddenly, crumpled up on the bed, her body gone slack, she looked ten years older than her age, a matron, a mother with a shapeless belly, her red hair in a thick braid, or else like an already mature nymphomaniac, outrageously painted (her cheeks were red, glistening with tears), pursuing the gigolo who—

Reine wept—but she always resembled something. Try as she would to feel the most sincere and personal of griefs, she seemed, in spite of herself, to impersonate a more universal suffering, a grief in its essence—motherless child, deserted wife, lovemaking without love, the fatigue of the indigent. (Robert recalled a verse of Baudelaire, on, he believed, the subject of Satan—But wasn't he being heartless, he wondered, to think of Baudelaire at this time?) Reine wept for all who weep; she shed tears for her worn-out old mother who scrubbed office floors at five in the morning; she wept for her father, stricken with fierce delirium, for Anselme and for Mélusine, for Jocelyn and for Gerry, she wept for Carol. She could condemn Carol and weep for her at the same time, without problems or embarrassment—something Robert could not do.

And rent with grief, she spoke with that childlike voice out of the big, sculptural woman's body and said with the most total sincerity the banal words of her songs: "I've at last understood—You need not speak—You don't love me any more; you've never loved me—It's better that we part without words. What good would that do? I will console myself, don't worry. We all manage to find consolation."

He let out a cry, as sharp as a knife.

"No. Not everyone!"

She raised toward him hurt eyes, divinely stupid.

"Is it your wife?" she asked.

No, not Catherine. He was certainly not thinking of Catherine. It was he who would not console himself, would never console himself for not being like her, like Reine, for being unable with a single word to reach the heart of the world and there bathe in love, there recover and be able to give some strength to others. He would never console himself for not having loved her enough and for even holding a grudge against her, against that big girl, beautiful and common, that second-rate cabaret singer, that stupid marvel; he would never console himself for holding a grudge against her because she could so easily touch, with such ludicrous means (a voice no better than many others, a face devoid of distinction, who performed turns in establishments without grandeur, in provincial towns, Besançon, Nancy, Limoges). Envious of that perfect gift. Her sublime athlete's hardihood, between the prix fixe beer hall and the badly heated hotel with damp sheets. "I gave myself utterly tonight," she would say with sweaty vanity, and it was true. No, he would never have that gift. Nor her indifference, either.

He knew that beneath her claims against him, which might appear mean and paltry, there was in Reine quite another thing, a proud passion, almost generous, for her "public," to which she wanted "to give" the best of herself, the peak moment of her strength.

But he would never be able to explain to her that Carol, too, had "given" them something beautiful that evening. Was it important?

"You are inspired by just anyone, except me," she said, however, with vehemence. "Might as well say there's nothing between us any more. You write a song for a girl who doesn't even have a voice, who sings off-key, and for me—"

"Why not?" he said, despairing of ever making her understand. "Anyway, we all sing off-key—"

"Me? I sing off-key?" she exclaimed, tragic and at the same time comic.

No, Reine, you don't sing off-key; you have never sung off-key. Perhaps not enough off-key. You love, you sing, you live without a flaw. And you are not a second-rate singer, even though you will never sing except in small towns such as Charleville and to a public of teen-agers in Longwy; you will never be a second-rate singer.

I am the one, no doubt, who is second rate; I am a second-rate writer and a second-rate lover. I will never do anything, professionally.

Discouragement overwhelmed him as he faced this woman who, with the worn-out words of her songs, was able to fabricate such a perfect grief.

And yet something within him protested. Something that resisted bitterness. A ridiculous little treasure, like the marbles and worthless premiums in the tin box of his tenth year; a little worthless secret, like the house with two exits where Anselme and he had played detectives; a treasure that he had been unable to share, a secret he had been unable to communicate.

"Perhaps you are right; perhaps it is better that we not see each other again," he said as if in a dream. "Marakis will still be able to write some excellent things for you—"

"Go, get out!" she said in a low, hoarse voice, the voice heard in melodramas. Melodramas are the real truth of mankind. Her hand clutched the coverlet. She was suffering shamelessly. She would suffer in front of a thousand people in singing one of his songs. She would not shut her grief away in a tin box, not she! She would offer it to anyone: to Marakis, on whose shoulder she would weep; to her mother, who would have "told her so"; and at Grenoble, Metz, Châtel-Guyon. All she had given she would give to anyone, without discrimination. Only, Robert reflected, she does not know it, and that is her strength. He felt like saying to her, "Believe it or not, I have never loved you so much." He did not say it because it would have sounded too cynical. And then, the word "love" was not exact. "Admired" would perhaps be closer to the truth.

Staggering a little from the shock, he descended the pretty stairway heavily. The tenants on the floor just below had had the charming idea of putting a duck out on their Renaissance balcony. The thought of never again climbing these stairs, panting a little, moved him inexplicably. It moved him more than the parting from Reine in tears. All the same, downstairs he paused on the threshold. A break with anyone is hard to endure at the age of fifty. Should he go back up? He hesitated. Then, no. Finished. Reine was a woman too high-minded for a writer.

III

The Silence

GOOD DEED

"You'll never guess who telephoned me at the office this morning! Robert!"

"Oh, I'm so glad," said Geneviève. "That misunderstanding was so stupid."

"He asked me to intervene at the ministry, to speak to Charlier in behalf of his old chap, the one who's been carrying out some archaeological digs in the Cotentin. It seems he's been doing that work without the proper authorization; he's been digging for more than ten years, and the municipality has only just become aware of the fact. Result: They're threatening to fill in the hole he's dug."

"Oh, that's not nice," said Geneviève. "But what has that got to do with Robert? After all, a subject is a subject. He can invent whatever he likes—"

"Well, you know Robert. He plunged blindly into this thing, on a sudden impulse; and now he's being preyed upon by a raft of people: the kid photographer, the old spinster, the museum guard, the mayor, heaven knows who else. And he is going to waste time now in phone calls, letters of recommendation, and so on."

"Yes, that's his boy-scout side," Geneviève said fondly.

"Scout, yes, you're right; there is a lot of the boy scout in Robert. And a writer cannot be a scout," said Bernard, joking beneath his air of severity. "However, we'll never manage to change him."

"Oh, that poor, dear Robert! Do you want to change him?"

"Of course not. But all the same—To start out with a novel and end up with a Good Deed—"

They exchanged glances of shared compassion, like parents of the Prodigal Son who has returned home.

CHARLIER

Charlier was languid in his gestures, marvelously well tailored, and endowed with beautiful gray hair. He was like a well-tended display window; no detail was neglected.

"Bernard, if you only knew how numerous are these discoveries, these inventions! They come to tell me about such things every day! But of course, since this concerns you and our friend Guibal—I assure you, this sort of thing is my daily bread. No doubt it all has its charm, its picturesque quality. But in the long run, you'll agree—I have in my employ a youngster, a charming youngster, who is a specialist in hydrography. Well! That poor boy spends hours every day reading papers sent us on systems for rainmaking, or methods of individual flight, or bombs that paralyze and ways to ward off —The War Ministry takes an interest in such things. But as for me, my interests are rather in the realm of historical and art treasures, the Cézannes that turn up in attics, primitives, dolmens—Recently, a fine fellow wanted to blow up the port of Cherbourg to uncover a prehistoric settlement—And to think, it's generally said that people nowadays lack imagination!"

"I'm all the more embarrassed to take up your time."

"No, not at all! If there's anything I can do—Since you are interested in this case, I shall examine it with the greatest attention—"

"I'm interested in it quite by accident," Bernard protested. "Simply because Guibal, an old friend of mine, has undertaken—But personally I will confess that these little provincial deliriums always make me rather uneasy. Those unhappy people who hold on to an idée fixe for years and years—"

"Yes, but," Charlier gently interrupted, "we must not forget that there is always a chance, in spite of everything—"

Charlier relapsed suddenly into a personal rumination, his fine but homely features softening. Then he shook himself awake with a charming toss of the head. "As I was saying," he resumed, "nothing proves that buried treasures do not exist under the port of Cherbourg, and this is somewhat the case with your—what's his name? Sorel. We cannot be sure. And in the case of Cherbourg, we will never know. A prodigiously valuable invention may turn up in the jumble of papers my young colleague is reading. Will he be able to recognize and decipher it? The task becomes all the more difficult, since most of these fanatics are self-educated. Their writings are full of errors in calculation, errors in language, which, my dear friend—Yes, the language is an almost insuperable barrier—Even in love—"

Again he seemed to become lost in thought. Bernard was somewhat embarrassed.

"Then you believe that it is possible that Gilles de Rais—that those Templars—Personally, I've always found it hard to believe that those secret societies and esoteric orders ever really existed. Even Freemasons, with their little aprons, their initiations—It all seems to me such a waste of time."

"That, my dear Bernard, is because you are a worldly man," Charlier murmured with a sigh, smoothing his hair. "A man of the world in the Pascalian sense, a man who belongs to the world. You do not believe in the importance of ritual, of incantations—But now, to return to your man, it would have been better had he applied in the first place for permission to do that excavating. True, the permission would no doubt have been refused, since he has no title to—Before dedicating his life—You say twelve years?"

"Twelve or even fifteen, I'm not sure."

"He must know, I imagine. Twelve or fifteen years alone underground—He must have kept account in days, in hours —What a wager! That, too, is Pascalian—"

"The essential thing is to know if there is really a—"

"No, no, my dear friend, no! It is not for me, with my functions, to say this; but really the question of the Templars, of Gilles de Rais is quite secondary. It goes without saying, I shall study this dossier; and if there is the least probability of interesting vestiges, I shall personally intervene with the minister. But that man, that confrontation for ten or twelve years—Why, during that time, he must have experienced a kind of mutation—"

"You really believe that?" said Bernard, yielding to the spirit of contradiction. "As for me, I imagine a kind of peasant digging the earth just as he used to plow it, with the sole difference that at the end of the furrow he hopes to find some gold."

"But exactly! Gold itself is a symbol. The philosopher's stone—Try to procure a little supplementary information on this affair of the municipal council. Those little administrative affairs are incredibly boring. I'll do my best; I'll do the impossible. For again one wonders if possibly, after all—"

"You think it will be very difficult?" asked Bernard, rising to go.

"Oh, not at all, not at all—I merely wonder if, after so many years, you see, if your man still hopes to find a solution —a material solution, if it's not beyond any kind of solution —But count on me, my dear friend, count on me."

Many people found Jean Charlier, attaché at the Ministry of Culture and heir to Charlier Textiles, insupportably affected and, to tell the truth, a little unbalanced. Bernard was not far from sharing this opinion.

MARSEILLES-RENNES

"Vivi's German" was thirty-four, and his name was Werner.

Werner was a football fan. He had wanted to see the Marseilles-Rennes game, and Vivi couldn't do otherwise than invite him to the house to watch it on television. "All the same, I can't oblige him to follow the match in a café," she said.

When he came to the apartment on the rue de l'Université, he immediately broke the ice by repairing an electric plug in Marina's room, leveling the legs of the bridge table, and gluing back on the head that had broken off the Venetian glass blackamoor. The conversation with the twins had started out so ceremoniously that they all three ended up in an outburst of laughter. Put at ease, he had then taken out of his leather pouch the photos of his mother, his little niece who was almost eleven years old, and finally his paraphernalia of handmade jewelry. He had explained his work, his difficulties. The twins were fascinated, and Manuel already imagined himself setting stones in his idle moments. He offered Werner the use of his bedroom as a workshop. Werner could use his auxiliary motor there (he dared not turn it on in the servant's room where he lodged, fearing the owner's anger). Marina, more reserved, finally forgot her airs of a well-brought-up young girl and sat down on the carpet in a yoga posture. When she lost her balance, Werner laughed so heartily that she lost what remained of her dignity. Then they all crouched down on the floor to watch the match on television.

Vivi remained apart, watching the formation of a family as if watching a bubbling saucepan of jam, waiting for it to jell.

. . . our friend, a few weeks ago, finally claimed to have uncovered a chapel, a ruined chapel quite like the chapel of the château, in which are twelve coffins, or sarcophagi, sketches of which I made after our friend's description and am enclosing herewith. The chapel also contains some ritual objects. Upon his insistence and at my own request, after having invited various persons, among whom was a former officer of Engineers, we followed our friend down into his tunnels. But having reached a depth of thirty meters and seeing the precariousness of the buttressing, we. . . . which means we have not, unfortunately, arrived at a certainty. The mayor, although not at all persuaded of our friend's honesty—

"Our friend! Our friend!"

. . . and it must be noted that Sorel's extraordinary state of maniacal excitement. . . . Even so, the mayor has proposed an eventual resumption of the excavations on a more rational basis, and he envisages obtaining a subsidy on condition that the discovery benefit the community. . . . Sorel, having refused the mayor's suggestion with violence that would seem to be suspect. . . . the argument became envenomed. The threat of having his tunnels filled in threw him into a state bordering on a mental breakdown. . . . Your efforts at the Ministry of Culture or any steps you could take with foundations that might be interested will be. . . . although salutary for our friend to be encouraged in his work which, it must be confessed, has led him to the verge of a perhaps dangerous obsession—

"Encouraged!" Catherine exclaimed with unexpected emphasis. "Encouraged! But he's an old imbecile, your parish priest! When you stop to think about those twelve years of the man's life devoted to that work—and now your priest wonders if he should be encouraged! Just when the poor fellow has reached his goal! I, too, would be excited if I were in his place."

Robert, Gerry, and Carol looked at her in surprise. Gerry still had the priest's letter in his hand. Carol stared at Catherine, who rarely gave way to such language. Robert appeared to be embarrassed.

"Naturally, Cathie, you are right," said Gerry, chivalrously. "But you must understand the poor old priest. After all, nothing proves to him—"

"Of course! Since no one dares to go down and see!"

"I'm not sure I'd go down myself. Forty-five meters underground, some tunnels so narrow you have to crawl through, and badly buttressed, with only the light of a lantern—No, what's needed is for Robert to—"

"Yes, it's absolutely necessary that Robert—"

They both stopped short.

"What do you want me to do?" said Robert in a weary voice. "Do you want me to crawl in those tunnels? Before I could manage that, I'd have to go on a diet."

"Why, of course not!" Gerry protested.

"That's not what is needed at all," said Catherine; and again the two fell silent, surprised to find they were allies.

"I appealed to Bernard. Bernard saw Charlier at the Ministry of Culture. What more do you want me to do? These affairs of municipal counselors, you know what they're like. How to get one's bearings, how to know what is happening exactly—"

"But you could find out what's happening! You could go down there, make the trip in the car—It's not at the end of the world, the Cotentin, after all!"

"Yes, you could go there, both of you, on a weekend," Carol interrupted in her plaintive voice. "Staying on in Paris, you end up by sinking into a rut."

"Oh, Carol, if you begin to take sides—Anyway, I have the feeling that I'll give up the whole thing, give up the book— I started out in too many different directions; some of them cancel out the others. I feel I'll never get disentangled."

"But that's another question! What we must think of now," said Catherine, speaking with passion, "is that unfortunate man. The book? To the devil with it!"

Again everyone looked at her, astounded. She flushed and

began to laugh, ashamed of her own vehemence, a relic of the past. What would Jean-Francis have said? She remembered the disdain with which he spoke of Robert's "journalism." And how he had said of Robert, "He still believes in direct contact with reality!" He had said that the other day, with pitying condescension. (I believe that was the word that spoiled everything. I couldn't help but think, And what you are asking of me; isn't it a direct contact with reality? And I laughed. How vulgar I am!) She had not been able to refrain from considering Jean-Francis a little ridiculous.

"And you are the one to say this!" Robert groaned.

"Why, yes. I want a direct contact with reality!"

And she laughed again.

But they could not understand why. Yes, Jean-Francis was a little ridiculous, all of a sudden, with his fine hands, his insubstantial words. Bach, the flute, a writer writes for himself—You, too, you only have to know what love is, she thought. Playing Debussy in front of a photograph. What am I doing here? she had asked herself. And as to him, what's he got to do with my problems? Both of us were a little ridiculous.

They had parted with dignity, emotionally stirred. (And at a distance, that scene was pretty comic!) "I hold nothing against you," he had said. "You are a woman who can love but once." After she had gone, he probably took up the flute again. Or wrote a beautiful poem. Who knows, perhaps relieved? Ridiculous, but touching. Yes, now that her irritation had passed, she found him rather touching. The little boy who declares he is "quite happy to play all alone." Me, too, I wanted to play all alone. And where did it get me? And that man down there, that unknown man, *all alone,* had foraged the earth, had tunneled for twelve or more years; and they were calling him a madman, a monomaniac.

"With all my heart," she said thoughtfully, "I can say I would have liked very much to know him, that man."

"Our friend is a monomaniac," the parish priest had said. And he was not basically wrong.

Catherine was indignant.

"But the same thing could be said of all creative people! And even the saints, if you care to go that far! Nobody can grasp all points of view at the same time. If you want to achieve something in saintliness or in art or politics or—"

She was about to say "or in love," but stopped short.

"It's impossible to live on all planes simultaneously!" she went on. "You simply cannot. And whatever you do, if you dedicate yourself to it, you must shut your eyes to everything else. Definitely. Look at Mamma. Everyone is always saying, 'She's a saint; she's perfect.' And it's true, poor, dear Mamma. But with that said, she doesn't understand a thing."

"You exaggerate."

"Not a single thing!"

Catherine got out of bed, where he remained, stretched out lazily.

"Yes, but your mother is an extreme case."

"Sorel is, too. And Cézanne. And Saint Francis of Assisi. One must know how to choose!"

That was what Geneviève also said. And had also said, "It's a working hypothesis." He thought briefly of Geneviève, with affection. Then forgot her.

"So, according to you," he said, raising his voice, for she had gone into the bathroom, where the geyser, that old-fashioned hot-water machine, was roaring like a volcano, "according to you, either one does nothing of account, or one is dedicated to something and doesn't understand anything else?"

"I suppose so. I think everyone has to choose!"

She called this out cheerfully. It was a sad thought, but she was happy because the dialogue that had resumed between them could be prolonged indefinitely, like those discussions of bygone times, the time of the little house called Olivette.

"It's heroism," he said, more for himself.

He had tried. He had tried to take a stand, had tried to choose. But he couldn't manage it. He was not a monomaniac. He was not heroic.

Marakis was a little embarrassed about bringing his songs to her. He was afraid that he would run into what he rather vulgarly called "a three-sided row." Not that he lacked courage, but after all, he had his future to think about; and as everyone knows, cabaret singers lose their dash, even lose their voice, when they have been left in the lurch. And so he climbed Reine's stairs, hugging his vocal scores like a miser hanging on to his money box.

"How kind you are," she said as she met him at the door. "I was very upset. I'm leaving on June twenty-fifth, and I absolutely must have something new to give. And Robert hasn't written anything new for me in the last three months."

She seemed to be preoccupied but not at all tragic. He was relieved. After all, it might just be a false rumor.

"I've got a bossa nova for you."

"Show me?"

He sat down at the piano. His black hair glistened, was rather greasy, and smelled of brilliantine. And she tolerantly told herself, That's not done much nowadays, but at any rate here he is—He had been in Paris only two years. A Greek export, from Athens. A good-looking young man, in his thirties, his jacket a little too nipped in at the waist, the necktie rather loud, his eyes dark and glowing but inexpressive. There was nothing particular to say about him except that he was healthy but vulgar. Reine was not so stupid that she could not perceive this. But what did it matter? On the other hand, that wave in his hair—Later on, I'll mention it to him. She wanted to make sure that he had talent and that his talent harmonized with hers. She waited until he had finished playing, then spoke.

"If you ever want to have a stage career yourself, then you should do something about your hair."

He was devoid of self-conceit. He liked music, his own humble music, easy and melancholy, his popular themes taken wherever he found them, but he arranged them nicely. His verses weren't bad either, and he would make an excellent accompanist.

"Would you like some coffee? A sandwich? We could go on working afterward."

He accepted with simplicity. He chewed the sandwich slowly, savoring each mouthful, now without a trace of uneasiness.

"It's nice here in your apartment," he said, wiping his mouth. "It's really nice. You and I are going to do some good work together."

She was sure of it. He inspired confidence. For a moment, a recollection made her sigh, but then she resolutely turned away from the past. Marakis asked no questions, calmly minded his own business. But after a moment, he showed her the photo of his mother and his four brothers. Yes, there is a race of man that shows family photographs, the Marakises, the Werners—

"I'm the only unmarried one," he said without emphasis.

Reine was wearing her cashmere dressing gown. It was hot. They worked late into the night, for Metz, Nancy, and Radio-Luxembourg.

1914–1918

"I really believe he's completely given up his book. And you know, Mamma, I find him changed. As if he'd had some kind of shock."

Catherine frowned as she spoke.

"What are you trying to tell me? He's come back to you. Does anything else matter?"

"Yes, as you say, he's come back to me. But I'd like to be sure—Well, I want him to be happy!"

213

"And what more? When a man came back from the war minus a leg, my girl—"

Catherine raised her arms to heaven.

"Oh, you and the years nineteen fourteen to nineteen eighteen!"

"Quite so. The years nineteen fourteen to nineteen eighteen. You're making fun of me. But I assure you there were men in those years who returned in a state of 'shell shock,' as we said then; and believe me, we women, we who hadn't gone to war, we knew very well that we could never understand. But it's not necessary to understand. The thing that's necessary is to love, to care, to—"

Catherine's mind wandered far from speeches such as this, piously retrograde.

And she told herself, "Oh, but I did go to war."

Because, in sum, the secret question had slowly come to maturity, disclosing itself in its scandalous nudity: Why, for so many years, have I been faithful to Robert?

Faithful. What does that mean? A constraint? A neurosis? Indolence? For as it turned out, I found I was incapable of being unfaithful, no matter how much I wanted to be—In short, I am congenitally faithful. It's a kind of infirmity. As for Vivi, she—

But the two sisters were very different. Vivi had always been the erratic one, the brilliant one, the foolish one. Vivi, who dared to say, when her husband Marc talked about his "apostolate" to the Third World, "Your apostolate is to make me happy. And not to go off to Brazil to work for the underdeveloped." And Catherine, in Vivi's place, would have accompanied Marc to Brazil. But then, Catherine was the serious and sensible one, who did well in school, chose a serious profession that ensured a pension; she adored her husband and was a good housewife. And fidelity along with suffering is a part of this panoply of the perfect wife. Mamma, the widow Germaine, the Mother—she is the dazzling proof; she derives her ostentatious happiness from self-sacrifice and

214

self-effacement. A woman preoccupied with homemaking, always having a broom or a piece of knitting in her hands; or else making no objections to following her military husband to barracks with beds swathed in mosquito netting; a mother making her own piecrust and correcting refractory geography lessons, vacating her cozy and beautiful apartment for her children in exchange for a modest two-room flat scarcely big enough to hold her, depriving herself of everything and benefiting by it. Radiant goddess of sacrifice, who always chose at table the least tempting morsels of meat, which are sometimes the tastiest. I tried to rival her, and what good did it do me? For, with the injustice of the gods, Germaine secretly prefers the foolish daughter to the sensible one, the frivolous daughter to the serious one, the faithless Vivi to the faithful Catherine.

Robert, too, might have preferred—No, because Robert has no preferences. If he seems for the moment to neglect Reine, it is not because he has begun to prefer me but simply because he does not prefer Reine. A very relative consolation. Some women would be content with it.

Catherine, when she had learned of Reine's existence, had sometimes mentally supplicated Robert, At least love the woman! As if that love could push back upon all women and upon herself their share of love—Yes, she reflected, I would feel closer to him if he were capable of loving as I love, even capable of loving another woman—As I love? Yet I left him momentarily; I betrayed him for a moment—oh, so briefly! Just the time it took me to go on foot from the boulevard Saint-Michel to the rue Delambre—Yes, there had been twenty minutes or a half hour during which she had not been fidelity incarnate, had not been absolutely a Penelope. But it was Penelope who had returned home, repentant, torn between tears and uncontrollable laughter, especially repenting the ridiculousness of having for a moment tried to turn herself into a Circe.

But am I Penelope? And who is Penelope?

PENELOPE

Penelope is waiting. Fidelity. The cloth embroidered by day and unstitched by night. She is the woman who at night undoes, thread by thread, the work accomplished during the day. Who, with her gold or silver scissors, undoes and renders futile the seconds of her life. All the same, that cloth was something! A kind of performance, a creation testifying to those long, terrible days, cold days, hot days, empty of love. And perhaps there was a detail in the embroidery, a flower or a bird, that really sang of happier times, when Penelope had nothing to do with being a symbol and example but was merely a woman who was loved. But the flower and the bird, after being done and undone, over and over, became meaningless. Penelope finally did not even remember that when she first embroidered them, sitting there alone in her room, she was thinking of her man, Ulysses. Penelope was no longer anything but a woman named Penelope, whose fidelity was simply gratuitous.

FIDELITY II

"I don't understand," said Vivi, "why you remain faithful to a man about whom you have so few illusions."

But Vivi was mistaken. I did once have illusions. One day he would understand that I was the one who loved him most. One day he would write the book he was capable of writing. One day we would be alone and happy together. We are now —for the moment—alone together. I don't have those illusions any more. Something has changed. Is it on account of my failure to carry out my resolve that day in the rue Delambre? Or his failure to write that book? The question is debatable, but the fact remains: We now have something in common—our two misadventures. This is rather sad, but it is also rather funny because I don't know whether my misadventure was in having ceased, even for a moment, to be faithful or in having failed in my attempt to be unfaithful, and he doesn't know whether his misadventure is in having been unable to write that book or in having undertaken it in the first place.

And neither of us knows whether it will be possible to return to our old ways—he to his philandering, I to my fidelity —as comfortably as one slips into an old dressing gown.

At seven-forty in the morning, the telephone rang. Catherine was in the bathroom, so Robert took the call, expecting it would be the twins.

"Hello? Robert Guibal?"

Catherine appeared in the doorway and gave Robert a questioning look. He put his hand over the receiver.

"It's Father Moinaud," he whispered, then returned to the telephone. "Yes, Father. What's happened?"

"Something very disturbing, Robert. Otherwise, I would not be telephoning you at this early hour. Anselme is in frightful trouble. He was arrested yesterday afternoon in the Saint-Pierre market, where he created a scandalous scene. I suppose he was a bit exalted. And now they're going to put him in jail! We saw it coming. We've had to put up with a great deal from him, except this!"

"We, we—Speak for yourself, my old friend," said Robert with great irritation. "I don't see what I, personally, can do."

Catherine redoubled her signs of curiosity.

"It's Anselme. They're going to jail him."

At the other end of the line, Father Moinaud was talking excitedly.

"What you can do is meet me immediately. We'll hurry off to the station-house infirmary, see the physician there, and explain to him the sad case of this boy—"

"Boy?" said Robert. "That boy is, after all, forty-seven years old!"

Father Moinaud became conciliating.

"Listen, Robert, my boy. I understand better than anyone

the demands of creativity. I know how busy you are, how overworked. But this is a matter of life and death for Anselme, who was your boyhood friend—"

"Very well, very well, I'll meet you," said Robert wearily. "I suggest we meet in front of the Latour-Maubourg metro station, in a half hour—But tell me" (for after all he needed to know), "what offense did Anselme commit in the Saint-Pierre market?"

"Anselme tried to persuade the women who were jostling and pushing to get at a pile of fabrics put on sale that their behavior was immodest!"

"Obviously!"

A half hour later, they were at the rendezvous. Robert had had his coffee and had calmed down.

"All this is going to end badly for Anselme," he said as he got into Father Moinaud's small car. "We'll not be able to go on rescuing him forever."

"Especially," sighed the good priest, "with his police record. And nowadays a sudden conversion like his appears to be, for most people, insanity."

"And frankly, isn't it close to insanity?" asked Robert.

"It's regrettable, very regrettable," Father Moinaud deplored as he started the car with a great rattle and roar. "It's very regrettable, but I believe you are right."

MONOMANIA II

"The other day we were talking about monomania," said Robert as he sat down to dinner in the kitchen. "Well, you know, Anselme is a typical case. Besides, that was the opinion of the physician, a worthy type, who will do everything he can—"

"But all the same, they've not let him go?"

"They'll keep him in the infirmary for a few days, on tranquilizers, then release him on probation. But don't

worry, they'll see him again! Father Moinaud has gone bail
for him, has promised to lodge him and to keep an eye on
him."

"Oh, poor Father Moinaud!"

"Yes, that will be a trial for him. He was so upset this
morning that he didn't even mention his manuscript."

"Oh, then this must be serious."

Robert smiled.

"Yes. After all, he couldn't let Anselme down."

"And the other one?"

"What other one? Oh, quite. Sorel? Are you as interested
in him as all that?"

"Yes, because I'm something of a monomaniac myself,"
she said mischievously.

He looked up at her in surprise, started to say something,
then thought better of it.

"Listen, if you're all that interested, I can send Mélusine
down there. I can't go myself, for I've got to work on a
mountainous backlog of manuscripts."

QUEEN MÉLUSINE

Lanky-legged stiltbird, Mélusine defiantly boarded the train.
She had arranged herself for this trip as she arranged for
everything. She had a little money on her, but she had taken
out of her eternal tapestry bag lined with mauve cotton cloth
a sandwich of *crudités* wrapped up in some Kleenex. Frugal
in her prosperity, she had added only an orange. Once comfortably wedged into a window seat, she might almost have
been taken for a respectable traveler, a pensioned school-
teacher, a retired governess of children who had grown up.
But her respectability was put in doubt by those tics that
make her twitch; she was too innocent even to dream of
trying to suppress them.

Thus, too, her way of walking made her noticeable. For

example, when she arrived at the outskirts of Boissy and walked away from the station after handing in her ticket, she strode away rapidly, with staccato steps, as if fleeing something or someone, and this made the stationmaster stand watching her until she was out of sight. From time to time, she came to sudden halts to stare as if meditatively at the signs posted up locating the municipal swimming pool, the slaughterhouse, the community center; and this made some passing schoolboys stare at her, fascinated. Then there was the way she went round and round the town square, taking note of the three cafés, the two hardware stores, the bicycle shop, the grocery store. She made this tour of inspection without haste, as if wanting to acquaint herself with this new territory. Her fragile figure, a little bent, seemed to hug the walls fearfully, yet her expression was peaceable enough as she passed the grocery store for a second time. Was she tempted by the low price on the cookies that were on sale? Then she paused in front of the presbytery, out of which was coming a clergyman, who looked at her in mild surprise.

Soon the two of them were seen to go off together, side by side, the round little parish priest, who was ceremoniously talking in his fluty voice to the strange woman, the old young girl, who seemed to be both arrogant and shy.

"No doubt," he was to say afterward, "Mademoiselle Rebec has her little manias, like everyone. But what culture! What erudition!" He had her opinion on many things. "What do you think of my clay artifacts?" he had asked her, and she had agreed that they must date from the twelfth century, "the period of Philippe Auguste." "And my monograph?" She had pronounced it "masterful!" And when the archivist had invited her to "stop over" at his house rather than at the inn, she hesitated only for a second, on account of the rather dilapidated state of her suitcase.

Soon the festival hall of Boissy was to witness a unique spectacle: Mélusine, teetering on her high-heeled buttoned shoes, losing and snatching up again her loosely crocheted shawl, giving a talk entitled "Boissy and Its Prestigious Past."

Her flat voice, typical of the solitary person no one ever listens to, rose in the silence, punctuated by the encouraging little coughs of the archivist, the nodding of the parish priest's head. Some schoolchildren shuffled their feet. The jeweler would be there with madame his wife. And over those few heads, piously bowed, Mélusine would reign supreme for forty-five minutes.

Collaborator—thus she had called herself—working closely with a writer of a certain renown, she represented in the eyes of the dazzled townspeople not only that writer but the magazines in which his opinions appeared and even his book publishers; over these people, for a couple of days, Mélusine was to exercise absolute power. Her dress and her stinginess would appear quite natural in Boissy, where there was no lack of old maids. She would be suspected of having "a nice little bit put by," and that would be all. Serenely, she would study the pottery artifacts of the parish priest and would pronounce them "of the very greatest interest," but she would give the pharmacist little hope for his manuscript, which he submitted to her, the labor of his lifetime: "The Mushrooms of Our Provinces."

"And so, Mademoiselle," the mayor would say to her, "you who are acquainted with the question, do you think the excavations of that unhappy man are basically serious? After all, I don't want to make myself ridiculous by sponsoring him."

"I must first judge the man; then I will give you my impression," Mélusine would reply with supreme arrogance.

Next day, she was to meet Pierre Sorel. The day after that, with two sandwiches and an orange in her tapestry bag, Mélusine would board the train for her return to Paris.

Mélusine would never change. She was doomed to be forever that old maid sitting on a bench, the one person who does not throw crumbs to the sparrows. She would always be that cautious madwoman who grimaces in the shadows as she pulls on her ragged gloves, would always be that mythomaniac, coldhearted and not very talkative, who deploys her opinions like pawns on a chessboard and who can recognize among a thousand replicas the authentic moldings taken from a Louis XV paneling, would always be that person peering through a magnifying glass at a page of Gothic writing or a newspaper picked up in the street. She would never change, would always be that spiritualist, that decent vegetarian, that malingerer who exploits her fragile looks and her decency, the very small capital life had granted her. The interest on that capital was minuscule: coffee with milk, a bed, an occasional cigarette.

This austere grasshopper, existing on little and accumulating nothing at all, never sang; and when she did hum a tune between half-closed lips, it was only for herself. She was the woman who rubs shoulders with phantoms and avoids people. However, this inoffensive and ridiculous old maid destroyed, with one sentence, the work of a man and perhaps the life of that man himself. But who could say what her motives were? Was it malignity, the trivial cruelty of a killer of flies? Or was it the harsh exigency, the magnificent acceptance of being nothing and needing to share that nothingness with others? Was she a grotesque and secondary figure like those gargoyles of Notre Dame, which are, after all, only rainspouts? Or was she merely inhuman, a destroying angel?

It doesn't matter. For although Catherine may have ceased to be Penelope, Mélusine would forever be Mélusine. She might be purity itself or even poetry: she would never change and would always be of no importance whatsoever.

CAVE-INS

No doubt they scrutinized each other, tried to plumb each other's depths. No doubt they could be said to belong to the same race. But she, from the age of twenty or twenty-five, those poor, awkward years, had understood. Suddenly and peaceably, instinctively, one might say, suddenly resting on her frail vanity of a young lady with diplomas, piano lessons, a useless education, she had proudly won her freedom to be nothing but a meager effort to survive. From then on, everything was allowed. She could range, in her reading, from sensational news items to works of the highest erudition; in her behavior, from devouring chocolate buns on a park bench, to visits in museums such as the Camondo, where she was the equal of the defunct banker-lawyer, whose spirit floated there in the fragrance of beeswax.

But then, Mélusine did feel some pity for all the sweat that had poured out, for those calloused hands that had drudged at a dream—foolishly, she thought, since he had only to reach out and seize it. She pitied those eyes that had peered into the darkness ahead when he could have just let himself be peaceably engulfed, without a struggle. No doubt.

But this is merely supposition, since no one will ever know what took place between Sorel and Mélusine at that encounter—if, indeed, it ever did take place. No doubt she very much wanted to show him how easy it was, that he had only to open his hands and shut his eyes—Or was she suddenly overwhelmed with wrath, with an aggressive and despicable envy at the thought of all those fifteen years of perfect emptiness, that ethereal creation, that invisibility which she herself had never been able to attain. We will never know. We will never know the truth about Sorel or Mélusine, or about the mayor, that corpulent worthy, that hunk of overbaked gingerbread, who had declared, "Since it is your opinion, then we will fill it all in. I'm not anxious to pass for an idiot, and besides, those tunnels he's excavated are dangerous, like all tunnels. *They could make the entire parish cave in.*"

"But, devil take it, what happened exactly? You should have warned me, sent a telegram, done something! Couldn't you have promised that brute of a mayor—?"

223

"I told him the plain truth," said Mélusine with a great air of offended dignity. "I told him there was little chance that you would obtain a subsidy and that the costs would certainly have to be paid by the commune—"

"But you're insane! You should have invented any excuse to delay the thing—"

"Perhaps Mademoiselle Rebec did not want to get involved," Catherine put in. She had been observing the old spinster closely. This was the first time Mélusine had been introduced into the boulevard Saint-Michel apartment.

"But it was necessary for her to get involved!" Robert exclaimed, purple with unexpected wrath. "I didn't send her down there to say amen to the brutes! You don't take into account those twelve years of work, those tons of earth excavated! And now there's nothing we can do!"

"There's still your book to write," said Mélusine flatly. Her fine hands were trembling as they tightly grasped the tapestry handbag.

"My book! But how can you expect me to write it now? As long as there was a hope—a topical event—People would be interested once the question was asked. Who knows, the book might have stirred up the ministry. But with the tunnels filled in by a bulldozer, how can you expect—?"

"The mystery remains entire," Mélusine said under her breath, staring down at her buttoned shoes.

"Naturally! Of that we can be sure! The mystery will remain entire under three tons of earth! And the unfortunate man who has lost his wife, his children, his employment—what recourse has he? You don't know what people are! From the sole fact that he no longer has the least chance of proving his assertions, they will take him for a visionary!"

"As to that—"

Catherine listened and said nothing.

Robert paced the floor, no longer controlling his inexplicable wrath.

"It was, however, easy to make those people back down! What would it cost them to wait? You needed to talk tourism to them. The tourists pouring in, the possibility of having the château designated—"

"Excuse me," said Mélusine, tight-lipped, "I went down there to talk to them about literature, about history—"

She paused, then added with a kind of harsh satisfaction, "The château is going to be used by a vacation colony or a youth hostel, I understand."

"That's the limit! To dislodge them now would be impossible!"

"They have given Sorel a fortnight to move out—"

"And you did nothing! Why, his life is in shambles!"

"Evidently," said Mélusine with a kind of placidity.

"And it's all the same to you! It can be doubted that you ever intended—"

"Robert, Robert," Catherine warned anxiously.

"The life of an unfortunate man is in shambles, and my book, too, by the same token; and you, all you can find to say is, 'Evidently'!"

"Oh, as to your book, I never really believed in it," said Mélusine, her eyes still averted.

"And don't think that I didn't know it," retorted Robert, quite beside himself. "I know very well that the only thing that counted for you was your pay. I don't blame you; I know the difficulties of your life. But what I can't forgive is that you gave the wheel a push to smash that poor devil, simply for the pleasure of torpedoing my work, or for I wonder what mean vengeance of an old maid—"

"Oh!"

It was Catherine who emitted this cry of indignation. Mélusine said nothing, absorbed in poking at her chignon with a hairpin. Robert collapsed in the battered old armchair.

"Very well, Monsieur Guibal, you don't need to tell me twice," replied Mélusine, trembling a little but proud.

She went toward the door, head high, catching her feet in the fringe of the rug, recovering herself, and finally left the room with a clicking of her wooden beads.

"Poor creature," said Catherine, coming back to sit on the

arm of Robert's chair. "How could you—?"

Robert did not reply but raised his arms in a gesture of discouragement.

"Although, to a certain extent, I understand you. She could certainly have been more efficient. And that poor man!"

"Oh, he mustn't be too much pitied. As crazy as she is, probably. Two of a kind."

His intolerance was so little like him that Catherine was dumbfounded.

"But—you're not going to give it up now?"

"Who would be interested in it now? A mystery that will never be solved—who would you expect to be interested?"

ANSELME'S DISLOYALTY

The physician had required Father Moinaud to pledge that he would "take in hand" Anselme's case. In sum, to a certain extent, what was required was for Father Moinaud to bring about a "deconversion."

Father Moinaud urged Anselme to seek employment. But Anselme was carried away by the lilies of the field. The old priest then tried to dissuade Anselme from pursuing his apostolate in public places (where he regularly had his nose punched). Anselme expounded on the wedding at Canaan. He then urged Anselme to observe moderation. Anselme preached endlessly on the money changers in the temple and on Samson with his jawbone of an ass and the Amalekites. Father Moinaud was not used to being paid off so lavishly in his own coin.

"To every one of my admonitions, he replies with verses from the Bible," said Father Moinaud hopelessly to Robert. "Why, it's almost dishonest!"

"Is the car in good condition?"

Robert asked the question curtly that evening, after his memorable fit of temper.

"Yes, dear. It only needs to be filled up."

"I'll have that done tomorrow. I'm going to run down to Boissy. It's all too stupid, really."

Next day he slept late. It was a Saturday.

"In such fine weather, I'd run into the weekend traffic on the roads, wouldn't I?"

He was asking for help, which she gave him.

"Yes, you certainly would! There will be traffic jams galore. In any case, you're not in a hurry, at least not so much that one day will make a difference."

"You're wrong; one day can make a difference!"

He was exasperated. But immediately afterward, he showed a kind of relief and proposed that they have lunch at Bagatelle. And that evening, they went to the theater, the last opening of the season. And there they ran into Bernard and Geneviève.

"What a bore," Robert groaned, "we'll have to speak to them."

Catherine privately thought that Robert had surely expected this meeting, since theater first nights and vernissages were the fishponds where Geneviève and Bernard selected their acquaintances, the people they cared to know.

"Catherine! What a lovely dress!" said Geneviève as if they had seen each other the night before.

"Hello, you rude and cantankerous person!" said Bernard to Robert. "Still as misanthropic as ever? By the way, you can stop worrying; Charlier has seen the minister, who is considering the case. . . . What? Too late? But you know it's never too late in such matters. . . . Filled in? Those tunnels? So much the better! Those gentlemen don't like to have their work interfered with. I'll bet Charlier will be very excited when he hears this! And we'll hear more about the Boissy affair and about you, Robert! While I think of it, you might do a nice article on the affair, the whole thing, with photos. You and I must talk this over."

Whereupon he slapped Robert on the back, as sincere and manly friends do in American movies. And after this encounter, Robert was unable to refuse a luncheon engagement— and expected Catherine to reproach him for it. But she said nothing, to his surprise.

The luncheon was at Bernard's apartment.

"How grown-up your children are! Valérie is now a real little beauty," said Catherine when the children had been led away.

"Yes, a wood nymph, a sprite," said Geneviève fondly.

"Like the Mélusine woman!" said Bernard, laughing. "I'll never forget your lady collaborator and muse, Robert! Always the same, aren't you? With your protégés, you could open a zoo!"

He so overdid it, laughing so broadly, that his geniality became almost vulgar. You felt he was on the point of taking off his necktie and painting his nose red. Robert was touched by this behavior, which showed, he thought, a real attachment. After all, he told himself, they've missed me—as if he were returning from a long journey.

Geneviève, with the thoughtfulness of a hospital nurse, suggested turning on the television for them.

They returned home dead tired. Sunday afternoon. And at this time of day, Robert reflected, Reine was no doubt visiting her mother, and Gerry and Carol would be watching the Sunday sports broadcast, and Jocelyn would be asleep, exhausted from an obligatorily volcanic Saturday night. Anselme no longer dared to come to see him—To what good this emptiness he had created around him? Perhaps they, too, missed him?

"I have some papers to correct," Catherine announced as she took off her jacket and silk shirtwaist and donned the more comfortable sweater.

"Really?"

"No, not really," she confessed. "But I detest Sunday afternoons."

He wondered how she had filled so many Sundays that he had spent away from her, with Reine and Marakis or at a football game with Manuel, or no matter what diversion that would take him away from the apartment, from Catherine and love and empty hours.

She replied to the implicit question as if he had spoken his thought. In the course of a week, she had found again the half-spoken language of seasoned married couples.

"I used to go to concerts with Jean-Francis. But I believe we're on the outs at present."

They exchanged an understanding glance of fleeting amusement.

"Suppose we both take that trip?" he said brusquely.

"To Boissy?"

"Yes, why not?"

"Well—the lycée—I'd have to give them notice. And then, I might be in your way—"

She had got into a tizzy. She telephoned Vivi to notify the headmaster for her. Vivi promised to do so and asked for details in an uncertain voice. Catherine could hear on the telephone the sound of hammering.

"What's that noise?"

"It's Werner, putting up some shelves," said Vivi as if utterly exhausted. You would have thought she had been subjected to a flood or fire. "He's repaired the fridge; he's repainted the bathroom," she added, as if announcing the last blow of fate. Catherine hung up, laughing.

"She'll end up by marrying that man," she said to Robert, who was cleaning his pipe as he sat beside her. "Mamma says that he's a very sensible young fellow, after all, and that he merely needs to find someone who will handle his wares. So, it's an unheard-of chance for her, and she seems to be in despair."

"I'm wondering," he said, "if I ever put up shelves for you."

A PARENTHESIS

Vivi had got used to disorder and worry; they were a kind of gymnastics, giving her keen and brief pleasure, such as are given by the constraints of certain sports. Being too slender and too overworked, too stimulated and underfed, unsure of the future, these were conditions that suited her; they made her feel young and alive. Happiness, on the other hand, weighed heavily upon her. She now looked like a tired young woman (the two or three extra kilos she now weighed may have accounted for this); she had bloomed into a beautiful woman, but a little overripe. Werner came to the apartment every two or three days, quiet and industrious. There was always something for him to repair, to do, always a football match to argue over with Manuel, a piece of jewelry to finish for Marina. He would say, "It's time for dinner." Or he would say, "Suppose we listen to music for a while?" And the roast or the music would be there, like important visitors, with Werner settled down in the armchair that had been vacant until then, taking up a great deal of space in the room. Vivi, who was used to eating standing up and listening with one ear to a few bars of music, adapted with difficulty to the new routine. She had a hard time digesting either the music or the roast. On the other hand, the twins were very satisfied.

"When will the wedding be?" they asked.

Werner laughed. His laughter was as hearty as a good soup.

"We must wait until Evelyn resigns herself to bring an end to this," he said indulgently.

She felt like a problem child among three patient adults, patient and very sure of themselves.

One night when she wanted to attend a concert of the visiting Strasbourg percussion orchestra, although she was ill with a liver attack, Werner backed the twins, categorically forbade the project.

The twins approved. She tried to revolt.

"But after all, I have the right to—" she exclaimed, almost in tears.

"We will go next Sunday, when you are well."

"Why, yes, you can go next Sunday," Manuel urged. And Marina, unconsciously cruel, said, "You're no longer a child, Mamma."

"But—"

"Really, Evelyn! If you go next Sunday to the matinee, it will tire you less; so what do you lose?"

Evidently there was no answer to this. What would she lose after all, except the fatigue and effort of this momentary childish urge to have her own way, above all things? She could find no argument, for there was none. She would soon not even know what she had won or what she had lost. Perhaps that was a very good thing.

"No," said Catherine, "you never did put up shelves for me. But some of your friends did."

She couldn't remember who those friends were. He had had so many friends! Everyone was his friend. He would enter into conversation with a delivery boy, would discover that the locksmith had a good singing voice, would sympathize with the conjugal troubles of the social security inspector—and oh, those endless halts in the concierge's loge! Indeed, his entire life had been one long postponement to the next day, like their recent weeks, a postponement of important things. If anything was important—

He responded to her unspoken thoughts.

"It's true, I've wasted a great deal of time, and I've made you waste time."

"Which brings us now to the same point almost?"

She had said this a little maliciously, without much reflection. The look Robert gave her made her bow her head, as if echoing his next words.

"Strange, isn't it?" she forced herself to say.

"Yes. I wonder—"

231

"What?"

"I wonder what point Sorel has reached. His wife gone, his children taken from him, no more money, no more job, no more goal, since from his viewpoint he reached it and simultaneously lost it."

"But after all, whenever we reach a goal, don't we at the same time lose it?"

"That doesn't sound like you. Usually you are much more optimistic than I am."

"But what I said isn't necessarily pessimistic. One can be relieved at not having a goal any more." And she thought, As for me, I was relieved to lose, at least in spirit, that tense fidelity, that tense waiting. And yet, I don't have that feeling of relief, and I wonder why not? She wished she could ask for his opinion, but they were not yet close enough friends or sufficiently indifferent to each other to talk with complete frankness. She merely said: "You, my dear, have never had a really precise goal. I mean, in the way that Sorel had one."

"No, certainly not." And he thought: Yet, I often had the feeling that I'd have a goal, or that somewhere in the midst of all those time-wasting activities there might be—But he merely repeated her words: "Yes, so here we are, at the same point. A little dispirited, both of us, it seems to me."

"Couldn't it be we've reached a point where we could really do something?"

"What, for instance?"

"We might go somewhere together—You know where."

The Sunday afternoon weighed heavily upon them. The study was silent. Even the sunlight coming through the window-panes showed up the dust and served no real purpose.

"I'm going to pack our bags," she said. "Otherwise, we'll never go."

"Well, I never!" said Madame Suzy, upon seeing Number 404 cross the courtyard together. Her husband, a pale little man, a tile layer by trade, took his nose out of the newspaper and raised his eyebrows questioningly.

"Monsieur and Madame Guibal, who are going out together. Looks as if she intended for once to give the lycée the go-by."

"Maybe there's a railway strike, and he's going to take her in the car," he suggested.

"Oh, no, there's no strike! I'd know if there was one!" said Madame Suzy curtly. "I tell you, they're taking a trip together, going to the country on this sunny day, like a pair of lovebirds. If only this could reconcile them!"

"Were they on bad terms?" he asked without much interest.

"More or less. He's a fine man, is Monsieur Guibal, but a womanizer. And she, too proud, much too proud. Besides, all these women who work—"

"And you don't work, you?" said the gnome, surging up from his wide-open newspaper in a feeble attempt to be aggressive.

"I don't call what I do work," said Madame Suzy, with a superb gesture, rejecting the upkeep of seven floors in the apartment building, the seven flights of stairs that she fondly polished, reducing her labor to the rank of an amusement. "What I mean is, work with the head. No wonder that she's frigid."

The pale tile layer renounced his newspaper to give, with a detached air of sagacity, his opinion on this sentimental problem.

"She—frigid? A woman who is so well dressed, even in the mornings! Always with her hair combed, even to go out for the breakfast croissants! You're crazy."

His argument struck Madame Suzy, by nature tempestuous, even snappish, but fair-minded.

"It's possible," she said doubtfully. "It's possible. Anyway, all's well that ends well, isn't it?"

"Got to think so," said the man resignedly. And, despondently, they abandoned the subject.

THAT WORD "END"

People dislike this word—not that they object to happy endings, but rather because they dislike having things come to an end. What, then, can they do? And from a realistic viewpoint, they have reason on their side. Things rarely end. Unclouded happiness, irremediable misfortune are rare. The most tormented, if the pressure of misery is relaxed for an instant, experience a brief respite, if only long enough to appreciate a cup of coffee. And the happiest—But that state of being is so infrequent! Anyway, the fact remains that Robert did not have the luck to hit upon a subject that ended really badly. His subject was an affair both intriguing and depressing.

All the same, one would prefer that, since it had to end, it should have ended with a victory; and in a picture-book story, the courageous seeker would finally, after many disappointments, establish the existence of his underground chapel and have his efforts crowned at the Académie des Sciences, immortalized at the Grévin Museum, or be made a member of the Royal College of Science. It remains to be seen what this revenge of Archimedes* would amount to after twelve or fifteen years spent underground. Or again, the revenge of Bernard Palissy.†

At any rate, there was no revenge in the case of Pierre Sorel. There was only a solitary man, driven out, uprooted,

---

*It will be recalled that Archimedes, mistakenly slain by a Roman soldier at the end of the Second Punic War, was "rewarded" with an honorary burial by orders of the Roman general Marcellus.

†Bernard Palissy, the sixteenth-century Huguenot, was executed for his religious beliefs and, centuries later, was honored by a ceremonial banquet.

deprived of his realm, torn from his landscape.

A landscape is contemplated, is painted; and on the canvas of the greatest master, the enigma remains entire, the question merely put. Only the worst painters appear to feel they have found a solution. Sorel, who was both painter and landscape, would not presume to propose one. Did he finally discover it? Or, blow after blow of the pickax, did he uncover at the same time the chapel, real or imagined, tangible or intangible? And did he know that the dream and the reality merged in this molehill, this buried cathedral, this concave creation which, nonetheless, he had nurtured, this subterranean and ethereal temple which is like a great organ, nothing but wind, yet, all the same, something, if nothing but tubes and tunnels, drafts of air in the mud, nothing but the impalpable, the invisible, the useless, and yet, chapel or no, discovery or no, folly or no, the cast of a church, Notre Dame du Vide? "Our Lady of the Void?"

Of course, a man was there, Sorel, a man of flesh and blood, forty-five or fifty years old, with a great deal of muscle and very little brains, who would stand there, stunned, bewildered, when the bulldozers of the commune—only two, but it was an army—advanced like armored cars and in a few hours blocked up all exits to his kingdom. Perhaps the man standing there was a rebel who bitterly rejoiced and snickered, "Now you will never know." Or else, he was a brokenhearted child, standing with empty hands and asking, "Why?" But are we forbidden to think that there was also a man in him who knew that something was being accomplished, a very ancient ritual of destruction which would carry him without effort, the man who had struggled so hard and long, to the summit of the useful and useless, the efficacious and the gratuitous, merging in a fugitive equilibrium? Did that man think that his story ended badly?

Would he unknowingly join Manuel's favorite heroes, Chaplin and Lucky Luke, solitary figures with all their worldly goods in a bundle slung over their backs, their hands empty? Would he become another proverb, a homely saying, as worn out as the soles of Van Gogh's shoes: "Money does not buy happiness"; "Poverty is not a vice"; "Who loses wins"; and "The first shall be last"? Utopian, high-flown words, the finale at which the well-born spectator weeps, although nonetheless convinced that the last will always be last and that it's better to win than to lose, except in the movies?

And even Chaplin and Lucky Luke, are they the modern equivalent of the pious images of yore, and can we be plunged into meditation by that bundle and that "poor lonely cowboy" as by the sandals of Saint Francis or the staff of the pilgrim?

Let us regard the image.

LUCKY LUKE

It is noteworthy that in the final glimpse given us of Lucky Luke in the comic strip (the cowboy "who shoots faster than his shadow" and who lays down the law), he is always shown, his mission accomplished, riding off across the desert alone (Saint Anthony?), and nearly always his back is turned to the spectator. Like Chaplin's Little Tramp, he no longer has, at the end, any personality; he has become transparent. Thus, they join the contemplatives, the hermits who "are and are not," and the motley crowd of unstable people, the failures, the homeless, and the uprooted—the unutilizables, or as social workers would say, "the unreclaimables." But how to distinguish between the transparent saint and the comic porosity of the drunkard, between excessive simplification and revelatory simplicity? Does the difference rest entirely in the eye of the beholder?

To decide this, we would need a simplicity lacking in the savant, a science lacking in the simple. And if there be a point where these extremes become reconciled, then it is no longer a literary problem.

They had not taken a vacation together the previous summer because Robert had accompanied Reine to the Midi in the month of July and only afterward had rejoined Catherine, who was staying with Germaine at her house in Normandy with Vivi and the twins. The year before that, they had been invited by Bernard and Geneviève to Saint-Raphaël. And the year before that—Oh, yes, Robert had had to finish a film script, and they had planned to take their vacation at Christmastime but could not because of Catherine's appendicitis. Yes, one had to go back six or seven years to their tour in Spain to find the memory of a vacation alone together—And even then, in Granada, they had run across Jocelyn, ashamed to be seen in such circumstances, for she was traveling in an organized group. "I joined this group," she explained, "because I wanted to see a small convent not far from here where there are some almost unknown frescoes by Zurbarán." And she had blushed like a young girl, while the busload of jolly moustached young men, not doomed poets, far from it, kept calling, "Hey, Liline! The bus is ready to go!"

"This encounter is going to spoil her vacation," Robert had said with amusement when the bus had left, with its passengers singing at the top of their lungs, and Jocelyn had squeezed into a corner trying to make herself invisible.

"Possibly," Catherine had said, "for she's a terrible snob!"

It was true. But in Jocelyn's situation, it was almost courageous to be a snob, and Robert would have liked to explain this to Catherine. Like elegance, which is a trifling quality in a rich woman who has only to pay the price to attain it, but which can represent an admirable discipline in the woman who has difficulty in making ends meet while forcing herself not to let this show. Once again, he had recoiled from an argument with Catherine because he knew that for her two kinds of elegance and snobbishness did not exist—nor two kinds of love. And she suffered enough from loving him, in spite of her principles, in spite of the idea she had of love. It was during that summer vacation that he had realized she still loved him and how she was struggling against it.

"I was almost afraid," she had said tenderly after the tumultuous departure of Jocelyn, "that you might ask her to join us."

And indeed he had almost done so, but he refrained from confessing it. Instead, he had exclaimed, "You must be crazy!" But once again, he had felt that he was betraying something.

That afternoon she had been happy. Following the siesta, they had visited a museum, had walked in a garden. And she, who was no longer very talkative, had chattered like a magpie and had laughed at everything and nothing, as if a little tipsy. And when she fell silent, it was a full and comfortable silence. The garden was sumptuous, sybaritic and at the same time self-conscious, with its luxuriant flowers strictly contained in well-kept flower beds.

Catherine had leaned against him as they walked, looking more Oriental than usual, with her lithe figure clothed in a gray and pink silk dress, and her air of modesty and refinement simultaneously excited and restrained his desire. Men, other men, regarded her as mysterious. And perhaps she was. That day he had told her he loved her. How many years ago was it? Six or perhaps seven years. Since then, he had never dared to pronounce the words. She would have been offended. He had said that he loved her as they stood in the midst of hyperbolic fountains and groups of little girls in starched dresses, dignified matrons who looked as if they were afflicted with severe liver trouble. He had told her that he loved her, no doubt a little bothered by the memory of a charming twenty-year-old Annie in the Dordogne, who was writing an epic novel, a girl of no importance to him but who was for Catherine an unpleasant recollection. He had told Catherine that he loved her, making something of an effort to convince her, for at that time she always had such an anxious, scrutinizing look in her eyes, as if the truth of his words must be weighed and tested, as if she were afraid to trust him. He had been troubled because he knew she was wondering to what other women he had said those words. And troubled because he really did love her.

Yes, one had to go back six or seven years to find the last time he had told her that he loved her. And when she had replied with simplicity, "Me, too."

And a couple of hours later, in the arbored garden of a restaurant, a catastrophe! Some of his friends were dining there. Exclamations, joyful cries! And she with her proper schoolgirl face, in the midst of an ambience of too much red wine and passably ridiculous guitarists—But he had enjoyed that coarse jubilation on the part of a couple of married journalists, not a little stupid, Xavier and Jacqueline Champion. He, a big skinny clown with a pleasantly lined face, a sportswriter; she, with the aspect of a seedy little housewife, but who "covered" show business and entertainments, could remain unmoved at a striptease performance and during risqué dialogue, as if watching a beef stew in her kitchen, writing lines such as "The nudes were not first rate," and "They urinated on stage, but that's been done before, in London." They were so glad to be in Spain! They were so glad to sample Spanish cuisine, so delighted with the sunshine and the cheap guitars! And Robert had wanted to prolong the evening with them, to talk about football with Xavier and flamenco music with Jacqueline. When he had noticed that Catherine was saying nothing and was nervously biting her nails, it was already too late. In their room at the inn, she had burst into tears, with dry sobs, a kind of suffocation that worried him. And when she recovered her breath, he heard, among incomprehensible babblings, the same old reproach: "No matter who—"

"No matter who!" Anselme exclaimed. "No matter who can preach the Word of God!"

Father Moinaud became flustered.

"Now, now, my boy, don't be so noisy! You'll get us into trouble."

"And no matter what hour is good! And no matter what place!"

"Yes, yes. But there are certain proprieties to be observed. The fathers go to bed early; a great many are now asleep—"

"Exactly! We must wake them up!"

"Wake them up for what, please tell me?"

"To announce the good tidings. To sing with them. To—"

"Anselme, that's enough," said Father Moinaud emphatically. "I would be willing to guess that you've not even had your dinner. I've put aside some fish for you, and I'll heat it up."

"That suits me fine," said Anselme with a wide and timid smile. "I'm very fond of fish."

With a sigh of relief, Father Moinaud went into the kitchenette. Ever since he had given Anselme lodging, Father Moinaud had had no life of his own. At any and every hour, Anselme created a scandal. And try as he would, the priest could think of no congregation that would accept the stuttering, unfortunate zealot. He put a little butter in the rice, added a tomato to the colorless fish sauce. In such ways, he tried to give Anselme some small pleasures, feeling slightly guilty toward him.

"But now, Father," said Anselme, who had followed him into the kitchen, speaking in a plaintive voice, "why don't you want me to preach in the streets? There have been others. Saint Philip Neri, Saint Francis—"

"I don't want you to," said Father Moinaud in a scolding voice, but glad to have his back turned as he bent over the stove, "because if it happens again, you'll get yourself put in the asylum."

"By the pagans!" said Anselme with dignity. "It's martyrdom. It's the modern form of martyrdom."

"Well, let's say that I don't want my choirboy to end up a martyr."

"Oh, you're surely not that attached to me," Anselme said gently as he slid the fish onto a plate and sat down at the table. "Besides, you have too much faith to drag me away from my vocation."

This display of self-assurance exasperated Father Moinaud, that old tyrant of classes in catechism, used to being obeyed by his youngsters.

"But what makes you so sure it's your vocation?" he said, wiping his hands. "And so sure you're not sinning by having overweening pride, or that you're not a bit insane?"

Anselme, his mouth full and some of the tomato sauce dribbling down his chin, looked at him with an air of gentle reproach.

"Don't we all have that vocation? Didn't the Lord say—"

Again he was going to quote the Bible! Father Moinaud felt close to exploding.

"No, no, I'll not say a thing more!" said Anselme precipitately. "But give me one good reason, one only, why I should be quiet, why I should hide this revelation I've been granted? Why?"

Why? For a moment Father Moinaud said nothing. Indeed, why? Because Anselme stuttered, because he was not good-looking? Because his nervous twitching gave him at times the aspect of a degenerate? Because he sweated abundantly as he talked, because there was a gap between his front teeth? Because his coat was too tight; his pants, too wide; and his expression, the evasive and humble expression of so many of the unstable and maladjusted, the semitramps, the drifters who live without any other resting place but the bosom of God?

241

Father Moinaud realized with grief that far from giving Anselme equilibrium, his conversion had accentuated Anselme's maladjustment. Persuaded that he belonged to the heavenly society, Anselme had ceased to pay attention to the criteria of human society. He was untidy and rather filthy, too talkative and too lively, too poor and too self-confident. And yet he practiced chastity, poverty, humility, and hope. It would be hard to discourage him. "And yet, that's my duty; I must somehow silence him, once and for all."

"You should not preach," he said slowly, after a pause, "because you don't have the gift."

"I don't have the gift?"

"No. Did you ever convert crowds of people at the Bon Marché? Or elsewhere? No. You don't convince. You feel your own faith very strongly, and I congratulate you. But you don't make others share it. You don't have the gift."

"And to talk of God, must one have a gift?"

"In-du-bi-tably! Otherwise, you do Him wrong."

"Oh! I do wrong to God?"

His voice was so much the voice of a grieving child that it reminded Father Moinaud remorsefully of the choirboy who, years before this, had asked, "If we win or lose the football game, does it matter?" But sometimes it is necessary to strike a drowning man in order to rescue him.

"Yes, preaching when you don't have the gift," the priest repeated as if to an obstinate child, "you do wrong God."

Anselme reflected, distressed but reasonable.

"It's not fair," he said. "It's not fair that everyone can't have the gift."

"You're right, it isn't fair," conceded Father Moinaud, thinking of his rejected manuscript.

An encounter between Anselme and Jean Charlier, attaché at the Ministry of Culture, would no doubt be interesting. Between extreme skepticism and extreme faith, there is only the thickness of a hair. Jean Charlier, as a boy, watching, with wistful admiration, his classmates playing football, must have said to himself, like Anselme, that to win or lose was of little importance. There would have been a bond of sympathy between the boy Jean and the boy Anselme. Today, however, Anselme's emphatic language and his sputterings would repel the fastidious dilettante, and Anselme would not fail to mention Sodom, Mammon, and Lucifer, at sight of the sumptuous office where Charlier wastes his time with distinction, sitting opposite a tapestry by Braque. Real encounters never take place.

THREE STARS

Toward noon, they stopped at a three-star restaurant not far from Alençon. Robert ordered the meal with that careful attention to detail that in days gone by had so exasperated Catherine. Days gone by—that was three weeks ago, when she had laid aside such prejudices, had experienced the slightly guilty relief of a person who has suddenly abandoned a rigid corset of principles. This time she took an interest.

"Yes," she agreed, "why not a Pouilly-Fuissé?"

She was fond of that wine; she was fond of Robert. Why not drink, why not love without constraint? But try as she would, since her ridiculous attempt to be an unfaithful wife, she felt—how shall I say?—she felt defrocked. The principle of her fidelity had collapsed; it was quite deliberately, even coldly, that she had made that rendezvous with Jean-Francis. But her body had refused to obey. So, then, it was not her body, her heart if you like, but her will that had commanded her? Then she was worth no more than Robert, whose squandering of himself and lack of seriousness she had so often criticized. Serious or not, it was a question of temperament, of humors. Suddenly, she confessed to herself that she had been, in effect, no better than he, and had made him feel that she was his superior. She had been armed with her fidelity as if with an entire panoply of weapons, and she recalled that he had never held it against her, indeed had even admired her for it. She blushed at the thought.

"What are you thinking about?" she asked, taking courage from the Pouilly.

"About this trip of ours. We are certainly a little ridiculous," he said with a sigh. "What could we expect to find down there? A poor devil who has wasted his life and would be unable to tell us why."

"You really believe that?"

"Why, it's obvious!" (Robert had forgotten his smoked salmon.) "He'd say, 'We had the i-dee that if we digged a bit down thar, we'd turn up a tray-shoor—' "

She laughed, on account of the Pouilly and the peasant accent he had put on.

"Oh, come," she said. "Peasants haven't talked like that since Molière."

"Well, I mean, the equivalent. What could a man say who has wasted—utterly lost—twelve years of his life?"

"And his wife?" she added with sudden aggressiveness.

"What do you mean by that?"

She sipped some more wine to give herself courage. It had been five or six years since they had gone on a trip together, five or six years since he had told her he loved her. And whenever she had said "I love you," it had been like a slap in his face. And as to their episodic lovemaking, the thought of those occasions made her blush, yet those embraces were supposed to have made their life together easier. And had not.

She observed him. Already he had lowered his beautiful eyes, with their long lashes, strangely feminine in that virile face, which was just a little fleshy. He had averted his eyes, expecting to hear some more of her eternal reproaches, more of her eternal attacks that wore him down without conquering him.

"I mean," she said, with deepening blushes, "that I now realize how often I've showered you with reproaches, and for no good reason; I've not made you happy."

244

"What are you saying?" he exclaimed, almost scandalized.

"That it wasn't worth while being faithful; it didn't give anyone pleasure."

"Well, if you'd cheated on me, it would certainly not have given me pleasure!"

She laughed, still with some embarrassment.

"What I mean is, I was thinking only of myself in being faithful to you. Of being worthy to be loved, more than being really faithful and letting myself be really loved."

"But it's admirable when someone tries to be perfect," he said gently.

"Then suddenly I was fed up with it; suddenly I detested myself, really, for forcing that kind of wife upon you."

"What are you trying to tell me, Cathie?"

She told him about Jean-Francis, briefly.

"And, you know, stupid as it seems, I don't, after all, regret—I don't regret having had that—impulse. And I don't regret, either, that I was unable to—"

"But that's still more fortunate!" he exclaimed, rather shocked.

He pushed away his plate; the salmon wasn't up to much, and he called the waiter.

"But it wasn't at all to revenge myself on you that I had the idea!"

"You call that an idea!"

"But that is what it was," she said, determinedly taking more wine. "After all, I didn't have the least *desire*—as it turned out!"

He calmed down and smiled in spite of himself.

"It was to shatter an idea I held, an idea that was too— too overwhelming, perhaps, the idea I had of love."

"In short, it was to please me?"

The waiter approached. Robert, upset, forgot he had intended to send the salmon back to the kitchen and, instead, ordered another bottle.

"You don't want to understand," she protested. "If I had taken a lover—" she had lowered her voice on account of the

245

waiter, who, anticipating a scene of passion, was loitering not far off near the sideboard, excitedly listening with all his might. "And if," she murmured, "I continued to love him—"

He understood. That would prove that he, too—He was irritated, amused, and touched by this naïve theorizing of Cathie's. Really touched.

"But you surely know that I love you. It was for your sake that I wanted to write that book, a futile attempt, but beautiful, all the same, just because of that—and still more beautiful because it failed. Basically, Sorel was to a certain extent you."

"Then why do you detest him now?"

The waiter, with glittering eye, brought the next course (sweetbreads for Robert, sole for Catherine), going away as slowly as possible, hoping to gather some scraps of sentimental dream. He was a quite young man, charmingly self-conscious, nurtured on the gossip columns of *France Dimanche*, which gave him a close acquaintance with Princess Margaret and the Marquise des Anges, whom he imagined to be rather close friends.

"I don't detest him; I detest myself," he said wearily. "Because I've not succeeded."

"Me, neither," she said. "I've not succeeded in being what I wanted to be. But maybe we've succeeded in something else?"

"Now that Catherine's problems are solved," said Germaine to her eldest daughter, "you ought to marry Werner."

Vivi struggled and slipped through Germaine's fingers like a fish in water.

"I can't marry Werner just to please—"

"But I'm not talking about pleasing me! Think of the children; they'd obviously be delighted. But I'm mainly thinking of you. You're in love with him, after all—"

"Yes," said Vivi uncertainly. "Yes. But just because I'm in love with him, is that a reason for me to renounce—"

"Renounce what?"

Yes, what? A frightened goldfish turned round and round in her head, trying to escape.

"I'd like to ask Robert's advice when he returns."

"You've monopolized Robert enough with your problems," Germaine decreed. "I sometimes wonder, even, if that hasn't contributed to separating Catherine from him. Oh, I'm not reproaching you. You were alone, helpless. But a husband is worth more than a brother-in-law."

Vivi tried desperately to find a viable argument. Taking a weapon from her mother's arsenal, she finally said, "There's the difference in age. And in nationality—"

"Oh, my!" said Germaine, seized with the same honest indignation that had seized Father Moinaud at having the Bible used against him.

The afternoon advanced.

"What do you say to our spending the night here at this inn?" Robert suddenly proposed.

"You don't want to keep on going?"

"I don't know," he confessed, "whether to go on or turn back. That doesn't seem to be the real problem."

"Me, too, I feel the same. You'll laugh, but when I saw myself there in Jean-Francis's building—this is the last time I'll mention it to you—ridiculously trembling in that elevator, I suppose exactly as I would have done years ago, I realized that my upbringing, my prejudices, all of that, counted as much as an—ideal, if you'll let me use the word, that ideal of fidelity I was so proud of, and I stopped being proud."

"But after all, there was the fact that you weren't in love!" he exclaimed, so loudly that the waiter, still present, shivered.

"That's true. But I would love you just as much if I hadn't decided, wanted—So, I don't deserve any credit."

"I don't want all that much to give you credit," he said tenderly.

247

Their hands met across the table. And violins softly moaned in the heart of the waiter.

"Shall we stay?"

"We could always take to the road again tomorrow morning," she said. "In one direction or another—"

At the street corner, Anselme stopped on the island for quite a while, admiring the policeman on traffic duty.

"What a fine thing it is," he said with conviction, "to make people obey the law."

The traffic cop stared at him briefly, then, seeing no ironic intent, merely an approving look on that long, pale face, he gave a reply.

"Oh, as for me, that isn't what I'm worrying about; it's just to keep the traffic moving."

"It's the same thing," said Anselme, now very sure of himself. "When there's an infraction, you blow your whistle, and the car stops. But those who are doing the right thing, on the contrary, you protect them from accidents."

"I do what I'm paid to do," grumbled the cop. "Are you or aren't you going to cross?"

"The red light is on," Anselme informed.

"I tell you to cross!"

"Even you can't change the law," said Anselme. "That's what's so beautiful in the law of God. Even He does not transgress it. Have you read the Bible?"

"I tell you to cross the street!"

"The light is still red. If God wanted to perform a miracle, He could keep it on red for hours at a time, so I could convert you."

"Convert me! You misbegotten missionary! What do you take me for? A little African Negro? Convert me! You cross that street in double-quick time, or I'll have you taken away in that police car down there!"

Anselme hesitated a moment, then sagely gave up. As he reached the other side of the street, he wondered sadly if Father Moinaud hadn't been right, that perhaps he lacked the gift. Discouraged, he went on his way, eyeing the public urinals on the boulevard Saint-Germain.

They made love timidly, self-consciously. Then Catherine fell asleep, her face hidden by her hair, like a masked bandit.

Robert, wakeful, let his gaze wander over the toile de Jouy curtains (why do all these three-star inns consider that fabric an infallible aphrodisiac?), reflecting that, after all, he had been the only man in Catherine's life. Quite astonishing. And that attempt with Jean-Francis, as he thought it over, almost filled him with awe. That stubborn fidelity was nothing more than love—a vocation. The only man in her life. The idea was as marvelous as those picture-book stories he had brooded over as a boy, stories of explorers coming upon deserted cities in the jungle. So, Catherine had been defended by all kinds of shames and inhibitions. And he recalled how, in their early days together, he had marveled at her gift for arranging flowers, her elegance, her perfume, her unexpected flashes of humor, her hidden sensuality, as persistent as a nocturnal fragrance—She was still the same. Body and personality intact. Almost adolescent, an Oriental purity. Even when holding a grudge against him, she had been unable to abjure all this. Was this love? The first and only man in her life—How moving! While I—But he did not feel remorse. Nor was he as reactionary as he seemed (or at least seemed to Vivi). For he would never dream of reproaching either Vivi or Reine— particularly Reine—for their free way of living and their past heavy with souvenirs. On the contrary. Few women had given him so great a feeling of virginity as had Reine. Much more than had the irreproachable Catherine, who—to use phrases so common in love stories—"gave herself," "abandoned herself." Reine didn't have to abandon or give herself. She was simply there, nothing more. For him, for Tixier, for Marakis, for her public. She was given (as one says, "Take a given number"); she did not give herself. And he thought, with a sharp pang, Reine, my sister—And he knew he would never see her again. He recalled once more Catherine's words, "I stopped being proud." He, too, long ago, had stopped being proud, of being sure of anything. Reine would always be proud, intact. Farewell, Reine. Farewell to the woman who never doubted. Catherine has rejoined me.

"I stopped being proud." True, she had said it with a sad and rather weary humor. But in this bedroom, with the gentle and hemmed-in view of a garden through the window, he suddenly, with the lucidity given by fatigue, heard again those words in a slow welling up of hope.

For her sake, I gave up what I believed to be simple and good, what constituted my garden, my true lifework, my own subterranean kingdom. But for my sake, she was ready to destroy her fortified castle, wanted to soil her clean page, wanted to tear her good child's apron. Can it be that neither of us was wrong? That on the contrary we have always been opposites but complementary, capable of merging without betraying our own natures?

He got out of bed and began to pace the floor. Catherine still slept. Somewhere or other Pierre Sorel was also sleeping, perhaps with futile visions in his head. And I, with a wealth of lost time, with a single step can rejoin them and tell them (one day, one instant, the duration of one word, having again become a writer)—I can tell them, "Be proud once more of what is lost—"

Thus he mused, gazing now at the little garden, now at the sleeping woman.

Downstairs, the waiter, blessed with a respite before the midday meal, was also daydreaming: about forbidden amours and about the pretty customers. Still a virgin at eighteen, through the fault of a widowed and domineering mother, he was obsessed by the procession of couples that passed through the inn, and to his mind all the women were beautiful, all of them desirable. Besides, he was perfectly right.

IN THE JARDIN DES PLANTES

"Mamma worries me," said Manuel, dragging his feet on the gravel path in the Jardin des Plantes.

"She's completely off her head at present," said Marina, shaking her pale, almost silver locks.

They were walking down the main driveway of the garden, almost deserted at six in the morning. An old man sitting on a bench in the sunshine was eating something he had taken out of its newspaper wrapping.

"Do you suppose that one day we'll be old like that?" said Marina in another tone of voice.

"My goodness, certainly not."

"Mamma doesn't think so, either. That's why she doesn't want to marry Werner. And one day she'll be all alone, like that old man."

Marina gazed at the little old man, who was now feeding the pigeons with the crumbs left over from his breakfast.

"When you're old, you're old," she said with conviction. "At least, when she had Uncle Robert—"

They had reached the entrance to the menageries. Automatically, Manuel took charge of the tickets.

"He has certainly forsaken us," he said, looking at but not seeing a fox that was turning in its cage.

"Phooey, what a bad smell this fox has," said Marina, tapping the bars.

"As for me, I like Werner a lot. How about you?"

"Oh, dear, this smell! Yes, I believe so."

"At least, Werner won't forsake Mamma."

"That's probably what scares her," said Marina, walking away from the fox.

Manuel followed, his eyes on the gravel. He hesitated briefly in front of a pushcart where brioches and chewing gum were displayed, then hurried to catch up with his sister, that fourteen-year-old woman. Then, abdicating his elder-brother status before her obvious superiority, he allowed his uneasiness to show.

"You really think that? But Uncle Robert—"

"Uncle Robert and Mamma are alike," said Marina with a doctoral air, "always involved in one thing after another."

"All the same, he hadn't the right to drop her like this."

"And what about Papa? Did he have the right?" Marina put the question in a muffled voice.

Manuel said nothing. His father had returned to Brazil to

render services to his compatriots. That indicated an ideal not to be denied. Mamma had not wanted to go to Brazil. Was she wrong? A woman should follow her husband. But even while he was still in Paris, Dr. Medina had rarely been at home, it had to be admitted.

Dr. Medina obviously shouldn't have married. When a man is married, he should place his wife above his vocation. That, at least, was Manuel's opinion, and there was merit in it, for the picture postcards his father sent him from Brazil made him wonder.

"He was mistaken in his vocation," he hazarded.

"And maybe Uncle Robert mistook his vocation, too? How simple and easy everything is for men!" said Marina, still walking ahead, without looking at the cages. Seen from the back, with her raspberry-red leotards, her denim mini-skirt, her shirtwaist, and her multicolored knitted vest, her hair so pale it looked bleached, you would say she was sixteen or eighteen years old, but she shrugged her shoulders furiously like a little girl, and Manuel's heart melted.

"Werner isn't like that," he blurted out.

"Werner isn't like that, and neither are you. But that's because he is in love with Mamma, exactly for that reason. Things always get so mixed up."

Manuel didn't know what to say. He wanted to help her, felt he should help her, since he was the elder of the two and a man, but he didn't know what to think. He didn't share Marina's acrimony. Grief, yes, he could feel, but he accepted life's imperfections with more resignation and courage as well. Marina's passionate revolt deeply troubled him. His sister—so pretty, while he (so he believed) was so ugly; she so quick, while he was so slow—his sister was a woman and therefore doomed to suffer. With this thought, his eyes were about to fill with tears when a joyous cry came from Marina and interrupted his reverie.

"Oh, Manuel! Do look at these adorable creatures!"

They were very young bear cubs frolicking together on the grass. Marina crouched down and called to the cubs through the wire netting.

"Pst! Pst! Oh, Mano, buy me some cookies for them, please?"

With a sigh, Manuel sacrificed the coins he had hoped to spend on cigarettes.

"Oh, Mano, Manolito! Aren't they adorable!"

Marina's voice was thrilling. The shabby-coated and rheumy mother bear was now suckling her cubs.

Manuel squatted down beside his sister. He felt the warmth of her frail body against him. In her ecstasy, Marina had forgotten all else. Manuel reflected that this furious little girl would one day become a mother, give birth.

"Yes, Marinette, it's lovely," he agreed.

He rested his head on his sister's shoulder. They snuggled together like the bear cubs. Never, never will I love anyone as much as I love her, he thought.

"Never, never will I love anyone as much as I love you," said Marina.

But she was the one who said the words aloud—and who was already aware that it wasn't true.

"And now what are we going to do?" asked Catherine, stretching her arms as she sat up in bed, half naked, clutching the sheet against her small, saffron-colored breasts. Breakfast had just been brought and the tray set down beside the bed.

Robert gazed through the window at the neat little garden with its flower beds and well-kept lawn. The bench under the tall tree, the quadrangle of aromatic herbs, the tables of weathered wood. None of the ugly garden furniture so often seen in country places of this kind, and at this hour of the morning, the waiters were elsewhere. It had the aspect of a charming private garden, a scene by van Eyck or Vermeer, perfectly ordinary, inexplicably artificial. The château would have that appearance—if he were to reach the château. It would reveal nothing more to him than this little bit of a garden, or Bergotte's wedge of a yellow wall, or Kafka's castle.

"What are you thinking about?" she asked, smiling at his absorption.

"About literature."

She laughed aloud.

"Why are you laughing?"

"This might be a scene in an American technicolor movie.

253

You know, the woman remains alone in bed, while he, the accursed artist, has already torn himself away from sensual pleasures to jot down some notes that will eventually be the *Eroica* symphony or to do a charcoal sketch that will eventually be *Le Radeau de la Méduse.*"

"That Géricault painting is not a masterpiece."

"It is for the Americans!" she said, leaving the bed, laughing.

She rummaged in the little suitcase and pulled out a black and white kimono. He turned from the window and went to sit beside her on the edge of the bed, where he poured himself a cup of coffee.

"It's the truth, you know," he said, without raising his eyes. "I wanted to write that book for you."

"For me—and for the others? The twins, Anselme, Vivi, and even Mélusine?"

"For you first of all. But for them as well. Of course, on a certain plane, it comes to the same thing."

"Yes," she said, "I understand. And whether you've written the book or not, it's also the same thing, on that plane."

"You think so? On that plane—But is that enough?"

She hugged him tenderly.

"We will never know, of course. We will never know. Just like the treasure. But as for me, yes, I think so."

And as he still hesitated to respond to her embrace or to her smile, she added, almost without effort, "All of your friends—We all think so."

"Then I gather we're not going to the château? We were just fooling?"

"No, not fooling—Let's say it was an excuse for a drive into the country."

"Tell me about it?"

AN EXCUSE FOR A DRIVE IN THE COUNTRY

They will have arrived at the château the following evening, or perhaps not until the morning of the next to the next day, because they will have given lifts to several hitchhikers (since he always picks up hitchhikers). Among these, there will have been a pale young man resembling Anselme, rhapsodic and blundering; a meticulously daft old maid similar to Mélusine; a lovely and empty-headed young girl like Carol; a young knight-errant like Gerry. And like Gerry, Anselme, Vivi, Jocelyn, or Mélusine, they will all have told snippets of their lives, their dreams, true or false; and all of them will have asked their benefactor to go out of his way by two or three kilometers; what does it matter? Then, one by one, they will have disappeared at the bend of a road or some hour of the day. But their house, their village, their telephone office (this for the old maid), the youth hostel (for the young man), the discount store or dress shop that will swallow up the young girl—all are merely façades, painted sets, dream castles. The Boissy château exists and doesn't exist, for dream castles are everywhere. Literature exists and doesn't exist, for each of the hitchhikers picked up at random will have said, after recounting a snippet of his life, true or false, "My life would make a book." And he, Robert, would agree with them, quietly and sincerely.

On the other hand, of course, it would be possible to obey Catherine's wishes (the earlier Catherine) and to continue on their way without stopping, and hence they would arrive that very day at the château, without any stopovers of a gastronomical or amorous nature, as, for instance, at this respectable three-star inn. They might possibly arrive not too late in the evening; Sorel might not as yet have followed his destiny, which was to disappear; and then they would not encounter, already installed, efficient and perspiring, the jovial little manager of the House of Culture, or the youth hostel or the Refuge for the Physically Handicapped. Yes, it could well be that on this bright and clearly defined day in May, they would finally meet Sorel.

"Then what?" asked Catherine, like a child.

Then there would be a hush, a silence cutting the words; there would be men of his own age who had frittered away their lives, each after his own fashion. Would they tell themselves this over a glass of vermouth-cassis or coffee and brandy? And then, might there not be felt an obscure fraternity, a fleeting harmony in the smoke-filled bistro, a precarious equilibrium where opposites briefly become coequals, a unifying moment for the perfect understanding toward which all life tends? If so, no doubt they would say nothing except plain and coarse words, plain and coarse like the none-too-clean goblets into which their wine was poured, well suited to the occasion. Of no importance. What would happen there would be beyond the realm of words. Words serve for nothing but to attain this silence.

"And stories, too, are they of no use?" she asked, again in that childlike voice, her amorous and nocturnal voice.

"One never knows till afterward. When they have ended. But all the same, they must be told. One must dig holes. Waste time. 'A treasure is concealed within.' "

"Within the hole, or within time?"

"Everywhere. There are treasures everywhere."

Reine would have said, "That's a theme." But now he banished Reine from his mind, since Catherine was at his side.